What You Have Tamed

Flame and Glory Saga, Volume 1

Jim Rose

Published by Jim Rose, 2024.

WHAT YOU HAVE TAMED

First edition. November 21, 2024.

Copyright © 2024 Jim Rose.

ISBN: 979-8992081817

Written by Jim Rose.

For Dee.

"Goodbye," said the fox. "And now here is my secret, a very simple secret: It is only with the heart that one can see rightly: what is essential is invisible to the eye."

"What is essential is invisible to the eye," the little prince repeated, so that he would be sure to remember.

"It is the time you have wasted for your rose that makes your rose so important."

"It is the time I have wasted for my rose-" said the little prince, so that he would be sure to remember.

"Men have forgotten this truth," said the fox. "But you must not forget it. You become responsible, forever, for what you have tamed."

-Antoine De Saint-Exupery

"The Little Prince"

Acknowledgments

To my wonderful wife, whose constant support has made this book possible.

To my parents, for their lifelong love and encouragement.

To my beta readers, Kris, Frances, and Kari, for listening to my insanity and showing me how I can make it crazier.

To my editors, Bailey of BA Editing Studio and Tere of Writer Garage, for pointing out exactly what was missing.

To my MFA classmates from SNHU, for being there to provide feedback without hesitation.

To the Flagler County Library Writing Group, for keeping my inspiration going.

To Messieurs Pfeffernusse and Stroopwafel for their endless vocal support and keeping those pesky lizards and squirrels away from me.

To everyone, too many to name, who heard I was writing a book and told me they couldn't wait to see it.

Thank you, everyone.

Chapter 1

IT WAS THE HOTTEST day of the dry season, and a boy was drowning.

The screams and splashing were not noticeable at first, flailing arms barely visible across the sparkling, dark turquoise water. His mother was screaming from the shoreline, near Lifeguard Station 33. Eira looked up from her book, first to the mother at the base of her station, then up to the horizon. Chucking the book onto the floor of her observation post, Eira jumped to her feet and snatched the neon gold flotation aid leaning against her chair. She squinted through darkly tinted sunglasses, struggling to gauge how far out the boy was.

A rip current must've yanked him out. And no buoy nearby for him to hold on to or give Eira an idea of how far out he was. Any situation farther than 75 meters, they'd need to call it in. She grabbed the radio from her bag. The Maritime Defense Command always has a ship nearby. All she had to do was switch to Channel 3 and request—the radio squawked at her. "This is Station 32," someone said. "Code 1, going in." To her right, at Station 32, the lifeguard there jumped, golden flotation aid strapped to his shoulder, following him like a cape. He high kneed through the soft sparkling black sand and jumped over the jagged golden boulders breaching through.

"Hey!" she called out, leaping from her observation tower. Her sunglasses flew off and landed on the bottom step. Eira left them behind and rushed to catch up to the other guy, her flotation aid bouncing off her back. He and Eira raced to the water, and he dove through the air and into the water a moment before her. Swinging her arms forward, Eira kept him in sight. While turning her head for

1

breath, Eira hissed a swear to herself. The other guy was faster. Her legs strained as she tried to kick faster to catch up to him, to surpass him.

They continued into the rip current, letting the rolling waves carry them closer to the boy. Through the sloshing water lapping at her ears, Eira could hear low words of encouragement: "I've got you. Here, hang onto this, start kicking. I've got you."

His voice had a depth that didn't match his lanky form. He pulled the flotation device under his and the boy's armpits. Eira struggled to maneuver hers to the front and paddle over to the boy's other side. It was useless, but a second one wouldn't hurt. Swim this way," he said. "Away from the current." Together, they went around the chaotic waves and kicked back to the beach. "Keep going, you're doing great," he panted out.

Eira didn't say anything, keeping her focus on the shoreline. Screams and cheers carried over the water as they got closer. Feet found the soft sand. Eira and the other guy stood up, hoisting the boy. A woman shoved her way through the crowd. She yanked the boy away from them and squeezed him in her arms. A brief applause from onlookers, then they dispersed. The excitement was over.

"Thank you," gasped the mother, refusing to let go of her son.

"Ma'am?" Eira asked. "Before you two go anywhere, can I take a look at your son? Policy says Emergency Health should be notified." She turned to the other lifeguard. "Call them for me?" He nodded and jogged towards Station 32 as if he hadn't just gotten his breath back. She was in control now. Eira knelt in front of the boy, checking his pupils and pulse. "That was really scary, huh? Do you know where you are now?"

To her right came a whirring noise, growing louder and louder. A dark green speedboat with Maritime Defense Command's logo displayed proudly on the side veered sharply shoreward. Neon green light bar flashed brighter than the sun. It slowed a few feet from the edge, and a pair of health-techs, in their soft blue overalls with bright neon sleeves and flotation vests. They rushed over to check the boy and questioned Eira and the other lifeguard once he came back from his station.

"You two saw him," one tech said, tapping away on his data tablet. "How far out was he?"

"I don't-" the other lifeguard began.

"About 70 meters," Eira lied.

The tech nodded without looking up at them. His holo tablet projected out of his wrist device and glowed blue as he finalized the report. "The kid's good?" he asked his partner. He replied with a nod. And before anyone knew it, they left. The boy went off with his mother, not a care in the world. Both lifeguards stood in the sand, unsure of what to do next. A mental checklist formed in both their minds, and they muttered each step aloud, nodding along.

"I...think that's it...?" he asked.

"Yeah, I think it is."

He outstretched his hand. "Reist Adeio."

"Eira Filodoxia." Her tone was suspicious, but she kept the handshake firm and her glare counted as eye contact.

He squinted at her. "Do you go to Southern too?"

"Yeah."

"Okay, *that's* where I know you from."

"Yeah. You dated this girl, Iliana. She's in my geography class."

He thought for a moment. "Oh, yeah," he said, with vague disinterest.

They stood silently for a moment, unsure of what to say next. "Well, I should get back," Eira said, pointing to her station.

"Yeah. Yeah, me too."

Eira picked her sunglasses, wiped away the sand, and risked a glance at the emotionless blur at Station 32. She looked back and studied the small waves rolling in as the events played back in her mind. Over the wind, children playing, and the impromptu volley-ball game, she hadn't heard the boy calling out for help. The mother's scream made Eira's blood go cold remembering it. After that...she strained to remember.

Eira had tried to call it in. It was what they were supposed to do, after all, as the junior lifeguards. She and Reist were only here for school credit. They did not have the lifesaving skills of, say, a Maritime Defense Command diver, and that had been hammered in during the three days of training they had to do.

So why had Reist jumped? He had the same training as her and had to've known better. But, while she was figuring out the right verbiage because they had always hyped on radio discipline, he had just...jumped. Reist had not hesitated and was off his station before her. He hadn't even climbed down; he had *leaped*. What did *she* do? She saw him, jumped, thought: *Mine,* and tried to beat him to the boy, to *her* victory.

His jump alone could not have been the sole factor. The more Eira reflected, the more obvious that became. When he hit the water, his skinny frame made him into a torpedo. There had been plenty built like him on the swim team with her last year. But he had never trained for endurance like she had. She had closed the distance while he tired himself out.

It doesn't matter now. He had made it to the boy first. She shouldn't criticize him for doing his job. Saving people shouldn't be a competition. But if it were, she would win. *Game on,* she thought. Eira pulled her sunscreen from the cup holder, reapplied the luke-warm cream, and wondered, *Is he processing this like me?*

Several meters away, Reist sat on a wooden observation post, toweling his face dry. He popped his sunglasses back on and leaned back in the chair, resting the back of his head against the smooth metal sign listing the codes lifeguards needed to know. Behind the tinted glass, he scanned the ocean; like a robot returning to his usual programming. But his gaze fell to his hands. They were shaking.

Reist flexed them into fists to settle them, but the rush didn't let up. Chemicals rushed through his veins as the adrenaline trickled away. He jumped back down onto the soft, black sand to pace around his observation post. His legs ached to run, arms demanding to swing. Reist shook the thoughts away and focused on the important thing. The innocent was safe, and the hero recognized.

Hours later, the next shift came and took over. Reist gave one last wave to the kid who took his spot, and joined the line of golden yellow swimsuits, all filing toward the closest hut. There was one at every tenth observation post. He glanced over his shoulder. That Eira girl wasn't far behind.

Inside the hut was freezing from the rumbling air cons. As soon as Reist walked in, he got hit by a gust of air that was supposed to keep bugs away. The floor was wet and jagged from the collective sand and ocean water dripping along the tiles. Reist went to his locker and pulled out his sandals and shirt. Eira's locker was on the adjoining wall. She pulled on her shirt, shorts, and sandals. She rushed towards the door, tossing her backpack onto her shoulder in time to beat Reist outside, cutting him off.

A momentary jolt of annoyance shot through him as she side-stepped out the door. When he walked out, she was there, staring at him. He stopped to stare back. She spoke first. "When do you work next?"

"Day after tomorrow." He held his small bag loosely over his shoulder, studying her.

Their glares matched, and she was the first to relent, offering a friendly smile. "Oh, good. Me too. See you then!" The last word was bubbly and cheery.

"...what was that...?" he muttered on his way to the row of bike racks. Reist unlocked his and popped off the wind catcher from behind the seat. It should have a good charge from the last couple of hours. He folded in the bike pedals and put both lock and catcher in his bag and made to go when a familiar, thunderous explosion erupted above his head. Descending into the stratosphere, roaring over the skyscrapers of Urbis, was the refugee transport.

Any sense of exhaustion in Reist dissipated. He twisted the throttle on the handlebars and soared into the bike lane. Reist swerved in and around commuters returning home from work or dragging small trolleys of groceries behind them. A few voices called out to him to slow down, you dumb kid, but how could he? It had been three whole lunar rotations since the last ship came down, and he refused to miss this one.

Following the same path he had taken a dozen times before, keeping the ship in view as much as he could, Reist pumped the battery again. His bicycle whirred meekly beneath him. Nothing like the rumbling of the ship's engines as the rear thrusters dulled from the brilliant red to a cooling blue. The spaceport was a little way out of town and would make Reist's trip home twice as long, but that was fine.

Like an angry beast of myth, the transport gave one last roar before softly coming down onto the landing pad. Reist kicked up a wave of dirt as he skittered to a stop at the perimeter glass walls. He panted heavily and sat back, waiting for the loading ramp to drop.

This was the best spot to wait and watch. Next to the landing pad was a depot, with a wide rolling door already open, and a line of city buses ready to take the refugees to the re-education facilities, then Servant School or wherever their skills would best be suited. Urbis couldn't have been the only city to accept the refugees, but the logistics weren't what was important.

Dropping with a groaning and heavy slowness, the ramp teased a brief glimpse inside. Reist pulled up his wristband and clicked it on. Blue holographic controls surrounded his wrist and upper forearm.

He hit a series of buttons and pulled up the camera. The more Reist zoomed, the fuzzier the picture got. It was meant for capturing moments in front of you, not from across an empty field.

Coming down the ramp, in an unorganized mess, were the humans of Efferus. Dressed shabbily, with dark hair and sundried skin, and each carrying only a single bag, they shuffled to the buses. Wherever the buses were going, they never stopped at Reist's side of town. The only Efferans he saw were his neighbors' city issued servants.

Still looking through the camera, a notification filled the holographic screen. Someone nearby was requesting to message him. Reist considered it, thinking maybe it was a refugee, and accepted. He had so many questions about what traveling to a new planet was like.

The message read, *You following me?* with a picture attachment. It was him, sitting on the bike, with his holo-device open. Reist's head shot up and he looked at where the picture would have been taken. Straight ahead of him, where the glass perimeter turned, was that girl, Eira.

He messaged back, *I always come when a transport comes in.*

Me too, she messaged back. *I like thinking about sneaking on board and seeing where it'll go.*

Back to Efferus maybe. Zenthara's closer.

Look at the logo, though. CDF, she replied.

Reist pulled the camera back up and snapped a picture of the logo for the Interplanetary Confederation Defense Force. He opened the chat with Eira just in time for her to say *See ya.* and watched her ride away on her bike. The buses were driving away too. Now was as good a time as any to head home. Her face was on his mind the entire way back.

EIRA HAD SAT BACK ON her bike and waited for the mass exodus from the beach to finish when the refugee transport blasted past overhead. She had chased after it, same as Reist had, but on a different route. When she had pulled up to the glass perimeter, she took stock of how tall the fence line was. Even if she stood on top of her own shoulders, it was still taller.

Then there was that Reist kid. Tall. Awkward. Oblivious. That was frustrating to see but could be amusing to play at. He had nice eyes. That counted for something, but what exactly she hadn't decided yet. None of her classmates cared, or seemed to notice, the transport when they came in. He did. That also counted for something. The first time she had watched one come in, she was a little ball of energy and so enthralled by adventure. She wanted to speculate with anyone who would listen. A year away from being a legal adult, that excitement hadn't let up. And now she has someone to talk to about it, finally.

On the ride home, Eira thought about how to be a stronger swimmer. She could rejoin the swim team. There were openings, and the coach liked her. But her ex-boyfriend, Thomos, had joined this semester. There might be friction there. She decided to sleep on it and map out how to be better next time. Hoping for a next time meant hoping for someone else to drown. In the moment, the pressure was infuriatingly terrifying. Afterwards, it was addicting.

Eira preferred the scenic route home. She enjoyed riding past the forest tree line before pulling up to the neighborhood gate. Eira waved her holo-device over the scanner. It beeped and opened the gate. She rode past the familiar homes and waved at the same neighbors. Several members of different boards of directors who own most of this region of Corvus, just out and enjoying their evening. As a child, it had never occurred to her the power they wielded with the same hands that waved at her now. One day, it had, and it was all she could think about behind the polite smile she gave them back.

Cuquas, the family chef, was walking along the sidewalk, past the neighborhood shuttle as it puttered away. The driver waved at Eira as she rode by, coming up to the house. "Welcome home, young lady," Cuquas said with a small bow, both hands full of grocery bags.

"Hey, Cuquas." Her tone was more familiar. He had been in the family's employ for several years. His formality with her, her parents, and Nana, was expected from his station.

"Might I get that for you?" He asked, nodding his head to her bike.

"No, I got it. Thank you, though." She shoved her bike to the small alcove of the garage, away from where her parents parked their cars.

"Very good, young lady. How was your day?" He followed her through the garage door.

"Pretty good. Saved a kid from drowning."

He gaped momentarily and regained his composure. "My word."

"Yep. See later." Eira went inside. He followed and split off towards the kitchen.

Her father was on the couch, sitting forward and glaring at the news report on the vid screen. They were talking about the increase in graffiti spreading out from the inner city. An angry red eyeball bore through the screen and into Eira's soul. She turned away. Her mother was on the back patio, in a lounge chair and looking at the lake that sat behind their home. Neither parent acknowledged her.

"Oh, I know who that is," said Nana. Her motorized chair whirred from the side room where she slept. Small and bony, a thick knitted blanket wrapped snuggly around her legs, she warmed the room with her smile. Beaming at Eira, she said, "Now what took you so long?"

"Still doing the lifeguard thing, Nana," she said. Eira watched Nana's face to make sure there was no confusion. It was hard to tell when Nana was being cheeky or if she had forgotten something else.

She had gotten better at covering her mistakes. Eira then eyed Nana's PICC line, snaking out of her shirt collar, resting lightly on her neck, and feeding into the med unit on her chair. The thin, clear, plastic tube rhythmically turned green as her medicine regularly pumped in, keeping her cancer at bay.

"Yes, yes. All your resume building and whatnot. Once you get to my age, you just can't be bothered anymore. It's rather relaxing."

"Sounds maddening, Nana."

"Yes, but I'm quite mad sometimes. Anything of interest today, honey?"

"Oh, the usual. Classes. Lectures. Saved a kid from drowning. Homework."

"What was that middle one?"

"Lectures."

"Thought so. Anything sticking? I always struggled to focus, would need your grandfather to repeat himself two or three times before I could retain anything he said. I hope you didn't inherit that."

"If I did, there's worse things, Nana."

"Sweetheart..." her mother slurred from the patio door. "You're dripping on the floor. Oh, bless it. Serva! Mop please!"

Eira rolled her eyes and sidestepped away from their housekeeper as she seemed to materialize out of the wall. "Sorry, Serva."

"No trouble, young miss," she replied with a bow, some of her dark hair already coming undone. With the force she shoved the mop around the spot Eira was standing, it appeared to be a healthy amount of trouble. The grip on her sundried hands tight around the handle.

"With me, hon," Nana whispered. She gave the news a stern glance and rolled her eyes. "Tell me about your day."

"I met a boy," Eira said under her breath. "It's probably nothing, but we'll see."

REIST TOOK THE SAME path home at the end of every shift. On transport days, he rode back to the hut on the beach, keeping the shore on his right side. Once he passed the hut, Reist swung a left and went straight through the business district. He rode through the last of the crowds of suits, leaving for the day to take the sky trams back to their own homes. Some days he'd stop by a department store to dumpster dive. Every few weeks, they threw out old mannequins and his sister liked to paint them. But not today. Reist was ready to go home.

There was a cutoff point he avoided. No one told him never to go there, but there was a primordial instinct that whispered in his ear that mingled with a curious perception. Most of the business district was well lit. Each skyscraper aglow with a dull amber as sunset turned to dusk. Just a few blocks past the last sky tram stop, the light dulled into dirt covered darkness. The only color discernable on this side of town was the angry red eyeball spray-painted on the side of the building.

It glared at Reist as he swung around the corner and out of sight. Three more turns and he would be home, a few more kilometers. He was riding into the familiar and comparatively friendlier atmosphere of his neighborhood. Suburban, two-story houses with front yards, each looking nauseatingly identical to the other. He knew which ones were which. There was not an inch of this neighborhood he didn't know.

Reist pulled into his driveway. He punched in the code for the garage door, and it rolled up just like the landing depot had, but smaller. Reist hung his bike on the hooks jutting out of the left wall. The back tire bumped off a mannequin propped against the wall, with multicolored wings painted across the formless face. He shut the garage door. Stepping directly into the kitchen and dining area,

Reist's dad was to the left, hunched over the stove, with clouds of steam billowing around his head. "Hey, you," he said, stirring the pot. "You catch that transport?"

"Sure did," Reist said, stepped into the living room, making towards his room on the far side of the house. His mom was sitting on the couch with his sister, Pari. On the vid-screen was a period drama they liked to watch together. He kissed the tops of both their heads. Pari hopped off her seat and rounded the couch.

"You smell funny," she said in her little voice. The small bells at the end of her pigtails jingled with every step.

"That's the salt water," Reist said. "I work at the beach, after all." That was still a weird thing to say. *I work here* made him sound so grownup. Accomplished, even.

"We always smell like that after the beach," she said, following him to his room.

"Pari, leave your brother be," their mom said from the couch.

"But he doesn't usually smell like the beach when he comes home," Pari called back.

Reist dropped his bag on the bed. "That's because I went in the water, little wing."

"You went for a swim? Good for you," their mom said. "I bet it was lovely out today."

"I went in because a kid needed my help," Reist said, stepping into the bathroom and shutting the door between him and the rest of the house.

His mom said nothing for a moment before calling out, "What?!"

Chapter 2

MORNINGS DID NOTHING to stimulate Reist. If it were up to him, he would still be in bed. But muscle memory made him vertical. He dressed, ate, and flowed with his classmates into school. Every morning, he split the school day up in his mind. Either in half, right at lunch, or further into fives based on each module. There never was a point where Reist felt fully conscious. He needed to be awake and aware, and he might as well have never used his eyes before.

First mod was Citizenship. He and his classmates pulled out the resumes they were to perfect and submit before the end of the semester. It was their last year of higher education, which meant internships and jobs should come shortly after graduation. With a diploma in hand, their resumes would be a formality. Extracurriculars, part-time jobs, and volunteer work are all done to be perceived as a well-rounded and dedicated worker.

Contributing to society was fine, Reist conceded; what was the alternative? He glanced at his classmates' resumes. Some looked better than his, but others looked similar enough to keep any anxiety down. As long as he was not falling behind, he could keep the peace in his mind by being average.

Instructor Rotkva pulled up the vid screen with a resume sample. "Right, everyone, this is a copy of a resume for Cannonics. You might have heard their name in the news..." Tired eyes scanned over bored faces. "No? They're reestablishing colonies on the Efferus moons, and the discarded pieces of the main planet...still nothing?"

No one said anything. Some didn't even look at the teacher.

With an annoyed sigh, Instructor Rotkva continued, "This person was accepted into a logistics role, and I want you to compare yours with this one. See how they broke this section off, keeping it short but concise? Look at the extracurriculars here. This part is important because each workplace will value different organizations. Debate is the classic choice for the legal offices. Speaking any of the Zentharan dialects can give you a leg-up in the shipping business. Their economy is finally catching up to us. Working with them wouldn't be such a bad idea. But, anyway," he said, flipping to the next slide. "So long as you can argue the relevance of whatever one you do, the sky's the limit."

In Reist's work folder, he kept the most recent copies of his parents' resumes, next to his own. They thought it would help, but he couldn't tell them it made the entire thing more daunting. The rational side of his brain knew it was because they had been in the workforce since they were his age. More life experience means more to put down, obviously. But the rational side was nowhere near as loud as the other part, the one that shouted he had failed before he realized where he was.

Reist shook the anxiety away—knowing it would be back to threaten him for not being awake and aware—and took notes. But he never used them. When studying for tests, he could glance over at them and vaguely remember what he was talking about, but not often. Memorizing facts and dates and names only did so much. Most of the exams he passed because he had recognized patterns in how they had been written.

The bell pierced his daze, and Reist gathered up his things and left the classroom. Second mod was mathematics, and his locker was on the way. A bunch of teens crammed into the hallway, and Reist walked his usual route. He reached for his lock to twist the dial when it happened.

A force rammed into his back. His face collided with the cold metal of the locker door. White hot pain splintered out from his nose to cheek and forehead. Anger shot through his arms. He shouted, spinning to face whoever pushed him and punch them.

There was only the regular stream of students, all coming and going from lockers and classrooms. No one was close enough to Reist to give the impression they might have done it. He looked around for anyone acting suspiciously. And his eyes focused on one. The back of a girl's head. Auburn hair, tied back, rushing away from him.

That was not someone late to their next module. The color stood out to Reist. The girl from the beach. What was her name? "Eira," he said, glaring at the back of her head as it vanished into the sea of students. He shook his head and went back to his locker. Third mod was next to second mod. Reist would need to grab the textbook for that class, too.

WHEN THE LAST BELL rang, and the entire school was flooding out the doors after fifth mod, Eira stayed behind. One of her classmates, Adrianna, had mentioned a couple of people getting together at the library to go over their resumes. The glass door swished open and Eira went straight for the middle table where other students had already sat down, resumes out and pens held aloft. Adrianna turned her blonde head and greeted her by pulling out a chair next to her.

"Hey." Eira gave a cursory greeting to the table.

"Hey, yourself," said a familiar voice.

She looked up and tried not to roll her eyes. "Hey, Thomos. Thought you'd be at swim practice."

"Switching it up this semester," he said with the annoying smirk he always had. Like everything was an inside joke. It never was, but someone else usually laughed along with him. Usually out of nervousness, which gave him another thing to laugh at. He had never admitted to this. Eira doubted he had the brains to think of it, but she had seen him do it enough times. "It's important to vary the resume, right? What sport are you looking to do this time?"

"Haven't decided yet. I'm still working with the lifeguards." Eira kept her voice light, cheery, and friendly. Tones and inflections painted words in specific lights. If Mr. Everything-Is-a-Joke didn't notice how much she never wanted to see him again, there was no joke.

"Oh, that's a good one," he said. "I should sign up for that. The guidance officer said some part time work would really fill out the rest of it."

"My uncle lets me work at his office after school," Adrianna said. "Inventory supervisor. A lot of admin work, but I think I'm good at it."

"I'm not all that interested in what I'm good at," Eira said. "If I'm good at it, where's the fun? I want something I suck at, so I can get better at it."

"You should do pole vaulting with me, then," Thomos insisted. "Get some upper body strength to balance out those legs of yours." Eira glared, while everyone else laughed politely. Thomos waved his hands and insisted it was a joke that everyone should relax and enjoy his wit.

"Hey, that's a *really* good idea, actually!" Eira responded, trying to control that balance in her tone so as not to sound angry or sarcastic. Keep them guessing. "Let's go do that, actually! When's the sign-up deadline?"

The stupid smirk had erupted into a beaming grin. "Uh, I don't know, but I'll find out. I think it's tomorrow morning?"

"Ah, that's perfect. Good looking out, sweetie." Eira bit back the urge to gag. Pet names made her gag. But if one made fun of him, it was alright.

They spent the next hour debating over fonts and formats, bickering about how to keep each one from looking too much like another. And argued about how certain words worked better without making the entire thing look ridiculous. Every passing minute, the discussion grew hotter and more animated. Eira kept peeking at the librarian, who occasionally glanced up from her computer, glaring over the rims of her glasses.

"I think that's my parents calling," Eira said, backing out of her chair and leaving before the table got too loud. She would need letters of recommendation at the end of this, and the librarian had several certificates at the end of her name, which would carry more weight than some teachers. She would do anything to stand out.

Her device had buzzed for real on her bike ride home. Eira pulled into her garage and checked it. Thomos had texted her. It read: *Yeah, the deadline is tomorrow by lunch time.*

She rolled her eyes. "I thought I blocked you..." she muttered to herself. She texted back, *Great!* and left it at that.

AS IF STUCK IN A SUSPENDED moment in time, Eira's father was on the couch, drinking and hate-watching the news. The camera panned over a group of men. Most looked like they were in their twenties and wearing hand-me-down clothes covered in grime and dirt. Each had a red bandana around their neck or tied to their forehead. They glared at the camera.

"Why we ever let those fucking Efferans come here," he said, "I'll never know."

"Language!" her mother hissed to him, before looking to Eira with concern.

"Oh, let the man say what he wants," Nana called from her room. "Better to be blunt than coy, I say."

Eira poked her head in the doorway. "Hey, Nana."

"*There's* my girl," she said, putting her book down on her lap. "How was your day, darling?"

"Uneventful. Just trying to figure out another club to join for the resume."

"I thought they weren't due for a while?" Nana asked.

"Not till the end of the semester, but a lot of us are workshopping them now-"

"To not worry about later, yes. It was the same with your father. They weren't really a thing when I was growing up. All we needed was a handshake from a friend of our father or an uncle's drinking buddy and that was enough." Her eyes lit up at a fresh thought. "Oh! What about archery? They still have that club, don't they?"

"Huh. Yeah, they do." Eira thought for a moment. "And there's the festival coming up too. Another thing to add to the resume to make me stand out. At worst, its participation in a regional event. At best, placing."

"Could be your own Princess Lucienne. Live the *Ravenguard* dream."

"I wish you wouldn't encourage her to read something so low brow," Eira's mother said. Eira and Nana both ignored her.

"That's a bonus, yes." She moved in to hug Nana. Habit made her check Nana's PICC again. It had the sterile new-plastic smell. Their doctor must've made a house call earlier. "Thanks for the suggestion. I'm going to see when I can sign up."

THE FINAL SIGNUP FOR the archery club was the same as every other team that season: the following day after lunch. This gave every student a chance to join at the last minute. Eira stepped up to the table and gave a polite smile to the coach. He slipped the signup sheet forward, not looking up from the news story on his tablet. Eira accepted the sheet and scanned the names. No Thomos, but she recognized a few names from class. One stood out the most. Mixed in the middle was Reist Adeio. *Trying to hide?* she thought.

Images of the beach, rushing through the soft and hot sand, the salty smell of the ocean that sticks to your skin for hours, all flashed through her mind. Her stomach twisted at the sight of his name. He had not hesitated. She had, and still didn't know if the boy had been too far out. Another chance to beat him presented itself to Eira on a sheet of paper. And no one needed to be in danger this time.

Eira signed her name and had a pep in her step until the last bell that afternoon. She gathered the textbooks for that night's homework and rode her bike to the beach. Depending on when tryouts and practice would be, she would have to quit or at least scale back her hours.

Her device buzzed when she parked her bike by the lifeguard locker room. The holographic wrist band expanded and glowed orange. Eira opened her inbox. Thomos had texted, *Hey, you sign up?* She rolled her eyes and texted back, *Sure did!* and left it at that.

She changed into the lifeguard one piece and kicked through the soft, black sand to her station, backpack on her shoulder. Reist was already at his spot, applying sunscreen. He glanced over, offered a nod and little else. That was fine by her. This was not the contest anymore, archery would be.

THERE WAS A CALENDAR in Reist's day planner. In between assignments, he tried to map out how the rest of the semester would go. He had signed up for archery club and pole vaulting. Reist's dad had done pole vaulting when he was in hi-ed and had broken a couple of records in his time. That was thirty years ago, and someone else had broken his records since then, but it still appealed to Reist to try.

Archery was his other option because there was a unique skill that Reist saw in the films he loved as a child. All the famous characters who shot arrows always had some sixth sense or special power that made them deadly accurate. The magic required to accomplish it was just secretly hidden away in their minds throughout the day. It was fascinating, and he fantasized about acquiring a hidden magic for himself and, maybe, winning first place.

Maybe he could go beyond Regionals and into InterPlanetary. He imagined what it would be like to climb on that transport and see canyons and mountain ranges across Zenthara or watch the fragmented chunks of Efferus ringing around the broken planet. Anywhere other than Corvus was fine by him. No matter how big the city of Urbis was, or the neighboring districts, they all ended at the Great Ocean, taking up most of Corvus's surface. So many more interesting places to go, and he had to be interesting enough to be worthy of seeing them. Maybe archery could get him there.

It was a new dream. No telling if he would stick it out or if he would have fun. That was a problem for the future, he decided. All the same, the excitement stirring in his chest when he had signed his name for archery club turned to a solid lump and dropped into his stomach the morning of the first practice.

He contemplated not showing up. *That's something people do, right?* he had thought. *What are they going to do? Track me down and drag me to the field?* Pole vaulting would've been safer, wouldn't it? His dad would be so excited and Reist would need that boost if he wasn't good at it. Everything could go according to plan that way. Archery didn't offer that security.

As the school day continued through, the lump rumbled, skating up and down his insides. The last bell rang, and Reist showed up after all. A small trickle of students flowed to the field after changing into loose clothes. Waiting in the center of the field were the coaches. Two were setting up targets and one stood by a table, hovering at waist height, with several bows laid side by side. No arrows in sight, but Reist suspected they were in the padlocked footlocker behind the coaches.

Students clumped into smaller groups; friends and classmates staying together. Reist gravitated towards Pressin, a classmate from his first mod. They gave each other a nod and crossed their arms in silence, waiting for the coaches to address them. A flicker of auburn hair appeared at Reist's shoulder. He looked down, and the lump in his stomach vanished. Eira gazed up at him. He could not identify what it was behind her eye: a threat, an invitation for a fight to the death, or a friendly greeting. He said nothing to her and looked back at the coaches. She copied him.

The first half of the session was about general safety and what to do if someone got hurt. There were several potentialities, and the coaches went through each one. And the second half of the session focused on familiarity. They passed the bows around, without arrows, for each student to feel the weight and the tautness of the string.

One by one, each student took a single arrow and shot. Reist grimaced at how bad his aim was. He meant for the center, but had hit the outer ring on the upper right side. Eira, as well as a few others, barely got the arrow to the target. When she had pulled the arrow back, and the feathery bit (the 'fletching' the coaches had called it) to her cheek, Reist stared. It seemed so soft. Eira loosed the arrow, and the string knocked a strand of hair to hang loosely at the corner of her eye. She turned to pass the bow off to the next person and met Reist's stare. Neither blinked as she walked back to his side.

This was a lesson in strength training, the coaches had said, finishing it with, "See you again tomorrow for the real session."

REIST AND EIRA DIDN'T say a word to each other. Not in the halls, where Reist had looked over his shoulder to catch her shoving him again. Not at the beach for their lifeguard duties. Not at archery practice.

On the morning of the 'real first practice', Reist was at his locker. He scanned the hall one last time before kneeling to get his books. The hall was just as packed as it always was. A pair of shoes came into view. Reist looked up. Pressin from first mod. "Hey, man," he said. "Are you going to the session after school?"

"Yeah, I think I am," Reist said, grabbing the next set of books he needed before lunch.

"I don't know if I am or not." Pressin leaned against the locker. "Wasn't really what I was expecting, ya know?"

"I get it. But first time, I guess? Gotta familiarize us with it." Reist did not know what he was talking about and knew it. But it sounded reasonable, like something an adult would have said. This time next year, he will officially be an adult and start a job like an adult. Might as well sound like one.

A force came at Reist's back, shoving his face into the locker. It was hard enough that his cheek scraped along the door latch. The slight but stinging pain shot up to his eye. Reist pushed himself out and shot to his feet, a single bead of blood forming along the bottom curve of his right cheekbone.

Pressin had his hands up. "Wasn't me." He pointed behind Reist. Spinning on the spot, Reist just barely made out the auburn hair vanishing into the crowd.

"Are you okay?" Pressin asked. "That looked like it hurt."

"Yeah. Yeah, I'm fine." Reist's voice had no emotion behind it, and his eyes darkened.

"Wasn't that-" Pressin began.

"Yeah."

"What in the hells is her problem?" Pressin asked. "I've never seen anyone do that before."

Reist rolled his eyes and answered with a grunt, grabbing his books. "Yeah," he said. "I'll be at archery today."

"HEY, HOLD UP!" THOMOS snaked through their classmates, rushing to keep up with Eira in the hall.

She didn't slow down, never did. The faster she can get through the halls, the better she was. "Hey, *keep* up," she said without looking back.

"Who was that guy? Was he bothering you?"

"None of your business." She sidestepped through a throng of students a few years younger than her. Sometimes that annoyed her, other times it was a challenge to slide past without them noticing.

"I didn't see you at pole vaulting yesterday."

"Could be because I didn't sign up for it." She still did not look at him. No matter how fast she tried to slide through the other students, he was still there at her ear. She opened her locker and kneeled to swap the textbooks from her bag.

"What? Why? You said you would." Thomos leaned against the locker next to Eira's, looming over her.

"And I changed my mind." She stood back up, keeping her eyes forward, and ignoring how she was a full head shorter than him. His shoulders blanketed her in shadow. "I've got practice. And I bet you do, too."

"What team are you on?" He insisted after her.

"Not pole vaulting."

He didn't let up until she stopped him at the girl's locker room. A teacher was nearby, watching with a suspicious eye. Thomos walked away, grumbling under his breath.

ONCE SHE CHANGED, EIRA slipped out the side door, facing the field. She rushed to the already formed procession of teammates, making their way to the practice field. No one paid her any mind, except for one person, glaring at her from further down the line.

Eira rolled her eyes at Reist's 'angry face' and kept moving, not realizing how fast she rushed past, until she arrived first at the coaches' table. Two coaches greeted her and the others, while the third was setting up the targets on the far side of the field.

The coaches began the safety lesson the same as the day before, and they were halfway through before Eira realized Reist was directly behind her. He was just as tall as Thomos, and she felt the breath from his nostrils going down the back of her hair.

It could be someone else, she thought to herself. But, no. She did not know all of her new teammates, but did a tally in her mind of everyone's estimated heights. And none of the taller ones would stand this close to her. And if it was Thomos rushing over, the coaches would have said something.

"Right," the head coach said, "we don't have a target and bow for everyone, so split up into pairs and we'll get started."

As everyone moved, it would have been the perfect time for Reist to shove her. Eira stepped with the rest of her team, daring him to do it. *Shove me*, she thought, *and I'll win.*

But it didn't come.

Everyone found a partner and shared the bow. Eira searched for someone standing alone, but Reist was still at her back, silently ushering her forward in line for a bow. The coach handed a bow to each pair, and Eira reached out to accept it. Reist took it and kept them moving to their target. Somehow, during all of this, he did not speak, look at, or even acknowledge her. *Just DO something already,* she thought. But he refused.

A coach came by with a quiver of arrows, announced the area was hot, and had them fire. Reist drew the arrow, aimed, and fired. He hit the bottom left corner of the outermost ring.

"Wow," Eira said, with a mocking musing behind her voice. "You *suck* at this."

"Said the one who can't hit the target." He handed her the bow. "Your turn."

They met glares, and Eira chewed her lip, accepting the bow. She grabbed an arrow and peeked over her shoulder. "Stop standing behind me."

"Shut up and shoot." Reist crossed his arms.

She struggled to draw the arrow. Her arm shook when she pulled the nock to her cheek. It had been easier to hide it yesterday. She cursed her stupid arms for embarrassing her.

"Wow," Reist muttered so only she could hear. "You *suck* at this. Maybe they have one of those kid bows. The ones with the suction cup arrows. That seems more your speed."

Eira pulled the nock back further and released. With a forceful and satisfying *frumph,* the arrow shot into the direct center of the target. She let out a small shrill of triumph. The nearest coach clapped for a moment and others on the team gave words of encouragement. She spun around to gloat, but Reist spoke first. "Bet you can't do it three times in a row."

"You haven't even done it once." She gave him the bow.

Reist took it, making sure not to yank it from her grasp. If she saw he was upset, then he lost. He stood back on the firing line and took in the scene this time, analyzing.

Looking at his forward foot, Reist counted the paces between him and the target. He tugged at the bowstring and tried to calculate how taut it was. *What am I doing?* he thought to himself, admitting he knew nothing about what he was trying to calculate. He wasn't even good at math.

A small breath of wind blew several somersaulting leaves past his gaze. *Hidden magic,* he thought. With a swiftness he didn't know he was capable of, Reist pulled the arrow back and loosed. It flew to the center of the target, planting itself to the right of Eira's.

Before he could turn, Eira said, "Bet you can't do it three times in a row."

Chapter 3

THE DRY SEASON WANED and moved on, and the fishing season was slowly approaching, and with it came the annual series of festivals. Reist was stretching his shoulders and staring at the dark turquois water with hardened determination. He stood in a straight line with competitors from other schools across Urbis. They faced the water, clad in school colors, with a semi-circle of arrows stuck in the ground next to each competitor's firing hand. Each arrow had a color and special marking that matched the competitor's armband. With fingers interlaced, he pushed his palms out and felt the strain on his back. *She* was several feet to his left.

Today was the first festival. The games would go on all day and well into the night, all the events overlapping with each other. The festival kicked off at the school, then went through the factory district before wrapping up at the beach later in the week. Behind the archers, up a small knoll, was the Southern Campus's field; Reist and Eira's school and training field. It was sectioned off to house the other events and smothered in cheers from the bleachers.

Standing atop the knoll to address the gathering crowd, the Southern Campus's archery coach activated his wrist device. A gold holographic box opened, showing the Founders' Festival script. He gave the microphone on his headset a soft tap and began.

"Millenia ago, our people sailed through the darkness of space and found this blue jewel of a world." His voice boomed out of speakers, hovering over the crowd, and louder than the crashing waves and heavy winds. "Making a new life here was hard for our ancestors, but they persevered. Renowned for their archery skills, they combatted the elements. Then, the only game they could grab were fish and birds, represented here."

Sweeping his arm wide, he motioned to the stationary targets stood out of the crystal, sparkling water, twenty meters out. Thick, wooden targets, the size of a person, and painted dark colors. "All competitors will fire at the stationary targets first. Those who score high enough will remain for the moving target portion. This signifies our ancestors adapting to this new world. Its gravity and rotation so different from their home world as they hunted fish. This section is a point system, where a winner will be decided.

"After," the coach said, pointing to a festival official. Dressed in blue and white striped jumpsuit and standing a hundred meters down the shoreline, next to a large, dirt brown crate, "will be the third and final section. Flying targets. Each one is a different size, and each offering a grant for the competitors' trade schools after graduation. This signifies our ancestors' developing skills before they moved inland to conquer the rest of the planet."

A quiet lull went over the crowd before he addressed the competitors. "Archers. Arrrrre yooooou ready?" Deafening cheers sent ripples across the water. Competitors on either side of Reist spun around and cheered back, pounding their chests. Reist turned and saw Pari sitting on Dad's shoulders, waving her little arms wildly. He could barely spot Mom's blonde head bouncing out from between the other onlookers. Reist smiled, and it fell instantly when he faced the targets.

"On my whistle," he continued with agonized slowness, as if he was eating up the tension, "you will fire until you are out of arrows. When that is done, you will run down to the final section. More arrows are waiting for you. Fire until you're out." He raised the whistle to his lips.

Reist flexed his fingers around the bow. His other hand hung limply at his side, as per the rules. He waited. Emotion rumbled down the stillness of the line from Eira. He could almost identify it as elation.

The bow creaked in Eira's tightening grip. For an instance she wondered if it might break apart in her palm. She shoved the thought aside and kept her gaze on the targets; fighting the urge to sneak a peek at Reist. Occasionally shoving in the halls kept him interesting, but he's not taken a swing at her yet. Oh, he had his quips and could push her buttons well enough. But he had not laid a hand on her. Once the games were done, she'd change that. He was still on the pole vaulting team, and they were competing right now. He chose to be here. If that wasn't an invitation for her to continue, nothing was.

The shrill whistle pierced through the cheering and heavy winds. Each archer grabbed their first arrow, aimed, and loosed. Coastal winds blew away most of the arrows, forcing everyone to adapt. Reist pulled the nock to his cheek and loosed. Sharpened tips drilled through the wood in a satisfying, soft *thunk. How would it sound if it went into a person?* He shook the thought away as the targets started moving.

They shimmied up and down, strafing from left to right and back again. Arrows filled the air. Reist found a rhythm; loosed an arrow, reached for another one, and fired again, and again until he was out of shots.

Whichever ones hit did not matter to Eira after she loosed the arrow. When one arrow flew, the only one that mattered was the next. One by one, the other competitors jumped back away from the firing line and ran down the track towards the water. Eira reached for the next arrow. She glanced down, saw she was out, just in time to spot Reist running past her. Eira bolted away from the line, focusing her mind on swinging her arms faster to force her legs to keep up with their momentum. She could barely hear the unlocking clicks of the dirt brown crate as the official tore the lid open.

A rainbow of multicolored mechanical birds erupted into the air like floodgates being yanked free. Some competitors had already found their spots and aimed their bows up. Reist and Eira were neck-and-neck until they broke away to find their marked arrows, stood up out of the grass. Reist could *feel* her on his heels.

Fat mechanical birds flapped erratically among smaller ones. Arrows flew through the cloud of machines, cutting them down. A line formed as each competitor stood away from their designated square and held their bows above their heads. Festival officials came up and down the line, collecting the bows.

Eira handed off hers and waited for Reist. They stood outside of arm's reach and didn't speak. If they acknowledged each other, the magic would fall, and their points wouldn't matter. The wait thickened the air with each second as the officials tallied scores. At final count, in overall points, Reist scored fifth out of the twelve contestants and Eira was sixth. However, Eira scored second in the number of grants received. Reist was fourth.

Officials led the competitors with the top three highest points scored towards the platforms and presented medals. Pressin came in second. Points mattered in the games, not the grants, but Eira disagreed. She would go home with money and could be left alone to enjoy the rest of the games as she saw fit.

The other archers broke away to return their colored vests and gauntlets before scattering into the crowds. Reist's messy brown hair stood out as he was anywhere between five centimeters to a whole meter taller than the others. Eira spotted him walking up the knoll, back towards the field and bleachers with, who she assumed was, his parents. He hoisted his little sister onto his hip, her little arms around his neck.

"Hey!" Eira called out as she ran up. "Good shooting."

Reist squinted suspiciously. "Yeah," he said, half-heartedly. "Thanks. You too." His voice came out more fully with the last two. "Oh, Mom, Dad, this is my teammate, Eira."

They all shook hands. His mom was the friendliest. "And you did rather well yourself, I saw," she said to Eira.

"Oh, I just did what I could. It's hard work keeping up with your son. He's very good."

...*what are you doing?* he thought, still looking at her. Pari put her mouth next to Reist's ear and muffled something. "Huh?" he asked.

"I'm hungry," she said.

"I know that meat vendor is calling my name," his dad said.

"Can you get me something too, honey?" his mom asked, motioning back to the shoreline. "I wanted to see the water skaters."

"I kinda wanted to see the pole vaulters, but I think their segment just finished."

"Sorry, Dad," Reist said.

His father waved away his apology. "I saw what was important. I'm good."

Reist gently lowered Pari to the ground. "I think the coach wanted to see us after the event. So, meet up with you guys later?" He ruffled his sister's hair.

"It was lovely meeting you, Eira," his mom said. "And good job again."

"Thank you, Mrs. Adeio," Eira said with a wide and friendly smile, which dropped as soon as the adults were gone. "Coaches?" she asked Reist. "Really?"

"'Oh, I'm just trying to keep up with your son,'" Reist said in a high-pitched voice. "Really?" He gave her a lingering look before striding away.

Eira rushed over, kicked the back of his leg, and then ran ahead, stopping a few steps away. He dropped to one knee for a moment before glaring at her, obviously biting back something unbecoming, like a swear word. *Say it, you coward.* She stood her ground when he closed the distance with heavy steps. People near them in the crowd turned. Eira knew what judging eyes felt like, but didn't care. *Say it for everyone to hear.*

There was a pleasant minty flavor that carried from his breath. "What," he panted, "do you want?" In the last few syllables, a growl rippled through his throat. Eira eyed his neck and bit back a gasp.

Her eyes remained vacant, and she shrugged. The frustration pushed its way through his shoulders, forcing him to step back and look around, as if the answer was bouncing around them that very instant. They made her bite her lip to keep from giggling. It became harder when he swore under his breath, audible enough for her and no one else, "For fuck's sake..." None of their peers ever swore. It was too low-society for their hi-ed institution.

That was enough of a response to satisfy her for now. Eira shoved his shoulder, doing it lightly and not hurt anymore of his precious manly feelings, "C'mon, I'll buy you a kebab. Your dad going on about the meat vendor got me hungry."

He answered with a stern and quiet acceptance, almost to show that he would like a kebab but wouldn't be happy about it. The meat stands wafted an aroma around him. Reist had skipped breakfast and was starving. They stood silently in line. His dad and sister were nowhere to be seen; either at a different vendor or had already gone to meet his mom.

Eira ordered and handed Reist the warm, densely packed wrap. As if to say, *See? I can be nice.* The closest event to them was the javelin throwers, and they wandered there to eat. The event had more rules than archery. "How did we miss this?" Eira asked between bites.

Reist shrugged. "Dunno. Think I'd worry about popping my shoulder out of place."

"Big baby. Wait. Are there weight classes in this?"

"Seems that way. See the color coding? Purple ones for the girls, and blue ones for the guys. Girls' ones look smaller."

"Shouldn't matter," she said flatly. "If you're not strong enough to throw a full-sized javelin, then get stronger."

Chewing thoughtfully, Reist looked Eira up and down, as if seeing her clearly for the first time. He looked back at the competitors with unfocused eyes and finally nodded. Pointing with his kebab, a line of oil slithering down his knuckles, Reist motioned to the men's class, "I don't think there's *that* much of a difference in weight between them."

"Okay, yes, there *is* a difference," she countered, "a small one that doesn't even matter, not in the grand scheme of things, at least. How heavy are they, anyway?"

"I think ten kilograms?"

"Oh, that is pathetic," Eira grimaced. A slow trickle of spicy sauce crawled down her thumb. She licked from base to tip and took another bite.

There was a glint in Reist's eye that vanished in a blink. "Could you throw that..." he double checked the flag markers, "fifteen meters?"

"Shit yeah, I could," Eira said, ignoring the twinge forming in her chest at the swear. A passing official stopped and stared. Eira apologized, and he skulked away, rolling his eyes. "Yes. I bet you I could," Eira repeated.

"I would love to watch the attempt."

"You're doing it with me."

"Fine," he said with an infuriating apathy. She studied his expressionless face and mused which spot would cause the most reaction out of him if punched. Eira saved his cheekbone in her memory and ate her kebab. She was halfway finished with it before she handed him the remains to finish for her. He had finished his and was drinking a fruit cider.

After the event finished, more officials in their white and blue stripes collected the javelins. They deposited them into a small cart, humming with a purring mewl, hovering a meter and a half off the ground. The proctor drove off with them. Eira moved through the crowd, trying to keep the cart in her line of sight. Reist was several steps behind her, walking casually and able to see above the sea of heads.

The cart parked next to the small, single-story, boxy building that was part coaches' office and part sports clinic. That many javelins wouldn't stay there year-round. They had festival markings on them, not school ones. With the day ending, the festival officials were to come by the next day to collect them for the next levels, or so Eira reasoned. She was leaning against the heavy road barrier, one of many in an extended line cordoning off the events from the rest of the world. Reist joined her and followed her gaze.

The coaches were hauling the bundles inside the building. "They'll be locked," Reist said.

"Yup."

"It doesn't need to be them," Reist reasoned. "There are others in there we can use any time."

"Yes, there are." Her voice conveyed no interest in this alternative.

Reist turned to look at her for a moment and turned back to the coaches' office-clinic. "They won't be in there long."

"My guess is they'll be gone by breakfast tomorrow."

"It'll be locked," Reist reminded her.

The grounding, crestfallen realization of reality crept up in the back of Eira's mind. What were they doing? They couldn't expect to steal the keys from a coach or break a window to get in, all for the sake of something stupid. Reist had to have realized this as well. His arm glowed blue with the holographic display of his wristband. He was watching a video.

With an inaudible sigh, Eira turned her gaze away from the coaches' office-clinic and down to her nails. They had been breaking off for the last couple of weeks. Tomorrow her mother will redo them and that was fine. A simple once over wouldn't be so bad, but Eira wanted a new salon. The nail tech she had kicked might still work at their usual place and refuse service. It wasn't Eira's fault; she warned them she didn't like her feet touched, but her mother insisted on the pedicure.

With tired eyes, she looked away from her nails and to whatever Reist was studying so adamantly. It took a moment for her to realize what it was. She straightened and stared at his face. "You're...what?"

Turning his device's screen to face her, as if to confirm her suspicions, "A how-to on lock picking," he stated simply. "I mean, we're still doing this, aren't we?"

Why was she staring at him? This was what she was pushing them towards. The least he could do was come up with a way to make it happen. The easiest way of dealing with people was to go with the flow. True, this was a step more like swimming at full speed ahead of the flow, but it was the same principle. *When faced with a choice*, he heard the quote from one of his favorite shows in his head, *which story would you rather tell: the time you did something interesting, or the time you could've done something interesting?*

He had never picked a lock before, but thought it would be a fun skill to have. There was always some seasoned, older person who had a random array of skills. All those skills, each another source of magic, had to start somewhere, right? Reist could add lock-picking and javelin throwing before sunrise.

She was grinning at him now. This solidified their plans in his mind. Happiness bubbled in his chest and nearly overflowed. Eira yanked his forearm closer to her and rewound it to the beginning of the video. She memorized every frame. "I can get you this stuff," she said when the video ended.

"They're pretty common," he replied. "I could grab them on the way over here."

"I'll get them," she stated, and let go of his arm. His motivation was making this happen. She'd have to contribute *something*. "So, when are we meeting here?"

Reist checked his watch. He knew when the last event was and guessed how long the cleanup would take. They would do well to meet up an hour after that, to be safe. There was a large suburb next to campus. Plenty of secluded areas back there to park. He had taken two of his previous hookups back there. If they needed to run and got separated, they could meet in one of these spots.

"Should I pick you up or do you want to meet here?" he asked.

"Let's meet here," she said. "If you bitch out, I'll still do it." She typed in her number to his device and called herself. "Now you'll get a picture of me proving how much of a bitch you'd be if you don't show." *Too many times. Scale it back, it feels too weird to say.* She could feel eyes on her.

It was never a good thing to hit a girl, no matter the circumstance. Whenever someone was looking to start a fight, one should walk away. These were basic principles Reist learned at a young age and whoever wrote them clearly never met this pain in the ass. After looking at his device, he pictured the home screen displaying a photo of her with a bloody and broken nose. He could wipe her blood on his lips and leave a kiss mark on her forehead.

Reist blinked and shook the image from his mind. *What the hell was that?*

Chapter 4

REIST HAD BEEN WAITING for half an hour. He had misjudged the traffic and had arrived at their meeting spot early. This had once been CEO Row, where the world leaders of Corvus all lived long before the campus was founded. But they had passed on, and their homes had lost value. A few houses in the Row had squatters or the elderly descendants of CEOs of the past still living in the family home.

Not the one Reist was sitting next to. A Community Leaders sign stood in the front yard, marking the house as a subject of historical significance. It hadn't been officiated yet, which meant the side alley between the house and a mess of trees was secluded, isolated, and ignored by everyone at this time of night. Reist was practicing on the lock he bought on the way over. With a pair of metal prods, he fumbled with the lock, feeling around inside for the mechanisms and imagining how they looked compared to the instructions online. It was less intuitive than he would have liked. Or maybe he wasn't as intuitive as he had hoped.

His device chirped. Reist put down the lock and tiny prods. Dull blue came out of his wrist device and wrapped around his forearm. He checked his notifications. It wasn't from Eira. Someone had replied to his post on a resume writing forum. He double checked the messages and confirmed, again, that he sent the correct street corner and time. She had ten more minutes. If she did not show up, he would leave.

Two how-to videos later and a pair of headlights emerged from around a corner. The vehicle slowed to a stop, pulling up behind

Reist's car. On either side of this road were the skeletons of future houses, abandoned and left to rot when the building contract ran out. The dark auburn hair was visible in the moons' light when Eira got out of her car and walked to Reist's passenger door.

"Hey, sorry," she said, seemingly without sarcasm. "I had to help put grandma to bed," she climbed in and pulled out two thin metal prods of her own. "Can I get some practice in?"

"Yeah." He handed over the lock. In the darkness, Reist studied the freckles on Eira's face. She had not...fully registered in his mind until now. Based on what little he knew about her. She was acting odd. Apologizing wasn't in her nature, was it?

Maybe it was, but not without an insult. And since when did she show such childlike wonder on something as frustrating as lock picking? Reist had had struggled with it and only got it open twice. The lock clicked open, and Eira's grin could have illuminated the car. "I did it!"

"Good job." How'd she do that so fast? "Now do it three more times and we'll go."

Welcoming the challenge, Eira closed the lock and restarted. It was soothing for her, holding something new, an embodiment of self-improvement, in her hand. Finding the right pieces to move and the right gears to align was so simple. She welcomed the distraction that kept the tears at bay. Nana was getting worse; she called Eira by her mother's name before calling for Popop. He had passed when Eira was starting pri-ed.

Before getting out of her car—well, her mother's car—Eira had checked her face for any sign she had cried. It was dark, he wouldn't see. The logical side of her brain would tell her there's no shame in crying over a relative's failing health. And yet, another voice questioned why she should mind her grandmother's fading. People die every day, and she knew Reist would repeat this statement in his low and frustrating voice and tone. He must have lost relatives, too.

The lock clicked open, and Eira grinned. She shut it again and the next two tries came more quickly. A light glowed warmly in her chest. Success, no matter how small, was always sweet and satisfying. It was like an obstruction in a stream pushed away for nature to take its course.

"Good job." He handed her a dark mask made of soft fabric and shoved another mask into his pocket as he climbed out.

The houses along the path hid in the looming shadow of the expanding trees. A tangled mess of thick, interwoven branches obscured the second floors. There were no sidewalks or streetlights in their path. The road had an older feel and look to it. It was like the roads in the historic district Reist's grandparents used to frequent during their reenactments. The reenactments were always an underappreciated side of the annual festivals, his grandfather had said. With increasing debate regarding the origins of Corvus and its citizens, some have looked to boycott them altogether. Reist hoped they wouldn't stop. The stories of the ancient star sailors always excited him. When Reist and his dad had built ship models together, his simplistic wonder imagined adventures led by historical figures and a couple he invented to make the boring parts more fun.

"How did you even know about this?" Eira said finally when they arrived at a wrought iron vehicle gate, nearly hidden away under foliage from nearby brush.

"The school buses used to run through here," he said as he put his back to the gate and knelt. "Now the food transports use it, and so do some of the cross-country runners." Eira stepped onto his knee and climbed up onto his shoulders, reaching for the top of the gate. She let out a little yelp in the nearly two-meter free fall from the top of the gate. "You alright?" he asked.

She nodded and studied the gate. "How...how're *you* gonna get over?"

Without a word, Reist took several steps back, away from the gate, and bolted forward. He soared towards the top of the gate, clasped it tight, and threw his hips backward. Using the momentum, he rose to the top and brought his leg over, slid off the top and landed next to Eira. Wiping paint chips and rust off his palms, Reist nodded to her and started walking. If Eira was impressed, she didn't show it. He'd have to do better to impress her.

There was an eerie stillness to the campus at night. To their left was the practice field sitting next to the expansive parking lot, and the gymnasium and main buildings stood beyond. To the right was the primary field and track, where they had competed earlier that night. Wind carried over the ocean on the far side of the field; a ghostly moan reverberated through the metal bleachers.

A small road snaked around the gymnasium, passing another building where Reist's first mod was the previous year and where Eira had anatomy class this year, before leading out to the main road. The coaches' clinic sat across from the gym and behind the first set of bleachers. They pulled down their masks. Reist clung to the shadows of the trees to his right and Eira followed suit. It was dizzying to watch Reist turn on his heel every few steps, turning and looking in every direction. By the third time he did it, they were several meters away from the coaches' office-clinic.

"Hey," Eira hissed, "you look right, and I'll look left. Okay?"

Reist nodded, and they stayed silent until they arrived at the door.

"I wanna try it," Eira hissed as she knelt, putting the lock—and, Reist noted, his crotch—at eye level.

One metal prod slid through the keyhole and Eira angled the second one up, probing and poking. She swore under her breath. It gave Reist an odd combination of disgust and liberation to hear her speak like that. His parents' disapproval of foul talk flickered up the back of his neck and veered to the back of his eyes. It was talk designed by and for the working class and the undesirables. Eira was attending this campus, same as him, so she clearly wasn't either of those.

"Want me to try?" Reist asked after Eira swore again.

"Want me to bite your cock head off?"

"I'll just stand watch."

"*Please.*" The words soaked in sarcasm and fermented in false kindness for several days. "You'd be doing me *such* a service." Another few minutes passed. The air between them thickened with silent anxiety, as if someone was watching them. Reist blinked away the images his brain invented of figures hidden in the bushes or behind trees. Each one looking to skulk out into the moonlight with dead eyes and gaping, rotten mouths.

The lock gave a *clank*. "*Yes!*" Eira stood and pushed the door open, offering Reist to go in first, "Please, *sir*, after you. I insist."

When Reist stepped through without offering a single retort, verbal or otherwise, Eira wanted to punch the back of his head. Manners be damned. She may have to shove him some more. He had responded to that quickly enough.

The javelins were difficult to find. They split up to search the offices, keeping the lights off, and hoped to avoid the attention of festival security guards that might be nearby. "This part of the festival is over," Reist reasoned. "They might not be working tonight."

"They might," Eira countered, "since the city's property is still in here until morning." She rushed through a set of lockers. "Or at least I would think so if it was even here."

"We saw them put it in here." Reist's voice was infuriatingly calm, but it offered a sturdier ground for Eira to walk.

"Well, when you're right, you're right," Eira muttered as she opened the last locker in the corner.

Approximately thirty or forty javelins were upright, tied in bundles of six. Each with the city's mark, a silhouette of a tower and village between a field of white and blue, along the middle portion of its length and the weight of each one stamped near the hilt.

Eira knelt to read the weight and picked out two of the heaviest set. Prying them out was tricky. Each bundle had been padlocked, and she had to maneuver the tips out from the locker to remove them from the rest. Behind her, Reist had already stuffed tiny field flags in his pocket and held a tape measure in his hand. He took one javelin, and they both crept outside, careful to shut the door quietly behind them. The road barriers set up as the cordon around the field were still in place. They slipped through the gap that acted as the entrance for the ticket booth and moved to the closest end of the field.

"How many of those did you get?" Eira brought her javelin down and leaned against it.

"About six?" Reist pulled out the small flags. "Yeah, six total."

"They're all the same color," Eira commented. They were all gold. She took three of them and pushed the tip of her javelin into them; six gold flags and three of them marked by a single and roughly made hole. "Ready?" any ounce of the foul mood Eira had before was gone as she hoisted the weapon onto her shoulder. Elation radiated off her like intoxicating steam.

"Ready," Reist nodded, copying her and dropping the flags to the ground.

"Three," Eira began.

"Two," Reist continued. They both mimicked the positions they saw the throwers using during the event.

"One!" Eira squealed.

Both spears pierced through the air for a glorious moment before the tips angled down and stuck to the ground. Reist swung his arm in a wide wheel, trying to stretch out his shoulder.

"That was, like, really heavy," Eira groaned. She picked up one of each kind of flag and handed Reist the one with the hole.

There was a moment of confusion when Reist took it, and she ran towards her javelin. He sped after her, unable to prevent the smile on his face. They shuffled to a stop where both of their missiles landed and stabbed their flags into the grass. His had gone farther, but Eira said nothing. Instead, she yanked hers out of the ground and ran back to their starting point.

A moment later, Reist was next to her. Both pulled off their masks and shoved them into their back pockets. They spared no time to catch their breath and jettisoned their spears once more. They repeated the process, wide grins never leaving their faces. Eira's second one landed closer to Reist's first, but his second was several centimeters further still.

They returned to their starting point. Reist held out a hand, panting. "Hold on," he said. "Just wait."

Annoyance bubbled through Eira's chest and into her hand, shuddering the javelin in a violent series of shaking, "*Whhhyyyy?*" she asked through gritted teeth.

"Just feel it for a minute," he said in a low voice. He sounded like a fraudulent life coach trying to teach the best way to be happy. The best way to be happy is to win. And he didn't realize he would never be happy if he kept stopping to 'feel it for a minute.'

Feel this, she thought as her fist collided with Reist's jaw. He fell back one step and stared at the ground for a long time. There was a satisfying sense of accomplishment that mixed itself in with a serving of pain and a dash of fear. His jaw was harder than she expected. Most people might've responded by now with shouting. Reist didn't move or utter a word. There was a noticeable pause in his breathing; a deep exhale a moment after the punch before it leveled out.

She pushed the fear aside, or she tried to. *Don't let him see you nervous.* "Do you wanna just feel *that* for a minute, honey?" Eira asked, her sarcasm more like silk than sandpaper this time.

Finally, Reist turned to face her. His eyes shook for a moment, not like someone about to cry. No tears; this was something new. It was almost as if there was something growling behind his eyes.

"Ready?" he asked, his voice void of emotions.

She nodded, and they hoisted the javelins up, and moving as one, sent their spears flying. There was no waiting for them to land; both teens ran forward. Spears stood upright in the grass; flags stuck next to the tips. Reist handed Eira the end of the tape measure.

Holding the plastic casing in one hand, he half jogged back to the starting point, the mechanical whirring sound getting softer with each step. He stopped and Eira knelt, placing her end next to the farthest flag, ignoring how much farther he was by comparison. He was a male, she hated to admit, so he was naturally stronger. The challenge was to see if she could do fifteen meters.

"What is it?" she called out to him.

"Thirteen point seven."

There was a moment's pause as she processed the information. Gritting her teeth, she grabbed a javelin in each hand and ran to him. Chucking them both to the ground, she yanked the tape measure from his hand and saw there, '13.75m' glaring back up at her.

"One more time," she demanded.

"Why?" Reist was infuriatingly indifferent. He might as well have been taunting her. "Do you think you'll get an extra meter and a quarter in one go?"

"I can at least get farther than you in one more go," she retorted.

It was almost satisfying watching Eira show a small level of desperation. If it weren't for the punch, he might not have cared, but her demand to prove herself his better beckoned Reist's interest to return. He smiled, and he leaned over to pick up both javelins. "Alright."

Eira snatched the spear from his grip and stepped back to her point. Reist stood next to her. Once the spears struck the ground again, Eira ran forward and Reist knelt to hold the tape measure. Her spear had gone farther still, but not by much, maybe eight centimeters. Reist's landed a millimeter behind his farthest flag. She pulled the end of the tape measure to align with her spear and crawled to the side when she heard the locking sound again.

Both of their spears were close. She pressed her face close to the ground and peered past hers to his. Whose was farther? There was maybe a hair's difference.

"Hey!" shouted a voice behind them.

She sat back on her feet and saw a hover cart with "Festival Security" printed in blue and white lettering, bumping into the barrier cordon beyond the track encircling the field. Reist was waving at her to hurry, pulling his mask back on. She shoved hers on as the two guards left their cart and yelled at them.

"Hey! Stop!" Reist was already at the weight room building by the time Eira's feet hit the soft rubber of the track. One guard was rushing to meet her and the other backed up the cart, obviously unable to move it through the small gap to catch Reist. "STOP!" the guard shouted, reaching for her.

Eira halted suddenly, stopping short of the guard's outstretched hands. She ducked and dove under his grasp and shot behind him, up the grass hill to the track entrance. Leaping over the cordon with the concrete coquina dug sharply into her palm, Eira ran. The road was in view. She was almost there. The low humming of the hover cart came closer, and hopelessness smothered her.

She was caught. Breaking into campus after hours. What was she thinking? After all, she had worked towards getting her pick of internships the following year, she lost to stupidity. *Nana's gonna hate me*, she thought. It wasn't Reist's fault. She should have said no. If he was smart, he'd be long gone. She wasn't smart.

But neither was he. Eira halted, nearly falling over, when the hover cart came roaring towards her. Reist was behind the wheel, flapping a hand at her, demanding she hop on. She rushed to him, the guard barely grabbing her shirt. Eira chucked herself onto the transport, into the nearest seat, and hit her head on an armrest. Reist did a rude hand gesture to the guard, and sped away, "Fuck confederali! Ribellio till I die, ye fuck!" Behind them, Eira's guard ran after them and gave up once they were several meters away. In the dimly lit shadow of the building, she could discern the second guard lying motionless on the ground.

"When we get to the gate," Reist said, "we gotta be fast. Climb on top, hop over, and run.". The rest of his words blurred in her mind, so she didn't argue.

The gate came into view, still shrouded in shrubbery, fauna, and shadow. Reist sped to it and yanked the emergency brake. Eira fell out of her seat and used it as a step to climb up to the roof and jumped over the gate. She landed at an awkward angle and felt a sharp pain in her left ankle. Reist landed next to her, badly. He stood and hopped on one foot. "Fuck, my fucking ankle," he whispered before leaning his weight forward. "Gotta move."

They didn't take the same route back. Reist pointed the way, and Eira followed. Her eyes jumped to every dark corner between houses. "Over here," Reist whispered, moving silently towards a garbage bin by a nearby driveway. He took his mask off and shoved it in the rancid container. Sweat glistened off his face when he stripped off his gloves. "I'll put these in one further down. You put yours in the one before that. Spread it all out."

"You think that'll work?" Eira's senses were slowly returning, but she was still jumpy.

"I don't know. It feels like the thing to do, I guess." They quietly made their way up the road, avoiding any houses with lights on and sticking to the shadows. Reist tugged at his black jacket. "Maybe it's too much if we ditch our coats, too. If we keep going, we should be gone before the cops show up."

Terror shot back up Eira's spine, splintering out, threatening to shatter her. "You think they'll call the cops?" Her gloves fell out of her numb fingers into a trash bin.

"Maybe?" He led them further down the road, making a left turn. "If they've called them already, I don't know how long they'll take to get here. But I'm hoping by the time they realize we came back here, we'll be gone."

They walked in silence for a time. "What did you yell?" Eira said finally.

"Huh? Oh," he brought his mind back to now, "that was some broken Efferan. Or my attempt at the accent, at least. I saw some gang tags for Ribellios on the drive in. I think it's their word for soldier. This way, if those guys call it in, that's where the cops will look."

Eira stared at him. Her expression was hard to make out in the dark.

"What?" he asked.

"Nothing, I just...I never heard you swear before. Well, not shout it at least," she said playfully, trying to smother her terror barely below the surface. "I didn't know you had it in you."

"I had to make it believable," he shrugged.

"Yeah, and what did you do to the other guard? Was he okay?"

"He should be fine...I think."

Reist recounted his side of the story. When he had made it past the student gym, he ran across the street and immediately ducked right. The hover carts couldn't turn easily. He had taken advantage of this by circling around the back of the cart and had yanked the guard out of the driver's seat. The man's head had landed on the curb.

"Oh," Eira said to herself. Their meeting spot was just ahead of them. "Oh, no..."

"I mean, he was able to sit up on his own...I think." Panic rose in Reist's throat, hearing her reaction. The realization dawning on them now their nerves were settling.

"Depending on how hurt he is," Eira began, "there's going to be some major blowback."

The metal of the car door was cold against the back of Reist's head as he leaned against it. "I hope my accent was believable enough."

Low rumbling reverberated through the silent darkness. Dim light illuminated the street, growing brighter and brighter as the rumbling came louder and louder. Reist and Eira both grabbed each other and dropped to the ground as two police cruisers flew past the intersection near where they had parked. Across the street from their cars, the abandoned and rotting homes, half-built and never finished, bore over them. The police didn't know what they did, but the ghosts won't forget it.

The cruisers grew quieter, likely turning into the campus entrance another few kilometers up the road. Loosening her viselike, clawing grip off Reist's shoulder, Eira tried to catch her breath. Reist didn't take his hand off the front of Eira's jacket. Both panting, their eyes met; faces inches from each other. But neither did anything. "Let's just get out of here, okay?" she asked, slowly rising to her feet.

"Yes, please." They separated, went to their cars, and left.

REIST'S PULLED INTO his driveway. His mom's car fit perfectly to his dad's. He had maintained the speed limit all the way home and obeyed every single traffic law. Mom was shorter than Reist, and he did not want her wondering why she was readjusting her seat and mirrors before work the next morning. So, the entire drive to and from the meeting place, he had his knees hunched up in front of the steering wheel and the radio set to an oldies station at a low volume.

He held the keys firm in his palm as he skulked into his backyard, locking the gate behind him, and climbing back into his open bedroom window. The bed creaked softly as he rolled in. Once changed into loose shorts and bare feet, he returned his mother's keys to their home in a bowl on the kitchen counter and climbed back into bed. He messaged Eira to make sure she made it back.

THE DRIVE HOME WAS trickier for Eira. Where Reist's window had the easily identifiable alarm sensor he could manipulate to keep it from going off, Eira's was better hidden. Her best option was through the sliding door on the back patio. It was overlooking the lake behind their house, so she would have to go up the side lawn and down the steep hill before climbing up the rickety wooden supports.

With it being this late in the evening, sunrise a few hours away, many of her neighbors wouldn't notice the car pulling in. She shut the headlights off two houses away from her driveway. Eira struggled to keep quiet when she turned off the engine, climbed out, and shut the door. The fence to her backyard clicked behind her and Eira saw the window to Nana's reading room. It was open. She jumped up and climbed in. The eeriness of the quiet darkness personified by the matriarch's rocking chair in the corner sat next to the bookshelf. Eira shut the window and slipped out the door, keeping the slow and steady.

She returned the key to the hook and slinked upstairs to her room. Eira changed into her nightclothes and laid in bed, staring at the ceiling. Her hands were still shaking. In the morning, she and Reist would know for sure if they got away with it. It was so stupid, but she did it anyway and he was there all the time. He could have left her to take the fall. Maybe he stayed to get her because he thought she'd implicate him. If that was true, she'd hit him the next time they're together for thinking that.

A dozen miles away, Reist was in between stages of sleep. He grabbed his device off the nightstand and returned it, disappointed. She hadn't messaged him. When he heard her voice, it was in the half-formed dream. If he fell back to sleep fast enough, he might just catch her.

Retrospect offered a new perspective. Reist snuck out to go meet with a girl. That should have led to many suggestive situations, but it didn't. He had never snuck out before. He never needed to. The memory of her crouched down, eye level with his belt buckle, made him want to sneak out again. Staring into her eyes made his chest tighten. He thought of asking her out, but she'd find some way to make it difficult.

Eira wasn't thinking about that. She was more concerned with something more long term. What was the real reason Reist came back for her? He had a head start. He was faster and clearly had some sort of contingency in place. With heavy eyes, she pushed the questions back to be saved for the morning.

Chapter 5

ALL THE NEXT MORNING, the news had back-to-back stories focused on the attack on security personnel assigned to the Corvic Festival Subcommittee at the Urbis Higher Education Southern Campus by two individuals believed to be members of the nearby Efferan gang. None of the local chapters took responsibility or made any comment at all. It didn't matter.

Every news station had a reporter in the pressroom of the Urbis governmental center. An empty podium took center screen, awash with silent chatter. Press representatives were gathering their notes, setting up their recording devices, and conducting sound checks. But when CEO Alexander entered, a blanket of silence smothered the room. There was no introduction and no warning. A darker skinned man with a commanding presence and piercing gaze, Alexander strode out in full uniform: black, button down, long sleeve shirt with a gilded name plate above his right breast pocket and above his left were several rows of ribbon, outlined in gold. His black tie had a golden clip; a keen-eyed viewer could make out the logo of the 75th Artillery Battalion of the Corvus Planetary Militia.

The Law Enforcement CEO for the city state of Urbis spoke from the dark wood podium into a bouquet of microphones. "Late last night, I was called into an emergency meeting with the rest of the Urbis CEOs to discuss the attack on security officials from the Festivals Subcommittee at the Hi-Ed Southern Campus. The Corvic Board of Presidents have also been notified."

Reporters erupted with questions, calling the CEO's name. Alexander raised one hand, and another wave of silence fell upon the room.

"The officials have provided their statements. One has been admitted into the hospital with a head injury and will be released later this morning. Though this specific incident was minor, with no apparent damage beyond this official, my officers will be investigating to confirm nothing else was stolen, destroyed, or otherwise damaged.

"However," he continued, "I and the other CEOs of Urbis have recorded a growing number of societal unrest by members of hundreds of Efferan gangs that exist on Corvus. We have sent a memo to the Corvic Board of Presidents informing them that we will be cracking down on these gangs. All citizens who have emigrated from the impoverished and scattered kingdoms of Efferus to the conglomerate city states of Corvus are free to do so, in accordance with the bylaws put in place by the Board of Presidents. And I do not discourage future immigration, so long as our laws are respected."

"Do you believe, Mr. Alexander, this to be the right course of action as an enforcer of the law, or because of your own Efferan heritage, sir?"

All the air left the room. The reporter who spoke stood up, unafraid of the penetrating stare boring down on him from CEO Alexander. "C. Gollon, Urbis Observer, sir. Are you aware of the images of your likeness across the city being graffitied and damaged, marking you as, and I quote, 'Blood Traitor'?"

"I was born here, Mr. Gollon. I am a graduate of Southern Campus, in fact. This incident has affected me personally."

"This is a matter of public record, yes, sir. And I empathize with you." Gollon's arm glowed blue from the hologram interface from his device. He scrolled through his notes. "Your mother was an alumnus from there as well, same as her parents, who paid for your education...and no records of your father." He looked back up at the CEO.

"Is that because, sir, your father's information was purged from your record because of his own Efferan gang affiliations?"

"I beg your pardon, Mr. Gollon?" Each syllable fermented in rage.

"Javelins were found on the field. Official festival ones. Did you not place in javelin throwing during your hi-ed days, sir? Odd coincidence."

The newsfeed broke away from CEO Alexander to footage of police handcuffing and chasing after people dressed in unkempt street clothes. All of them with red bandanas either tied to their foreheads or upper arm.

"Sorry, we had to cut away there," said the newscaster's voice over the footage. "We will keep reporting as more information comes in. The many kings of Efferus have issued statements, and the evening report will expand on that. Stay tuned."

Reist sat back on the couch with a sigh that was heavy with both relief and worry. His dad peered over the kitchen counter. "Alright there, bud?"

"All good, Dad." The lie came so quickly. Each inflection pressed in just the right way to sound truthful. "Just heard about last night and want to see if the festival will keep going or not."

"Oh, I hope so," his dad said. A small puff of flour followed him as he placed the newly formed rolls onto a cooking sheet. "Did you hear from your coach? Maybe there might be a slot for you to compete in pole vaulting?" Optimism wafted around the kitchen, mingling with the flour.

Reist raised his wrist to activate the device and made a point of checking his messages. He had not asked the pole vaulting coach anything, had barely spoken with the man. The device chimed, and Eira's name filled the screen.

"Speaking of..." his dad said hopefully, shutting the oven and cleaning his hands.

"Nah, it's Eira." Reist scrolled through the inbox. "Oh, yeah. There was a mass message. There's a makeup event day after tomorrow for pole vaulting, early afternoon." That made his dad happy. Reist left the couch and ducked into his room, checking Eira's message.

See the news? She asked.

Yeah...all good, I guess?

I guess, Eira said. *Wanna meet up to work on resumes together? I want a set of eyes that isn't a teacher, know what I mean?*

"Change of topic," Reist muttered. "No big deal." He typed back, *Sure. Just not the day after tomorrow. I'm competing in the festival then.*

Wait, is there another archery slot I didn't catch?!

Reist paused for a moment. *No, this is for pole vaulting. I skipped out on the first one, but enough people were doubling up on teams. This is a makeup competition.*

Cool. When is it?

He forwarded her the mass message from the coach.

MILES AWAY, EIRA READ the email. It was weird he had not mentioned he was competing, but there had been a lot going on since yesterday. She had tossed and turned all last night and decided sleeping was *not* happening. To make better use of her time, she had set up an online folder and uploaded her resume there. She sent an invitation to Reist's inbox so he could upload his and they could work on it whenever they couldn't meet up.

Her father was on the back porch drinking a whisky with Nana while Cuquas waved away the smoke from the grill. Inside, Eira's mother was following Serva, the housemaid, around the house, correcting her. No one paid attention to the news besides Eira. *For the best*, she decided. Reist's little plan had worked, and no one was looking at the students.

Cuquas put the food onto four plates and shut off the grill. Eira stood to watch him rushing past the couch without looking at her, towards where her mother and Serva disappeared to. The cook cannot speak to the homeowners unless spoken to directly. The servant was the go-between for the homeowners and the other lower servants. If Eira's family had a wider staff outside the servant and the cook, then the responsibility would fall onto the head butler. But her family was only upper middle class, there were only the state issued housekeepers. They had a groundskeeper until a few years ago. Her father had not explained why they fired Giard, or where he was now, but Eira noticed how closely her father was watching the stock market and how frequently he grimaced.

Her mother emerged, followed by Serva and Cuquas, and Eira joined them on the back porch for dinner. Serva took the plates and put them in front of the family. Dinner was ready. That was what Cuquas had rushed to say. Eira rolled her eyes at the decorum and pulled up a chair next to Nana, bumping her knee against Nana's med chair. She eyed the glass cylinders, stood upright below the armrest. The green med gel bubbling ominously before pulsing through the plastic tubing going from the top of the chair, and into Nana's shirt, to her chest.

Before Eira started hi-ed, Nana's med chair, a bulky beast on wheels had whirred angrily, far different from the low humming it is supposed to do. Sputtering, as though several thick pebbles bounced between cogs and gears. It had ended this series of ugly sounds with a *clunk*, like one of those pebbles was stuck in a chain link. Eira had watched with nervousness as these noises began and finished. She and her grandmother had made eye contact; the confused and scared younger eyes had met the frightened elder ones as they slowly flooded with pain.

The medicine had kept Nana's cancer at bay. It needed to be introduced carefully and slowly. The machine's malfunction had caused the chemicals to overflow Nana's body. Scorching poisonous hellfire had spread throughout her body. It stayed in her system a long time before emergency medical came to transfuse her blood and cleanse her organs. On the really bad nights, Eira would climb into bed with her grandmother and read to her.

The favorite one they always came back to was *From Far Away*, a historical fiction saga of a Covic heiress from yesteryear, heavy with child, surviving the bombardment of the monstrous Mier Republic before the Confederacy was founded. There was a complicated romance with a Zentharan smuggler who was unapologetic about his lack of morals. He had no heart of gold but loved children; he was a survivor and always came out the other side looking as dashing as ever. On first reading, Eira favored the dishonorable Mr. Hovmester for his ridiculous nature. As she grew older, there was a heavier focus on what little nuggets of knowledge he could offer about how morals only existed to hold people away from their true potential.

There was a chapter Eira had been certain her mother forbade her to read, but Nana didn't care. That night, Eira had received *the talk* well into the early hours of the morning. Eira had rushed back with new questions for days after. Mrs. Filodoxia-Elder's attitude was always matter-of-fact and carefree, just like the swashbuckling rogue of the pages.

In fact, Nana quoted Hovmester when Eira's mother had approached her about the reading material she was allowing Eira to consume. "Shielding the lass from knowledge will do her no good in the future. Or would you rather she stay a fool forever?"

Mrs. Filodoxia had spluttered for a moment at the implication of her daughter being a fool. Nana had winked at Eira before reminding her daughter-in-law that Eira had been wearing bras and having periods for some time now. Emotions and hormones were ablaze and damn it all to the dirt. She didn't have a lot of time left and why not impart as much experience as she could into a ready to receive mind? When her father came in and got the same reply.

The last part of her argument had struck a chord with Eira before she could bury it back where she could address it later. Did Nana need to make a point about how old she was? It wasn't exactly a secret. People grow old and die. It didn't make sense to bring this up when they could focus on other things. It was Nana's suggestion to approach Reist, not with words, but with fists and a silent challenge.

"If he's worth your time," she had said one night in the dimming twilight of her antique lamp shade, a wedding gift from *her* grandmother, "you'll know. He'll make himself known to you here," she pointed to Eira's head, "and here," she pointed to her heart. She paused for a moment and nodded, admitting as an afterthought, "And somewhere else too, but," she rolled her eyes and finished sarcastically, "we're not supposed to talk about that..." Nana gave her another wink, the same wink she gave at the dinner table now.

The grilled fish was soft enough to cut with a vegetable fork. Eira's parents had stopped correcting her using the wrong utensil. Her father would berate and scold her until the veins in his neck threatened to burst and the most it did was make her Nana giggle. Serva arrived at his side to offer a small glass of whisky off the wooden platter. Eira's mother took a glass of wine.

The smell of their dinner lifted into the air to mix and mingle with the smell of their neighbors' as they sat on their balconies as well. Without looking at her father, Eira knew he was glancing at the Aemulus family to her right. Thomos was over there and had been texting her all day.

"Was talking with his father the other day," her father said. "The boy's got trade schools throwing money at him to attend. He broke your school record of five meters on the pole vault."

Didn't notice the grants I earned, did you? Eira thought, but didn't say. She cut her fish with a soup spoon.

"Not that it matters now," he said. "You chose archery. It is a dying sport that is mostly for show. There's little actual skill in it. I think you should have gone for something else. Maybe should've kept up with rowing. Make Regional."

"You're welcome to best me in a few rounds, Dad," Eira retorted. He waved away her challenge as a waste of time.

"We know that for a fact?" her mother asked. "His scholarships, I mean." When left unchecked, Eira's father would push and push. As a child, Eira had accepted it; not anymore.

"Mm!" He sipped his whisky and gave a low exhale. "Spoke to his father at the last Association meeting." Every homeowner in their development needed to attend a Housing Association meeting once a lunar cycle. "The boy's been part of two sports since year one, never the same ones, mind you. Every season, he's been busy with one group or team or something. He's already got an acceptance from the Tech sector."

Eira's dad looked at her, and she stared at the glistening condensation on her glass. *Here it comes...*

"Wasn't that the place *you* were applying to, honey?"

With a forced smile, she looked up and said, "Uh huh," then returned to her meal. "Serva, could I get a straw for my soup?"

"Do *not* get her a straw for her soup," her mother said sternly.

"Might want to temper your expectation," he said, "with so many like him throwing their names in, they might not notice you."

"That's okay, Dad." The false cheer in her voice *had* to be obvious. These days it was difficult for even her to notice anymore. "If all else fails, I can just go join the Militia. I'm sure they'll find *something* for me to do."

The table grumbled with subdued reactions, carefully held back so as not to be heard by the neighbors. They were several meters away in either direction, but voices carried, especially, over a lake. Her mother gripped her fork with a small gasp. Her father choked on his fish. Nana, however, stifled a surprised and bemused grin that treaded dangerously close to being a cackle. She sipped her water, eyes bouncing between her son, daughter-in-law, and Eira.

The reaction was enough to satisfy Eira's ego, and she allowed herself to enjoy her father's backpedaling, mixed with her mother's carefully masked begging. "No need to be so hasty," he said.

"Really, Eira," her mother added, "you're so smart, there's no need to sell yourself so short."

"Your talents can be much more useful in any of the other sectors," he continued.

It's not like you have anything to brag about me with anyway, Eira thought to herself, remembering how the fieldball shin guards always fell to her ankles when she was a little girl. *You didn't care about my success then. Why now?*

Eira motioned to the living room with the tail end of her fork. "With how many Efferan kings up in arms now? We'll need all hands on deck if they decide they're not too happy with us. Or have you not been watching the news?"

Her father grimaced and waved the matter away as though it were an unpleasant smell. "They're a whole planet away and they can barely present a united front. We've no need to be worried about them."

Nodding, as if to consider this point with great thought and enthusiasm, Eira slowly chewed and swallowed her food. "You're right, Dad. Absolutely right. I should go for Law Enforcement instead."

The response of polite disgust repeated itself. Nana tried to pass a small titter as a cough, but neither of Eira's parents paid her any mind.

Eira shrugged. "There is a *lot* of gang activity around here and it is only going to get worse. If we don't have to worry about a war with another city state, maybe we should be worried about trouble on the streets. Not everyone wants to be part of the Attendance Academies." No one looked at Serva. She had all but vanished from the family's notice, but Eira saw her lift her head slightly.

Motioning to the living room again, Eira continued, "I was just watching a vid the other day about how some refugees believe attending to be beneath them," she continued quickly to prevent her parents from speaking up. They glanced towards Serva but said nothing. "Some of them were kingsmen back on Efferus and were exiled here," Eira said. "Maybe they figure if they can't make it here by legitimate means, being a self-established criminal king sounds better."

"Eira, please," her mother gasped, "think of your grandmother's heart!"

"Yes, dear," Nana replied with such dripping sarcasm, it was unbelievable her parents did not hear it. "I'm so fragile these days."

Chapter 6

ON THE DAY REIST WAS competing in the pole vault make up, festival security was tighter than during the archery competition. On the opening day, it was a free-for-all for parking, and everyone could come and go as they wanted. Now there were vehicle checks upon entering the campus, and pat downs before coming onto the field. There were more festival officials stationed near the entrance to usher the athletes towards their sectors and show the spectators where to sit.

Reist stiffened as he strode towards the security tent with his family. Eira was already waiting there and waved them over. If she can be calm, he could too. He could already hear Eira's voice in his head. *You're only suspicious if you act it. If you pretend you've done nothing wrong, they won't see you.*

A few feet from her was a team of squat, bulky, and stern looking men in the festival blue and white stripes. They were fairer skinned than the bronze and freckled Corvic people, or the more sundried skin of Efferans. *Zentharans?* Reist wondered. Their heads turning from side to side, constantly scanning the crowd.

"Hello, sweetheart," his mom said to Eira before swooping in to hug her. She took in her regular clothes and asked, "Not competing today?"

Eira gave a smile Reist only ever saw her give adults. "No, ma'am." She pointed to him. "Here to show support." She gave Pari the smallest of waves, as if trying not to overwhelm her.

They all stood in line, and Reist was separated when he showed the code the festival officials had emailed him. Both the Zentharans had an earthy smell that wafted up to Reist's nose. The taller one was a head shorter than Reist and led him by the arm to the same student gym he and Eira had run past what felt like ages ago. He couldn't help himself and risked a glance at the spot where the guard had fallen. It was such an unsuspecting, unmarked, unimportant spot. But he could still see the shadow forming there. He went inside to change.

The crowd was smaller than during the festival's main event. Most of Eira's neighborhood threw a block party this time of year, and she had no doubt both her parents were close to passing out on a neighbor's lawn. It was absolutely not because of the news reports of gang activity intensifying after the festival attack. Not at *all*, Eira tried to convince herself.

With the crowd being smaller—maybe a couple hundred people instead of the several thousand from before—there was more room to stretch out on the bleachers. Eira joined Reist's family at one of the higher spots. His father was on the edge of his seat, eyeing the standard and taking a guess at how high the pole was.

"Looks like three meters." He was unimpressed. "The kid can do that, easy."

"I'm sure he can, dear," Reist's mother said. With a note of seasoned and patronizing patience, from what Eira could pick up. They spoke to each other so differently than her parents did. It was both refreshing and foreign.

"I heard one kid set a new record at *five* meters." Reist's father said. He lifted his chin and turned his head from one end of the field to the other. "I wonder if he's here, too."

"It's a makeup day, hon," Reist's mother said. "They need to start somewhere and build up. Let the boy do his thing. He already has some grants stored up from the other day. This is all extra."

"He might need that extra," he said. "Have you seen how much more the IT schools are now?"

"I saw. And that's okay. We can help him if that's what he wants. He might declare a different school, a cheaper one."

"I know..." he said. "I just-"

She patted his leg. "I know."

"Why are we so high up?" Reist's sister, Pari, said in her little voice. She had been fidgeting since they sat down.

"It's better up here, sweetheart," Reist's father said.

"I wanna go down and see him though..." Pari whined.

Before Reist's father could reply, Eira chimed in. "Ya know what? I do too. Mrs. Adeio? May I take Pari down to the track? She won't leave my side."

Reist's mother smiled at them both and nodded towards the fence at the bottom of the bleacher steps. "Go on. Just be loud for our boy."

"Of course," Eira said with a grin. She patted Pari on the shoulder and they rushed down the steps.

At the bottom of the bleachers, they found a gap in the crowd along the fence line. She looked back to make sure Reist's parents could see them and gave his mother a wave. Pari stood on her tiptoes to peer over it. Eira squatted to put her head level with Pari's. "Okay, now where's your brother?"

"I don't know...Everyone looks the same."

"Could it be," Eira made a show of looking across the field and appearing shocked, "that weird-looking guy over there waving at us?"

Pari hopped to look better over the fence. "It is!" She hopped a few more times, throwing her arm over her head, giving everything she had into the wave.

"Here, let's try this," Eira said as she hoisted Pari up and placed her down to sit on the flat wooden cover of the glass fence. "I'm going to stand behind you like this, okay? So you don't fall. How's that?"

"Much better." Pari looked up at her and gave a very serious nod.

"Very good." Eira matched the tone and smiled inwardly. She looked at Reist and heard the soft, metal clicks of a lock being picked, the low whistle of a javelin soaring through the air, and him shouting *"Fuck confederali! Ribellio till I die, ye fuck!"*

Her eyes shot to the security guards pacing up and down the track. The nearest one gave her and Pari a look. A tinge of paranoia mingled with fear. *Did they hear my thoughts?* She shook off the thought. They were getting leered at by security because there was a child sat unsecured on the top of a meter tall fence. But she had someone older watching her and was obviously (at least obvious to Eira anyway) too cute to be scolded.

These new guards were so much more...imposing than the ones from that night. Those other two had been slim and out of shape. If Reist or Eira came toe to toe with these, they absolutely would not have gotten away. Her eyes lingered on the thick, calloused hands and wondered how easily they could crush a windpipe. Or what that would sound like.

Ok, what? she wondered to herself.

"Well, look who's here!" came the cocky and arrogant voice of Thomos, tearing Eira away from her thoughts. "Came to see me break my record again?" Hands on his hips, and chest out, Thomos was trying to embody a proud citizen of excellent stock for everyone watching. He gave a wave to spectators taking pictures. "That's right," he said to them. "That was me." Breaking the record for a five-meter vault made him eligible to compete in Regionals.

"If you already placed, then why bother competing?" Eira asked. Reist was walking towards them from the field. "I can find you some pompoms."

"Some nice blue ones would be really pretty for you," Pari said, far too innocent to be aware of Eira's attempt at a jab. There was a scattering of chuckles around them.

Thomos laughed too. "I'm trying to re-break my record. Whatever my top score is will be what I go to Regionals with."

Reist strode past Thomos as if he wasn't there. He pressed his forehead to Pari's and nuzzled her nose until she giggled. "Hey, you two."

"Hey, yourself." Eira wrapped a hand around Reist's head, glanced at Thomos for a fraction of a moment, and pulled Reist in for a kiss.

It was meant to be a quick peck, but it lingered. Specifically, Reist lingered, pressing further into the kiss. He grabbed her shoulder, holding her still until he pulled away, taking some of her breath with him. This little moment spurred cheers from the surrounding spectators. As well as a look of disgust from Pari and a glare from Thomos. "Good luck," Eira gasped.

"Yeah." Reist said breathlessly. "You too. I mean. Wait. I. Yeah." He took another beat to regain composure. Rustling Pari's hair a little at first, Reist waved to his parents and returned to the field. His gait was slow and confused. He looked back over his shoulder once more before returning to where the other competitors crowded.

Thomos stood in place for another moment, goading Eira to look at him. She refused, finding something far more interesting to look at on the field before bowing her head to chat with Pari.

"Blech," Pari said, sticking her tongue out.

"It's good luck," Eira said with a giggle. "I'm serious."

A festival official with a whistle and a gold holographic pad projecting from his wrist called for all competitors to circle around him. Thomos gave Eira another look before giving up. With a wave to the rest of the spectators, all of whom had already forgotten about him, he turned and jogged to join the circle.

Reist was only half listening to the official. He caught enough to know it was a talk on general safety and all of it he had heard from the coaches at the start of every practice. Between classes, the constant hammering of resume writing, two different sports practices, and part time work at the beach, it was a wonder Reist could keep in any information at all.

He nodded along and said, "Yeah," or "Yes, sir," with the other competitors. Reist had always been good at blending in with the crowd. It was why he did not blink when coming back onto this field after the other night. But he was fighting hard against the temptation to walk directly over the spot where he and Eira had stood. Whoever set up the runway and height for the pole vault event started it directly on the spot where the javelins had landed.

It called to Reist. He refused to look at it, but energy radiated from it, making his heart want to burst from his chest. An image of him and Eira dancing on the spot formed in his mind. Her kiss was still fresh. First, they twirled to a slow ballroom tune, then the scene dimmed, and they were embracing. Sweating and grunting, colliding and swirling through each other, each demanding and refusing submission.

"Any questions?" the official asked. No one said anything. "Good." He read his data pad. "We do this alphabetically. Reist Adeio. You're up. Followed by Thomos Aemulus."

As the rest of the competitors went to the tent at the corner of the field, Reist stayed back to get a better look at Thomos. He did not have any classes with him. The only time Reist had ever seen him was at practice and thought Thomos was the mouthy sort. It had irritated Reist he had the skill to back it up. That went against how Reist saw the world.

Thomos stepped towards the bleachers and extended his hands to accept the applause. Reist's eyes fell on Eira and Pari. They gave Thomos an unimpressed look, but Eira's was more...irritated. Reist pursed his lips. The feel of hers was fading. Eira looked at him and made a face. Turning on his heel, Reist went with the officials to chalk up and collect the pole. All the way, he was thinking about grappling with Eira.

"How high do you want to set it?" an official asked.

"Five meters." Reist tightened the straps on his wrists.

"Um. Are you sure, kid?" the official asked. "That's a Regional record. A pretty new one."

"I know." Reist smacked his palms together to level out the chalk. "Five meters, please."

"Uh, yeah. Alright. You get three tries to make it. You can ask to lower it on the second one if need be." His forearm glowed blue as he spoke into his device and informed the announcer.

Hoisting the pole towards the skies, standing directly where his and her javelins had landed the other night. She, his parents, and Pari pierced through the polite clapping with their whistles and screams. Running over the javelins' landing spot, past the victory and anarchy that came so frighteningly natural to him, Reist heard the nauseating *clack* sound the security guard's head made when it hit the ground. Planting the pole in the box, Reist swung his feet up past his head, turned and...hit the crossbar with his hip.

He bounced off the soft padding as the crossbar reverberated off the side rails and rolled towards the small crevice between the rails and standard. Reist jumped up and rushed back to the front of the runway.

"-at's alright! Give it another go!" came a voice that sounded like Mom from the stands.

Reist accepted the pole from an official and began the approach run again. Flashes of Eira's lips, a bloody nose, and the horrid red eye flipped through the front of his mind. Shoving the pole in the box again, Reist took off, swung up, turned and...felt the heat the crossbar had collected that morning emanating onto his stomach as he cleared it.

A rumbling, guttural shout erupted from Reist's mouth as swung his fists in the air on the way down to the padding. He shot up to his feet, and the applause washed over him. Reist's parents rushed down the steps when he ran to Eira and Pari. Both girls were crushed in the ensuing group hug, but neither complained.

It took an official putting his hand on Reist's shoulder for any of them to know he was there. "All competitors need to be at the tent," he said. Reist nodded and turned to go. But Eira gripped his arm to pull Reist in for another quick kiss before he went.

The Thomos guy was coming out of the tent as Reist came up. "Not enough to take my girl, you need my record, too? That's cute," he said with a laugh.

Reist gave him a confused looked. "Who're you?"

When asked what height he wanted, Thomos asked for five and a half meters. He tried and failed twice before begrudgingly bringing it back down to five meters. He failed again and stormed back to the tent. One corner of the tent had a cool section of shade where Reist stood comfortably with arms crossed. He eyed the crowd as Thomos skulked past him. *Don't know why he's mad. They're still cheering for him.*

One by one, the competitors left the tent and tried their heights. Eira helped Pari down from her perch and motioned to Reist's mother that she was taking Pari to get a snack. Did she or Reist's dad want anything? Mrs. Adeio waved; *No, thank you.*

Leading the girl by the hand, Eira eyed the end of the barrier stanchions on the other side of the fence. The track surrounding the field was for festival officials, security personnel, and some police today. But Eira allowed a lingering glance at the spot where she and Reist were the other night. Learning how to pick a lock from a how-to he had found and deciding on the worst idea they could think of. A shudder went through her chest. They should never have done something so stupid, but they needed to do it again, she decided.

Eira guided Pari through the crowd and spotted Mr. Aemulus, Thomos's father, eating a kabob with her father. As if flowing from the river of memory, she could hear her father complaining about how poorly she did during the fieldball match. *Wait,* she halted this train of thought. *I haven't played fieldball since I was seven.*

Blinking her vision into clarity and banishing that horrid memory to the back storage area of her mind, Eira looked at the two men again. It *was* Mr. Aemulus eating a kebab, but with an older man wearing the blue and white striped jacket of the Festival Subcommittee. Eira slid past them, holding Pari's hand the same way Nana had when she found seven-year-old Eira, hiding behind the bleachers and crying.

Eira shook away the memory again, but Nana's voice came through. *"He's got too much of his father in him, little wing,"* Nana had said to Eira. *"But I'll be damned if he'll break you the same way my late husband broke him. Not you."*

Despite her best efforts, a single tear fell from Eira's eye while she waited in line to order food for herself and Pari.

"I'M SORRY." EIRA WAS rarely ever sorry because there were so few things she ever apologized for. "But I don't think I heard that right."

Reist shrugged and repeated himself. "I'm not going to Regionals."

"And why is that?" Eira had crumbled the food wrapper in her fist, which was propped on her hip in an indignant pose.

Motioning to the dispersing crowd vaguely, Reist said, "One of the officials told me Thomos was going to Regionals because this was the only team he's been on this semester and gets priority."

Reist's dad audibly winced. "They didn't let you two have a tie breaker?" As it stood, both Reist and Thomos had vaulted five meters.

"Didn't even come up."

"Oh, I'm fighting that." Eira looked around the crowd for the nearest official to shout at. *I'll be damned if he breaks you,* the voice in her mind said.

"Don't," Reist said. "I don't want to go to Regionals, anyway."

"What?"

"Honey, can you go bring the car around?" Reist's mom said to his dad. She looked down at Pari next, "Why don't you show me where this yummy looking kebab is?" The three of them faded away into the crowd. Eira did not stop glaring at Reist.

"What do you mean, 'what?'?" he asked.

"If you're good enough, *why* don't you want to go?"

"Because we don't need any extra eyes on us right now," he said under his breath, closing the gap between them.

"They don't know," Eira growled. "Fight this. Being a Regional competitor will look better on your resume. Why are you so set on mediocrity?"

"Don't." His tone felt like a slap. "That Aemulus kid. Is he your ex?"

Eira scoffed at the question. "He wishes." He stared. "Okay, fine, he is. So what?"

"Why did you kiss me in front of him?"

Eira's eyes lost focus. She knew exactly why, but the synapses between brain and mouth were short circuiting. So she shrugged.

"No." Another verbal strike. "Why?"

"I...I wanted to piss him off. Okay? Happy?"

His eyes darkened as Reist leaned in. "Give me a signal next time. I'll join in whatever games you got. But *never* make me a piece on your board. If I am less than you, leave. Got it?"

Eira dared not look away from his shrouded stare; all defiant defenses torn asunder. "I got it."

"Cool." It was like a storm cloud dissipating. Reist sounded almost cheery. "Wanna go piss him off more? If we put an image in his head, we can make him stumble at Regionals."

"You." Eira struggled with her words. "What?"

"I said I'm down for whatever games you got," Reist said with a shrug. "They're fun. Just not in front of Pari, okay?"

Eira blinked twice. "Deal."

Chapter 7

THE MORNING AFTER THE pole vaulting make-up was when the news reports changed planetwide. In the Adeio household, there was an established routine. Their dad prepped everyone's breakfast while their mom went to wake up Pari and Reist. Once Reist was awake, his muscle memory took him the rest of the way. This included keeping Pari from sneaking back to bed while their mom got ready. One morning, she had carefully hidden herself under a pile of clean clothes waiting to be put away.

While the family continued their routine, the news ran on the vid screen in the living area. Every morning, the story of the hour usually centered on the Economic Market with regular wanderings to local stories around Urbis and traffic. But the morning after the festival make-up, the smooth and droning voice of Filip Remas, the lead newscaster for longer than Reist had been alive, began his report with, "Dear viewers, we will run our usual programming through the chyron at the bottom of your screen. For the next hour, on behalf of your safety and all the Corvic citizenry, please listen closely to what we have to say."

The screen cut up the middle. Filip Remas was sharing the screen with footage of a man with pale and sickly skin, a dark gray beard, and hair draped on his shoulders in rows of jeweled braids. His eyepatch was the next noticeable feature, then his crown and fur cape. Long and spindly fingers gripped a podium of dark wood. He shook his forefinger and fist at the crowd. A burning red eye took up the center of his chest.

"The gentleman you see on your screen," Filip Remas said while the footage next to him continued without sound, "is King Arrabbiato, of what remains of the southern continent on Efferus. He is calling for, and I am quoting him, his people to remember their warrior pride, stand up to the 'godless and clanless Toffs', which is an emasculating slur, in charge of Corvus and Zenthara. He is also calling on the other kings across Efferus to establish an embargo on Carburantium."

The right half of the screen stopped showing King Arrabbiato and showed the usual rising black lines on a green background of the Economic Market. Except now, the lines were dropping and turning red.

"Oh, no," their dad said. "No, no, no, no, no."

"Time for school, kids." Their mom rushed to the closet and came out with containers. She grabbed random foods from the fridge and sealed them in.

"It's too early," Pari said, rubbing her eyes. "Why is Dad so mad?"

Reist took the containers from Mom and led his sister by the hand. "This just means we can enjoy a walk now. Isn't that nice?" Their mom mouthed a thanks to him, and he nodded back.

"I guess."

They were halfway to Pari's pri-ed school—it was on the way to Reist's hi-ed—before Pari started again with her questions. "I don't know, little wing," Reist said, walking beside his bike, keeping his gait slow. "Looked like a lot of boring grownup stuff, though."

"The guy on the news was angry, too."

"Yes, he was."

"Was that grown up stuff too?"

No, that was me being stupid, Reist thought. *Break one lock. Crack one head. Say one stupid thing because I didn't want to get in trouble and the planet's economy is supposed to plummet?* "Sure is, little wing."

—————⊬⊬⊢⧵⧵⊬⊬————

PROFESSOR ETAM'S HISTORY class had the midterm presentation topics listed on the presentation board. Students could select the topic, Professor Etam assigned the partners. Reist's partner was Ina, a blonde, hazel eyed girl who kept to her trio of friends near the front left side of the class. Eira got Haemus, a dark-haired boy who had scored second place in the festival quarter finals as a javelin thrower.

Ina had stage fright and held no qualms about telling Reist about this when he planned their presentation. They picked—Reist picked—the ancient mythologies of Efferus and their influence now. Haemus was content to allow Eira to take control of the direction of their assignment. She chose the xenopolitical impact the pre-Confederate arms race between Corvus and Zenthara had on the modern day.

"It took him until the third research session before he made a grab for my ass," Eira said, stretching her back. She was next to Reist, warming up for archery practice. The team made a circle around the coaches.

They began the next stretch. Reist said, "Mine constantly messages her boyfriend and looks like she's going to have a panic attack at the idea of talking in front of the class."

"You should make her give the whole presentation," Eira said. She put a hand on his shoulder, and he on hers, for support while they stretched their quads.

Reist made a fake cough. "Ina? I'm so sorry," his voice was quiet and strained, "But I think I'm coming down with something. You'll have to present for us."

"Do it."

They dropped to sit on the grass for the groin stretch. Today they were starting with sprinting intervals to kick off the rest of their workout. "It's all in the slideshow," he replied, pulling his heels in tight. "All she'd need to do is follow along with the main points."

Everyone stood and filed over to the usual starting point for the first lap. Reist would come to despise the rubbery smell of the track all his life. For Eira, the smell was inconsequential.

There were only nine members left on the archery team. Now that credit counted towards the resumes for this year, there was little point to stay on a team. The coaches split them up into threes and sent each trio down the track. Reist and Eira always made their way to each other when this happened and the unlucky third cycled out.

It was an open secret the coaches took bets on who ran fastest. Reist had longer legs, but Eira had a mind for strategy. At the initial release, Reist ran as fast as he could, but burned himself out by the halfway mark. Eira did the opposite. She found a good pace and wait. When he slowed, she caught him.

Whoever had run slower would have to make it up on the target to win. Neither Reist nor Eira could explain their point system. They never agreed to it, but it made sense enough to them. Practice followed this pattern throughout the first semester, and it showed no signs of slowing into the second. "Whatever you two are doing," the coach said, "keep it up. If the festival started today, you guys could have gotten the championship, easy."

The sun was setting, and most of the team was leaving. Reist and Eira stayed behind to help pack up the equipment. All the hover carts returned to the Festival Committee at the capitol. Eira and Reist followed the coaches from the furthest end of the field to the coaches' building. They both snuck a glance at a specific and innocuous patch on the field and pointedly looked away from each other.

The inside of the coaches building looked different in daylight and far emptier without the extra festival equipment. "Hey, thanks," the coach said, taking the equipment from them. Reist and Eira left and made for the parking lot where they locked up their bicycles.

Before stepping off the sidewalk to cross the parking lot, a chill ran down Reist's spine. He turned, very suddenly, to stare at the side wall of the coaches' building. Eira followed his gaze and an icy wave trickled over her chest. "Irrepresivi" was spray painted onto the surface in deep, blood red. The circle of the p was a deep, angry eye, staring at them in accusation. How dare these two children return to the scene of their crime?

It was not the breaking and entering, or even the assault, they should be ashamed of. Oh, no. It was the false witness they had placed. The eye knew this. Just as the ones who painted it must surely have known as well.

"Come on," Reist whispered, and they turned away from the eye as it threatened to burn through their backs.

There were no witnesses that night, Reist told himself. No one saw their faces. Eira repeated this whenever they talked about it. The gang activity in the neighborhoods surrounding the campus was nothing new. They had unearthed enough research to prove this.

New statistics were coming in all the time, and the gang tags had been increasing since that night. Experts being interviewed on the news and claimed it was the festival that pushed the Efferan gangs over the edge. They were ostracized on a planet that celebrated its own culture and excluded, even mocked, theirs. Of course, they would lash out. It was a cry for attention, simply put.

"Hey," Eira said. "I can hear your brain rattling. Talk to me."

Reist glanced back at the burning red eye. "How much of this would be happening if I didn't do that?"

"You were thinking on your feet," Eira said. "I think it was impressive. And you weren't alone there either, ya know."

"There are riots, now embargos, and the Market was tanking this morning."

Eira brought her hand up to Reist's chin and lifted it. "Hey," she said, "stop that. Urbis is too big a district to care about a non-life threatening injury done to one guy. You didn't kill anyone. And that tag isn't the first one we've seen, right?"

"Right."

"This has been going on for years, babe. It is way bigger than us. Too big for our dumb asses to stumble into causing. A spark to light a fuse, maybe. But this is a mess that's been building."

"One night," Reist mused. "Barely, what? A couple of hours? And we might have turned everything planetwide in a single direction."

"Again. You are overselling our impact *way* too much."

"Yeah, maybe," Reist said, and allowed himself a small grin. "Goals though."

Eira considered and nodded. "Goals though."

Chapter 8

PINCHING THE BRIDGE of his nose, Reist struggled to keep his eyes open. Eira sipped her caff and resumed her flurry of keystrokes. The computers they commandeered at the far corner of the library seemed to be the only source of life. At this time of night, most people would be home, enjoying supper. Datapads stacked at an angle by the keyboards, humming lowly, screens glowing.

"What're you working on...? That's not your resume." Reist asked, blinking away the exhaustion. On Eira's screen, she had bright white documents with empty sections she was filling in.

"Side project for something else. I'll tell you later. What have you got so far?"

"Alright, how about this?" Reist said, scrolling up to the top of the paragraph. "'Individuality has been the key driving force for Efferan culture, with the Monomyth resting at its heart. The earliest sign of this was Kynrathe, the Avatar of Vengeance. Records of the original author remain unknown, but his has been a story to shape the culture's very foundation. Forsaken by his father to be raised and sacrificed by rivaling sister orders, dark magics believed to surround the boy's fate. With his resurrection from beyond the Shroud, Kynrathe ascended to godhood and continues to watch over the people of Efferus from a throne of bones, drinking melted brains and blood-'"

"Is that last part necessary?" she rolled her eyes at him. The bags under her eyes were more pronounced in the monitor's glow. She had been up since yesterday, same as him, each pushing the other to finish everything before the break coming up.

"It's interesting," Reist shrugged.

"It's gratuitous. But if you want to keep it in, that's fine."

Reist returned his attention to the screen, "'The belief of resurrection continues in each of Efferus's other myths,' blah, blah, blah." He scrolled past two other paragraphs. "And... 'Initial death is necessary for deification, as it sheds the human flesh for the new life to be breathed back in. Simple death does not cause this, as the glory surrounding the death would be what gains the gods' attention. The more noble and glorious the end, the more likely the gods take notice—'"

"Do you have to use 'glory' twice there?"

"Well, what's another way of saying 'glory'?"

Rubbing her face in frustration, Eira replied, "Dude, I don't fucking know." Reist didn't flinch at the swear like he used to. Now he felt a light thrill. She shook her head and stared at the words on the screen. "How the hell did we get anywhere with Cibun, man? I mean, it's fine for boats, but it's a wonder we haven't poisoned the oceans with it."

"Told ya it was nasty," Reist nodded, remembering the report he wrote previously on the chemical composition of their planet's original fuel source. "Kybunic's no better."

"But it took us getting to the closest moon to find that shit," Eira shrugged. "Makes for a helluva explosive, though. I had a nice segment over," she said, and scrolled through the paper, "here, about it. 'When Dr. K.S. Andra founded the Kybo Space Station on the moon it was named for, she submitted her findings through published science journals. In them, she theorized the wartime application for them and rued the repercussions her discovery will have brought,' and just like that, we figured out how to make bigger and meaner bombs and Dr. Andra's granddaughter went on to reinvent the ocean cleaner and blah, blah, ocean labs, blah. Underwater volcanoes."

WHAT YOU HAVE TAMED

"I think I saw a vid on that. Pretty good, won a few awards," Reist said.

"I'm so sick of this shit, man." Eira drained the last of her caff and pushed the little cup into the trash bin. "This ain't even doing it for me anymore."

With two keystrokes, Reist saved his work to their online shared folder. He leaned over and made the same motion on Eira's keyboard. She didn't object but gave a small pout, stuck somewhere between relief for the end and disappointment in accepting defeat. "Where's that side project of yours?" he asked.

"I'll save it. I'm not ready for you to see it yet."

Reist gave a shrug and returned the datapads to the librarian. Eira gathered their bags, waiting by the door for him. There was a low buzzing in Reist' bag. She rummaged and found Reist's wrist device. He had taken it off to ignore the constant buzzing of news stories. "Dad" was calling.

"Hey, Mr. Adeio," she said to the blue holographic circle on her palm.

"Hey, kid," he replied after a brief pause, "where's the other one?"

"He's putting stuff away. We're done at the library."

"Just stay there, okay? I'm coming to get both of you."

"Okay." She didn't ask any further. Her exhaustion bred an annoyed apathy. "I'll tell him."

"I'm a few minutes away. Hold on." The call ended with a soft, low boop in time for Reist to appear from around the corner of an aisle several feet away.

"Your dad's coming to get us." She handed him his device and bag.

"Oh. Okay." He rarely asked questions.

If it was blind trust or Reist was secretly another drone like everyone else, Eira still couldn't tell. He was the one that found a way to break into the coaches building. He showed no objection to committing a felony and thought quickly enough to get the blame off them. By that same token, his resume writing was incredibly dull. He had no interest in the leadership roles for the Tech or Logistics divisions, but wanted a desk job that offered quiet solitude. Give him the tasks and let him be. That was what he said made him happy. The token turned again. This couldn't be true because she's caught a glimmering sparkle of glee in his eye when she bests him.

The challenge called to him the same way it does her. Reist clearly saw it, but then they're apart for a day and he returns to the definition of domesticity. *More trips outside the house should do him some good*, Eira thought. *Let him be away from his parents for a while.* They meant well, of course. Eira would never say Reist's parents weren't loving and kind, but he followed them so blindly. Too often, she asked for his thoughts and heard his dad's opinion. When she asked him why this was his opinion, he tried to paint it as though it was the same as hers. Pressed further and the spluttering words turned into, "I don't know." To which she replied, "That's a good start."

When asked about his little sister, there was a light behind his eyes Eira rarely saw elsewhere. Pari's successes and failures fascinated him like he was watching something grow in real time. Eira silently wished for a sibling of her own, but she had Nana, and that was more than enough. Regret threatened to climb into her brain and yank her away from what she was going to ask Reist to do, knowing full well it meant her leaving Nana and him leaving Pari. But that would be the next step, with or without him.

A TEXT MESSAGE READ, *Outside.* The blue hover-mobile hummed just past the sliding double doors, opening a hatch for Mr. Adeio to wave at Reist and Eira to get in. They buckled in and Mr. Adeio left the car park. His gray-blue eyes blinked into the rear-view mirror and back to the road. "You two hear what's happened?"

Shaking their heads, Reist and Eira had differing reactions. Whereas Reist was tired and showed a curious disconnect from the rest of the world, Eira sat forward and listened intently. She had better access to the energy reserves, so rarely found in a person's self-control.

"Big gang war broke out," Mr. Adeio said, lowering the volume on the radio. "Well, not *gang* gang, I guess. Gangs *are* involved, but they were fighting the police not too far from here."

"Oh, shit," fell from Eira's lips before she could catch herself.

Without a blink, Mr. Adeio began again, "Oh yeah, it started not too long ago, and that half of the district is cut off now. Which is why we're taking a detour." The on-ramp to the motorway was alight with red taillights. "And so is everyone else, apparently. *Great.*" Traffic crept by a few centimeters at a time.

While on the motorway, Reist and Eira gave each other a series of looks. She gave him a look of concern and he shook his head. "What?" She pointed out the window, and he turned.

A column of smoke rose less than a kilometer away from them. Reist nudged Eira, and she followed his gaze. That was Centre Street, if the glowing gold sign for *Gilded Piscis* was any indication, at the corner of 19th Street. Reist's parents took him there for a celebratory dinner when he joined the pole vaulting team. His dad had found all the old photos of his competitions. The small restaurant offered a quaint and familial setting, despite the thick Zentharan accents of the owners and employees. They had come over with their meals and commented on the old photos of Reist's dad and how striking a similarity he and Reist looked.

The sign struggled to shine through the smoke, but the golden light flickered. Sparks flew up from underneath the fish mascot, Mr. Pi, on the sign, holding the restaurant's name up with his fins. The metal beam holding up the sign bent inward and fell to the street, casting Mr. Pi into darkness.

83

Eira's and Reist's gasps made Mr. Adeio look over. He slammed his palm on the steering handle and shouted, "Why aren't we *moving*? Grab your bags and stay low, kids. We might have to run." Neither of them could peel their eyes from the sight unfolding under them. Smoke hung ever-present like a silent god watching the violence growing at its feet. Figures in the unmistakable black uniforms of the police were retreating from the wave of red scarves and gunfire.

One police officer stood out to Reist. This lone paragon stood in ebony armor against the crimson tide and shot his weapon towards the enemy. One of the gang members held a fire in his hand. The Molotov cocktail exploded, and the holder erupted in flames. From this distance, the sight was bush shaped before the violently swinging arms broke the facade and the man's screams carried to Reist's ears.

All the time, the lone officer was there, behind one of the patrol hovers, still firing towards the ever-growing flood. His fatal mistake was turning his head to find the nearest comrade. A spray of blood erupted from his face, the blow pushing his head back, and he fell onto his side, dead.

People climbed out of their hovers to watch. Some stood on top of their vehicles as the mob pushed through underneath them. Through the underpass, they chanted "Irrepresivi" like a war cry. Gunfire was the battle drum, ushering the invading army into paradise to set it to the torch.

Panic and fascination mixed on the motorway. People stood at the edge of the overpass to watch the firefight continue, cheering when armored hovers bustled around the corner to unload their cargo of assault teams to attack the rebellious Efferans. Others left their vehicles behind and ran.

The three of them were still in Mr. Adeio's hover, who was beside himself with confusion, anger, and fear. Should they stay or leave? And what would happen if they couldn't outrun them? Reist and

Eira said nothing. They watched the scene play out and held hands, but not in fear. The acrid odor of the smoke mixed with the smell of burning meat and in the cacophony of screaming and gunfire, there was an elation in Reist's chest and the smoke god smiled on it all.

Chapter 9

THERE WERE OVER A DOZEN tabs open on Reist's web browser. The chair let out this annoying squeak when it leaned back. His eyes lost focus for a moment and he looked away from the news article about the gang attack beneath the motorway. It had been a week, and they had identified the last body. The officer Reist saw die was Sgt Harold Mutatio. His face was up on banners with the others who had died that day. One of the other tabs was an article about other skirmishes in other districts. Another had a story about a police raid on a gang hideout. It said local, non-Efferan youths were rushing to join the gangs.

There was a paragraph regarding the reaction from the Efferan kings. Many were silent, but others swore allegiance to the Screaming King. Fighting is in their nature, they said. Human nature, in fact. Their scripture established this and the rest of the Confederacy was overdue for this most holy lesson. Reist had also found some Efferan language tapes.

The next tab was the Economic Market. Reist didn't know how to read it, but tried to learn it so he could predict his dad's mood that day. It was going to be another bad one. He switched to the next group of tabs. All of them were recruitment pages from the Law Enforcement Offices, the Planetary Militia, and the Confederate Defense Force. Each page had the physical requirements and job descriptions. The police and the militia offered much of the same: stay close to home but travel the planet; be it on another corner of the Corvic Continent or across the planetwide ocean. There were logistics and technological duties, but not to the extreme extent the Companies had. One person in the online forums mentioned he used the militia as a steppingstone towards one of the corporate jobs. That was something Reist could sell to his parents.

The CDF had more options to move around. Several bases across each planet in the Confederation, including the colonies; more intense training and specially designated schools. Trade schools, essentially, but militarized. Reist didn't realize how much this fascinated him until he looked at the clock. Two hours had passed. The remaining tabs were all the combat positions and their requirements. He sent Eira a list of links and wrote, "*Check this out.*"

The links were stories about heroic acts and dangerous missions by the CDF. Reist ran his fingers through his hair. He checked his messages. Eira left him on 'Read'. He closed the tabs and pulled up the midterm presentation. It was mostly done, but needed more. The doorbell rang. Reist heard his mom say something and closed the door. Someone was coming towards Reist's room at the back of the house.

Eira stood in his doorway when he turned. Her hair was pulled back in a ponytail and her face was flushed. Sweat patches made a half-moon at the middle portion of her top and dark splotches across the rest of her shirt. There was still a headphone in one ear, and the other was pinched between two fingers. Her device glowed purple on her wrist. The screen was on a page that looked like one of the special forces stories Reist had sent.

"What is this?" she kicked the door shut.

"It," Reist began and paused, trying to find the words, "looked like something I wanted to show you."

"Why?" Her face was expressionless. "You show me this shit in the middle of my run. Now tell me why."

"Did...did you run here?"

"The path I use is a couple of kilometers from here. Now talk."

"I was following the news. I wanted to see what was happening with, well, everything."

"Right." Eira crossed her arms.

"And, well, I don't get it. Why are they fighting? Here," Reist said, pointing to one of the news articles. "Statistically, most of the gangs are full of people who were born here. Half can't even speak Corvic, but they were born and raised here. Ultimately, this is their home as much as ours, right? So why fight their own homeland?"

"I don't care." Eira held up the screen on her device and pointed to the special forces story. "Tell me why you sent me this."

"I'm getting to that. Just go with me on this. They, the gangs, I mean, must know this will hurt them to fight, but they must. They have to. Like it's a calling. The fighting could be the calling. Maybe the end result they're hoping for is the calling, but I have to think what they feel when they fight is what I felt with you that night."

Eira did not budge, except for a small twitch on her face. "Go on."

"I don't want to sit around when there's shit going on." Swearing was becoming gradually more frequent with him these days. "I like, um, I dunno. Responding, I guess? When something's happening. I like how much stronger I feel after pole vaulting and archery. I like the competition too. But fitness is a perishable skill—"

"So be a fitness instructor. Or a coach. Join the Festivals Committee."

Reist shook his head, "No. That's not enough. I like responding. Doing the lifeguard job gives me a feeling of importance-"

"Be a lifeguard then, full time. There's bound to be jobs for, I don't know, beach safety? Be a rescue diver for Maritime. Or a cop."

Again, he shook his head, "Still not enough. That feeling is scattered few and far between long stretches of a ton of nothing. We know that, and the cop forums I've read say the same thing."

"Then what?" Eira shook her device's holographic screen at him. "Long stretches of a ton of nothing never bothered you before."

"It's also not a calling."

"What does that even mean? Why this? Why combat? Somewhere away from home?"

"We were helpless," Reist said. The sentence fit well in his mind, and he followed the path it led. "We could have died there like livestock. We didn't know how to respond or where to go or what to do. And I don't like that. I want to know what to do in that situation. So, I think that could be my thing. To know what to do."

"Emergency response then," Eira said with a shrug. "There are forums for that, too."

"Forums for people who want to stay civilians. But, I don't want to hear secondhand how to survive that shit. I want to *know* how to. I want to *live* it and be good at it. And I want to keep moving, but if I keep moving around the same stuff, the same areas, it'll drive me insane."

"Still," Eira said, "you can be a cop. We saw the riot guys. You can do that."

"That's not enough." Reist didn't realize he was telling all this to the floor. He met her gaze. "I want more."

They locked eyes, both refusing to blink.

"I need your shower," she said finally.

"Sure," he said, "I'll lend you some clothes."

"Your clothes are huge on me."

"And?"

"Valid point." She turned and opened the door. He followed her out and told his mom Eira would use his shower. She offered the invitation for her to stay for dinner.

—✝↘\\↖✝—

MRS. ADEIO LENT SOME of her bathing products and a stack of fresh clothes, then shut the door. Steam rose and Eira climbed into the shower. Afternoon sunlight spilled through the rectangular window above her head, illuminating the tiles off the white shower liner.

With a deep sigh, Eira allowed the floodgates of her mind to open. The thoughts, scenarios, and backup plans fell into place. Her subconscious had done the heavy lifting prior to this moment. Until now, it was important she not suggest the idea of CDF enlistment to him. This path stuck in her mind nearly a year and a half ago. Her father had always helped her plan out her life with a single-minded vigor. His suggestions had always felt like commands. Being a good little girl was the easiest thing in the world until the flaws in her parents' logic had become clearer and clearer. She lathered the body soap into her washcloth and scrubbed.

The generation before her lived in interesting times. Domesticity offered them a breath of fresh air and a safe place to build something that would outlast them, leaving their mark behind. Naturally, they wanted that peace of mind for their children. It was not what Eira wanted, not yet at least; not for a long time, if it ever came at all. She rinsed the suds off.

There was a thrill of competition and a passion for selflessness. More importantly, there was a love for self-improvement. When Eira emerged from this shower, she saw the muscle definition in her legs and abdominals. The other night, she had taken a second mirror to admire her back and glutes. Pride became something deeper. Struggling to become better was addicting. The thrill of success was good as well, but it lacked a lasting effect. Resting on her laurels disgusted her.

Eira's father was a proud and competitive man and wanted her to reach higher than he had. Wanting the top spots in business was a good goal to have. Ten years on and she can still hear her father complaining to his friends about how slow his daughter was, and how lucky they were to have sons. Nana had taught her how to use that anger as motivation to be aimed at whatever she wanted, like those top spots.

But what happens after she gets there? The low hum of the air conditioning and soft buzzing of office lighting mingled in with forms and admin reports about...whatever. Her biggest threat was going to be a paper cut or a jolt of static shock.

The paycheck would make the struggle worth it, but the breath of fresh air her parents guarded so closely sounded horrifying to her. Climbing the corporate ladder lacked a more elegant and primal sensation. The hi-ed drama would continue into the business world and coworkers would discourage fistfights, just like teachers do. *So much faster, though*, Eira thought.

The clothes hung loose on Eira's shoulders, and she tied a knot on the pajama pants to keep them steady. Reist was in his room. Two plates full of food rested on his bed. Mrs. Adeio came up behind her. "Oh, hello, honey." She gave Eira a glass of water. "The boy said you two were working on your resumes still, so I decided you two can work better in here than at the table. Lemme know if you need anything," she beamed and closed the door for Eira.

Reist stared at the door for a moment. "She likes you."

"I know. A closed door. What a scandal." Eira kept her tone level. It was important she remain aloof to how this conversation would continue.

They sat for a moment, Eira on the bed corner and Reist in the chair, eating. It was weird for Reist to see his clothes on someone else. Eira was practically drowning in his shirt. A stray droplet of water trickled down her neck, from behind her ear, to her collarbone. The shirt absorbed, but Reist didn't stop staring.

"So," she began, "why CDF? Why do you think they'll have more?"

The chair squealed as Reist leaned back to hit the keys on the computer. The webpage changed and there were two long columns of duty titles Eira recognized as the CDF recruiting site. "Look at all these. I could go do, literally, anything I wanted. CDF hires by contractual obligations, so if one job doesn't work, there are other places they can put me. Why be a fitness trainer or law enforcement here when I can be one up there?" He pointed to the ceiling. "Why bother with the shit that's here when I go up there and get a bigger picture?"

First bump in the road. Eira leaned forward. "What shit down here?"

Another click and the screen changed to a page memorializing the police who died the week prior. "They call these guys heroes. And, sure, they were. But what does that do now? They're dead. People went on with their lives and, honestly? That scares the hell out of me. So, my thoughts are 'Don't be in that job' because I don't want to die. But," he opened another page, showing statistical graphs, "then I see the rate of accidental deaths this year alone. Look how many were in the kitchen or the bathroom. There was a chance you were gonna die by the time you finished that shower."

"Where are you going with this?" she asked, half wondering, half hoping, he was on the same path as her.

"Why die doing something mundane when I can die doing something awesome?"

"Being a great worker can be awesome," she countered; a feeble attempt, even she admitted to herself.

"I could go into my cubicle and file away reports. I'd be good at it. It's what both my parents do," Reist continued the thought, "Then what?"

"There's plenty of stuff on your off time you can do," she said. "There's the laser tag leagues, there's fitness competitions. You can get your thrill of awesome anywhere else around here."

Reist's face dropped. "It's not the same. Look, I'm sorry if this upset you." He moved to close the tabs.

A jolt of panic gripped Eira's chest. She kicked it back and swallowed, reclaiming her calm. "Hold up, hold up. Go back. I'm not upset. I just want to understand."

Their eyes met again. Reist sighed, "I had no idea I would do as well as I did in archery, or even pole vaulting, for that matter. But I went out there and I tried. And I got better. Working at it, improving on it, and *being* better. Just *deciding* to be better. It feels amazing. That transformation I see in myself when I look back. I want *that*. I want it more and more and this here?" He re-opened the page discussing CDF basic training. "Imagine how I'll feel when I look back on this accomplishment. Or the one after that. I want something that will push me and open my mind. But I *cannot* get that here. I can get it here." He pointed to the screen. "I want this."

There was a low rumble trickling its way up Eira's spine. The plate clinked when she pushed it away. She stood and took his plate, putting it on the bed. She sat in his lap and turned to the computer, signing in to her email. Reist's arms instinctually went around her waist. It was the smell that drew him deeper. He pressed his nose to her back. It wasn't his soap, but it smelled amazing on her.

She had requested the form and filled it out months ago, and kept it saved in the "Drafts" folder. Last week, she made a second copy, and put Reist's information in it. Double clicking both forms, they each filled out half the screen, side by side. Eira waited as Reist read them both. The CDF logo was prominent in the top right corner of each. Minutes dragged by and his arms linked around her waist. "You clever bitch."

"Do you really want to do it?" She turned her face away, hoping to hide the redness she felt rising in her cheeks. "Or was all that a crock of shit?"

"I'll sign this right here, right now."

"Same," she said. "Go back to section nine."

He did. "Yeah, that's a bunch of numbers and letters. What *is* that?"

"It's a specialty designated code for a duty position, SDC for short," she began, "look it up."

His arms left her waist to type the SDC into a search engine. Reist did this thing where his head rocked backwards when he got surprised. He thought he could hide his reactions, but he couldn't hide that, not yet.

"Recon?" He looked at Eira.

She nodded. "The exact job you texted me."

"Whoa, wait, hold on." The chair squeaked again. "That's too high up. I don't even know if I want that."

"Oh, quit being a wimp. It's like you said, if you flunk out, there are other jobs they'll give you because you're on contract. Why not try for the hardest thing there is?"

"Because what if I don't make it?"

"So? Failure is awesome. There's no limit to how many times you can try. And what if you *do* make it? Think of *that* accomplishment you can look back on."

As if all the weight left him, Reist dropped his head to the back of the chair and paused.

"You," he said, "are evil."

"I know," she said, and kissed him.

Chapter 10

REIST AND EIRA LEFT the plates on the corner of the bed and sifted through stories written by former Recon members. All information on current Recon missions was deliciously and infuriatingly absent. There were stories from when the Confederation was founded, but stories from the war against the Mier Republic were still classified. There was a constant reference to "winning hearts and minds" that made people laugh.

More digging and they found old footage from a documentary about the training courses. Men and women not much older than Reist and Eira stood in formation with white shirts and their surnames painted on their backs. A voice shouted from off camera, and they all shouted back in unison. It cut to footage of these trainees carrying bulky backpacks through a wooded area. Text appeared in the center of the screen, "Advanced Combat School- Camp Unia, Zenthara."

"Shit," Reist breathed. "How many damn schools are there?"

A moment later, Eira got the answer from her device. "Ten. Over three years' worth of training."

"We'd be dedicating ourselves to *three years* of training?" Reist asked, already portraying exhaustion on his face.

"Yep," she said.

Reist shut his eyes and sighed deeply. "Yeah, alright. Let's do it."

Reist paused the video and pulled up the contracts. Their future glared at them, testing their resolve. He scrolled down to the signature block and clicked it. A press on the finger pad and retinal scan later, and it was signed. A moment later, so was Eira's. They stayed in her "Drafts" folder on her email, "We can go in with them during the break and turn them in face-to-face."

"They're gonna love this." Reist didn't need to say who 'they' were.

"By the time we'll get a date to go in, we'll be adults," Eira replied. "It'll be our choice. And we can back out and any time between now and then." Reist could hear the silent challenge in her tone. He pulled up the physical requirements for Recon members again. They studied them for a moment.

"Which of these do you need to work on?" Reist asked.

"The run," she said right away, with a grimace.

"Same," he replied, matching her tone. "I hate running." He gave a sigh and searched for cardio routines. "Right. Archery team isn't going to do this sorta stuff for us."

"Then we'll drop it and do it ourselves," she said.

"We can use the track for some of these. The rest are calisthenic and lifting."

"I see the list too," she replied. "Let's do this tomorrow. Test ourselves and make a journal or something."

Hesitation reared its ugly head towards Reist again. *Why try when you'll just fail? Stick to what you're good at. You're naturally gifted at something. Why not stay with that so failing remains unlikely?*

"After school lets out," Reist agreed.

Eira nodded and stood to collect the plates. They left Reist's room and made for the kitchen. Mrs. Adeio stood at the sink with Pari, who was holding a towel. The little girl gave Eira a curious glance. It wasn't the kind Eira would come to expect from the little sisters of her previous boyfriends. *Ugh, did I just...?* she thought. There was nothing territorial in Pari's gaze, but a mild intrigue.

"Thank you, dear." Mrs. Adeio accepted the plates and utensils and added them to the small, dwindling pile in the sink. "How's it coming in there?" she asked.

"Oh, really great," Eira replied, forgetting for a moment she and Reist were supposed to be working on their resumes. They had finished them a week and a half ago. "I think we got them just about right."

"That's great, honey." Her tone was always so upbeat and pleasant. How does one maintain that? Eira had never met anyone like Reist's mother. And how did none of that rub off on him? Reist took after his father too much.

Eira pushed the negative thought away. It would hurt if he didn't follow her into Recon, but there'd be other relationships. *But building one with him sounds* really *nice.* If he stepped through the door with her, she'd have a partner. If he didn't, then he did her a favor by giving up before she truly got started. Feeling the air was growing awkward, Eira stepped away, towards the back porch. Maybe Mr. Adeio needed some help.

In size, the Adeios' porch was smaller than Eira's. But it still felt homey. Plants and flowers hung to offer a splash of color and pleasant scents. There was a wicker table and four chairs and a rocking loveseat. Mr. Adeio was brushing the grill with a heavy hand. He was of average height but broad shoulders and back. Reist had inherited those, Eira had noticed.

Both Reist and his father shared the same single-minded, determined look whenever they were at work. There was a contained focus, like they were already mapping out what the next step would be. Such a unique opposite to Reist's mother.

"Can I help you with anything?" she asked.

The stern, concentrated face peered up at her and softened instantly, like a magical, special effect. "No, I'm almost done here. Actually, that rag in front of you. Could you throw that to me?" A hand towel, riddled with holes, was on the wicker table. Eira picked it up and underhand tossed it to Mr. Adeio. He caught it with a lazy hand. "Thanks."

Reist had once told her about the significant relationship between throwing and catching. When he was younger, there had been
a bizarre and indescribable disconnect between him and the other
kids. Until one day, on the playground, some of the other boys had
been playing catch. At that moment, in pri-ed, Reist still had many
years before he'd bloom. He was clumsy and kept quiet, so sure if he
said anything, it would label him as odd. And yet, at that moment,
while he was so confident in the belief of his own insignificance, a
voice had cried out. *Watch out*!

Little kid Reist had turned and saw a ball arching up through the
air and coming at him. With reflexes he didn't know he had, little
Reist had caught the ball easily. His classmates exclaimed, impressed,
and called for him to throw it back. He did, and he described it like a
grappling hook. He had tossed not a ball, but a connecting end away
from him and to someone else. It was like a tube linking two buildings together and real, human interaction could begin.

It was just a game of catch, dude, Eira had said to him when he
told her this story.

Not to me, he had replied. That was when he started feeling like a
person.

At this moment, between Eira and Mr. Adeio, she could almost
see what he meant. Maybe he felt it, too. Mr. Adeio wiped his hands
on the rag and closed the grill. "Resumes coming along well?"

Eira may have hesitated if they hadn't made the connection. But
she didn't. "Absolutely," she replied with all the confidence she could
muster. It was true, after all. She was sure about it and couldn't help
acting like she was on top of the world. Getting to the top was another matter, but you must start somewhere.

"Good," he said. Leading the way inside, he continued, "I gave
him a copy of my original one and one of my more recent ones to
start off with. But I guess the format has changed somewhere be-

tween starting my first job and this one. Made me feel old when I realized I've been working at the same place for eighteen years."

"Twelve for me," Mrs. Adeio added. The dishes were drying, and Mrs. Adeio took the dirty rag to the washer. "I really wish they'd streamline those things," she said. "They were so silly when we started, and they've only gotten more complicated since."

"The kid's diploma should be enough," Mr. Adeio nodded. "*Maybe* a letter of recommendation from a teacher or two. The rest can be built on later."

A soft touch drew a line across Eira's lower back. Reist emerged from her peripheral. He had refilled both of their cups with ice water. Pari was still by their mom, her eyes barely able to peer over the countertop to study the pair of them standing so close together. Reist's mom asked her something.

"What?" Eira asked.

"Would you like to stay for dessert?" Mrs. Adeio repeated.

She paused. "Sure. That would be great." Her last boyfriend's parents were nowhere near this nice. *Ugh, I did it again.*

Dessert was cake. Mr. Adeio attempted to replicate a cake he saw on a baking show. "We can pack up some for you to take home too," Mrs. Adeio offered.

As much as Eira loved Cuquas's cooking, it lacked the certain mystery ingredient Mr. Adeio brought to the kitchen. She asked for another serving and they were happy to oblige, while also giving Reist an additional serving, though he didn't ask for it. "The boy will be hungry again later," Mrs. Adeio commented. "He's got a black hole in that belly of his."

Mr. Adeio asked Reist about the resume. Eira tried to listen in, but Pari suddenly appeared by her side. Light feet seemed to be a genetic trait of this family.

"You were at the contest with my brother, right?" Pari asked.

'My brother.' She didn't use his name. There's the territorial nature Eira saw in siblings. "Yes, I was," she replied. "We watched him compete, and we got lunch together, remember? Your brother and I are on the archery team together."

"And you two kissed."

"Yes, we did."

Pari nodded as though there was some solemn bit of information. She gazed up at Eira again. "Are you his girlfriend?"

Though he was facing his father, Eira saw Reist tense. He wasn't standing straighter because of pride or showing off. Reist was *fully* capable of showing off. Eira was witness to each irritating incident. But this was more...in preparation; the way someone might keep a door held in place before an oncoming horde.

"Yes," Eira nodded. "I am."

Reist relaxed. His parents *had* to have seen this. She couldn't have been the only person to read his body language this easily. These people live with him, raised him. *Why put a name to it?* She wondered. It was too common. Too familiar to call them boyfriend and girlfriend. Was Eira going to sail into the blackness of space with her *boyfriend?* No, there was a childish notion entangled with that word. And within that notion was a vein holding a virus of expectation.

People build relationships. A boyfriend would eventually become a husband. A husband meant family, children, and a tiny house with pets. There are far too many questions to tie in with that. You can't build a family while lugging your way through another planet's atmosphere. You can't have a child in a war zone. *Well. You shouldn't,* she thought, *but that* would *be kinda bad ass.*

Eira and Reist can discuss that later. For now, keep up appearances of normality until they take that step and go to basic training. Although Reist visibly relaxed when she confirmed it. Disappointing him would be a problem. *No,* she told herself. *This is good.* She can talk to him about it later and if he acts weird about it or steps away, then she'll find out if he will stick around sooner rather than later. It's a win-win for her no matter what, and that was how she was going to look at it.

They kept chatting for a few more hours. Eira took Reist's bowl and washed it. There was still the matter of appearances. After this, Mrs. Adeio offered to drive her home. Eira accepted, and they were out the door. Reist climbed into the backseat with her. There was a passenger seat. Why didn't he sit up there? There was more leg room after all, but maybe he caught on to her signal and was looking to keep up appearances.

Eira gave Mrs. Adeio the directions and before long, they stopped on the curb in front of Eira's house. Reist climbed out and walked her to the door. The overhead light buzzed hotly and gave Reist an uncharacteristic halo. "I'll see you tomorrow," Reist said, "babe."

Eira glared piercingly at him. "Text me when you get home," she said, "toots."

Reist moved closer to her, arms opening, and Eira resisted the urge to punch him. He *had* caught on and was making fun of her. Eira wrapped her arms around him. He rocked their hug back and forth, and some of her resolve chipped away.

Back in the car, Mrs. Adeio smirked at Reist in the passenger seat. She pursed her lips and made kissing sounds at the air. "Aw, too embarrassed to kiss your girlfriend in front of your mom?"

Rolling his eyes, Reist said, "I didn't want to be too forward too soon." Though that excuse was rather hollow. They kissed in his room. And Eira started it. It hadn't been a particularly romantic moment either. Based on the vids and books he's ingested over the years, people like to kiss their significant others in tender and touching moments. And kissing old girlfriends had never given him any feeling. *Maybe romance*, he figured, *should take the back seat for a while.*

The car moved forward, and the familiar streets passed in the night's shadow while Reist replayed the moments in his mind's eye. They talked about their future adventure. It spurred excitement in his chest. The unknown can be startling, even petrifying in its mystery. But having someone next to you, unafraid and unfaltering, was comforting.

More importantly, Reist had clarity. There was no more uncertainty about who he was or what he was good at. He was going to be a fighter. He was going to be one half of a team, unafraid of the great unknown. Reist wanted to kiss Eira just for that. He made a note to do it tomorrow. *It doesn't feel what I thought romantic should feel like,* he thought, *but it makes sense.*

EIRA WAS DISPASSIONATELY welcomed home with a vague greeting by her mother and the classic grunt and nod combo by her father. Nana, however, made an appearance. The motorized chair came, buzzing and whirring all the way out from the back room. She wore her usual cream-colored housecoat with her old and patchy blanket draped across her lap. A book rested there.

"Oh, there you are," she said to Eira. "Did you run around the whole continent? You'll need some good food to replenish all that." Nana gave her a once over, taking in the oversized boy clothes. "And you went thrifting."

Eira held up the cakes. "I stopped to have dinner at a friend's house." Do *I correct myself?* "I got us some cake to share."

"Oh, that's nice," Eira's mother said with a noticeable slur. She took them and lifted the lids. Apparently satisfied, she went to shove the containers in the fridge. Both servants must have gone home by now. She rarely ever opens the fridge herself. "Honey, go change. You look like a vagrant."

Nana rolled a little closer and spoke in a low whisper, "Which friend was this, dear? My memory isn't quite what it used to be, and keeping track of names might help me keep the ol' noggin going a little longer."

"Reist," she said. "We're on the archery team together and he's a lifeguard with me at work."

Her father didn't look away from the news report. Her mother nodded, satisfied by the additional information. Someone from school is a recognizable and safe connection. Having a job and an extracurricular activity worked in Reist's favor here, as well as having supporting parents to feed an additional child on a whim.

Nana, however, did not allow the matter to pass unnoticed. Though she would not openly question Eira about a paramour in front of her parents, it didn't stop the knowing look behind her eyes. Nana seemed to know everything, making Eira think she was clairvoyant. It supposedly existed over in the Mier Republic with other mental advancements, but that was all rumor.

Though, if anyone outside the family would suggest Nana got these advancements herself, there would be little doubt. With a slight nod, Nana beckoned Eira to her room. Inside was Nana's bed with a bookshelf and a small writing table along one wall. A lamp illuminated one corner on the opposite side of the bookshelf where she would park the motorized chair. There was an extra chair, old and wooden, where Eira always sat.

"Little wing," Nana said. "This young man wouldn't happen to be the same one we've discussed?"

A little smile betrayed her face. "He is."

"Oh, good," she backed her chair into the corner. "I liked this one. How do you like him? A boy with nice parents mustn't be taken for granted."

Eira nudged the wooden chair closer to Nana and sighed. "Remains to be seen. We were playing with some ideas for the future. A future together."

"Mhm," she nodded knowingly as ever. "Building together is good. But don't lay any foundation too soon. You're both still so young."

"And it's a great asset I can use," Eira said, reciting one of Nana's previous points. "But...I'm excited, Nana. About this future. It'll be better if he can keep up. I know he can, but whether or not he will? I don't know yet."

"If he can't keep up, little wing, then he's not the right model for you and the upgrade will be around the corner," she said. "I've been around for too long, yet not long enough, and I'd rather have some of that time back from the occasional idiot I ran with. But," Nana began, "when you're ready, I'll be happy to meet him."

Before going into the recruiter would be good, Eira decided. Once he signs the final line with her, then he'll be ready to meet Nana. *And the parents too, I guess.* A small buzz came from Eira's device. Reist had sent her another article about Recon.

"Interesting," Nana said.

"Huh? What is?"

"You're beaming," she said simply. "That him?"

Eira paused, pushing back embarrassment. "Yeah, he's researching more about the future options I mentioned."

Nana nodded with an approving smile.

REIST SCROLLED THROUGH Recon forums. He created a guest login and made a vague guess at the security question. It was an essay question about an experience that would prove he was Recon. After watching enough videos online about the training schools, he typed in an answer that might suffice. Whether the answer he gave was creative or believable enough, it didn't matter. Reist was in and he lurked through each thread of discussion.

One thread focused on games, another followed sports statistics. He pushed further and found some references to previous missions. Each of these threads was restricted, closed to only the members who founded it and whoever they invited. Reist rewatched the training videos.

The recruitment website boasted a 95% fail rate. If it was meant for gatekeeping, it worked. How long would Reist make it through the training? Would he flunk out of the first school, the second, or second to last? That would be the worst thing: failing near the end. If he started something, he wanted to finish it. But he wouldn't be alone. It was a fact he had to remind himself of. How tough *was* Eira? She was a reliable lifeguard and teammate, but is that enough? Reist paused the training video.

In the video, it showed trainees carrying massive logs; trees, really. Reist saw them grimace as they struggled through every agonizing step. They each started as something else. None of their information was available. Their uniform normally had a name tag sewn over the right breast pocket. But these trainees had theirs removed. Reist leaned in and saw names torn off, the same with the ranks on the upper parts of their sleeves.

Instantly, innocuous information about each trainee came to Reist's mind. All imaginary but made the video feel real. This one was an accountant, that one was a mailman, this other one wrote for his hi-ed newspaper. They each could have been in any number of other locations but they sent themselves to...Reist double checked the location...Advanced Combat School- Camp Unia, Zenthara.

Something sparked in Reist's mind, and he researched something he wasn't completely sure about. A moment later and it was confirmed. Gravity on Zenthara is much higher than on Corvus. Which meant that tree they were carrying must have weighed several hundred more kilograms than it would if it were taken down in the woods close to Reist's house. How horrific would that log be? How would Eira respond? He sent her the link, wanting to see her reaction.

"Whatcha lookin' at?" a little voice came behind him. Pari had shuffled into the room, in her pajamas with wet hair. Mom always ached about Pari drying her hair, but it was too much effort, according to the little girl.

"Research for a paper I'm writing." The lie came quickly and with zero thought.

"Are they in the woods?" She shuffled over to his shoulder and studied the screen.

"Sure are." He pressed play.

Shouting came out of the speakers again, and Pari winced slightly at them but adapted quickly. She and Reist were similar in that way. It was the first, and would not be the last, time Reist wondered how well Pari would fare on the battlefield with him. But each time, including now, he shoved that thought away. She'd be so much better following their dad into computers. The image of her on a shooting range wasn't bad, but in combat? It gave an empty feeling in the pit of Reist's stomach.

"I wanna go to the woods," she said, ignoring the sneering faces of the instructors and the shouting cries of the trainees.

"Maybe we can go the next day I have off," he said.

"Mom won't like it."

"Mom doesn't have to know," he replied. "I'll do our laundry before she and Dad come home."

The mention of clothes reminded him of the small pile in a plastic bag by the foot of the bed. Eira's sweaty clothes. She forgot to take them with her. When Pari leaves, he'll toss them in his hamper and return them this week.

"Really?" Pari asked, eyes alight with glee. "We can play Alien Hunter?" It had been a long time since they played that together; before he started hi-ed at least. He'd been increasingly busy ever since. If he wasn't doing homework, he was at work, or at archery.

"You bet we can." He matched her excitement. True, he'd rather spend that time in the solitary quiet of his room. Too much energy spent around other avenues and people. He'd need a recharge soon. But maybe making his little sister happy would give him the mental boost he needed. Things were simpler when he was younger and making fake laser noises in the woods was all there was in the world.

Their mom came in and told Pari it was time for bed. Reist gave his sister a hug, and she shuffled away, dragging her feet. Before she stepped out, their mom spied the computer screen. The Recon videos were still up. "What's that, honey?"

"Research for a paper." The lie fit well.

"Huh," she said flatly. His mom eyed him for a moment, and he kept her gaze without expression. "Okay..." she said next, before stepping out. "You should invite your girlfriend over for dinner again." She was halfway out the door now. "It'll get you out of this room once in a while. And I won't always be as nice as I was," she said with a wink.

REIST WAS TOO RED-FACED to speak up when he and Eira approached the archery coach. It was because of this she did most of the talking. They were handing in their resignation from the team, stating a change of priorities towards their futures. When the coach accepted it without question, and commended them for coming to him like adults, a weight fell from Reist's chest.

"You worry too much," Eira said when they stepped out of the coach's cramped and stuffy office and into the cool breeze. "This is just the first stop, too. We got to go to the beach and do the same thing."

"I know, I know," he said.

"Oh, yeah. And I signed us up for an internship at the hospital, too."

"What? Why?"

"Nothing crazy. Just nursing assistants. It'll be good for us. Know how to patch someone up before we go to the medic school. We'll be ahead of the others."

"Huh. Yeah, that makes sense," he said, trying to change the topic. "Right, so, each lap is a kilometer and CDF fitness test has us doing two and a half kilometers. Recon is ten. Which are we doing?"

"Ten. Duh."

"Yeah, I thought that too." His thumb swiped on the holographic screen. "Minimum time is-"

"Nope, shush with that shit," Eira said. "Let's just do it without knowing the time and work off of that."

They dropped their bags on a bench and spent about five minutes stretching. It didn't need to take so long, but a silent anxiety infested the mental bridge they shared. Anxiety twisted and squirmed, threatening to transform them into the mundane and average. It scorched away when Reist and Eira made eye contact and nodded. They stepped away from the bleachers and brought their toes to a white painted line with "00.00" on it. Devices beeped and timers set.

"Ten kilometers," Reist said. Each lap being one made all of this easier to digest. Three CDF runs, plus a little extra. It would sound more impressive in his mind and bolster him until the end.

"Ten laps," Eira said. Kilometers sounded so daunting. She would finish one and realize how much more there was to run. Laps sounded smaller. Laps crushed under her heel.

"Three," Reist said. Thumping in his chest thundered through his ears.

"Twoonego!" Eira ran.

Keeping count is easy, but counting the laps during a run was harder. Hitting the 'lap' button on Reist's device kept him true, otherwise he'd be unsure if he was on lap three or four. *Kilometer one or two*, he corrected. The first two laps were the toughest to push through. Soft whispers tingled at the bottom of his mind, telling him to stop. *Hey, don't stop running now, just stop at two and a half,* it said. *That'd be fair, right? Work up to ten another day.*

Eira was next to him. And there's no way she'd let him live that down. It took until she started the fourth kilometer—*Fourth lap*—that made her question why this was a good idea. They had never run further than a lap or two at a time for practice and the farthest she ran at a time was five kilometers. Once. Now they took on the colossus that was twice that. Each convinced of the other's prowess and stubbornness. Neither was giving up while the other was watching.

The final stretch of the last lap was coming up. As soon as they cleared the curve, Reist, the bastard, began sprinting. Eira shot a swear word at his back and fought to catch up. He had kept pace with her the entire run and *now* he wanted to show off?

She pushed until pain sliced through her lungs. She fought to ignore it until she crossed the 00:00 line. Reist was already walking the curve, hands folded on top of his head, and struggling to slow his erratic panting. Eira stopped sprinting after the 00:00 line but slowed to a sweet spot between running and jogging. Her ankle swung out and struck the back of Reist's knee. He fell to all fours with a coughing shout.

Spinning around to face him, Eira grabbed Reist by the jaw and lifted his head. "Were you holding back?"

"W-wha-what?" He panted.

"That was some crazy sprinting you did, fucker," she said. "Were. You. Holding. Back?"

Reist shrugged. "I didn't want to burn myself out."

"So, you keep pace with me for nine and a half kilometers and at the last stretch, show your dick?" She shoved an accusatory finger in his face.

Reist slapped her hand away. "It's called finishing strong," he said, standing up and glaring down at her.

"It's patronizing," she said, meeting his angry stare. This mean-mugging glare works on house pets and weaklings. Not her.

"If you're faster than me," Eira began, "then be faster. This is for the both of us. You're doing me *zero* favors by holding yourself back."

Reist was still panting. His eyes bounced off far away corners and surfaces before returning to meet Eira's with a shrug. "We're in this together," he said.

Her frustration lowered a level. Eira was still mad, but at least he could explain himself. That was a start. "Yeah." She shoved him. "We are. But that doesn't mean we hold each other back. If you're faster, then you're faster. It doesn't mean you're leaving me behind. And if you do? I'll catch up."

They began walking, keeping to the track.

"I've never run that far before," he said.

"Me neither," she said. "And now we have. Means it won't be so scary next time."

He nodded and grinned. They can do this. He wrapped an arm around her shoulders in a one-armed hug. She gave a sickening grimace at the affection. They were both sweaty. Reist didn't care and tried to hug her. They playfully, and weakly, chased each other for the rest of the lap.

Chapter 11

"WHY ARE WE HERE AGAIN?" Reist asked.

"Officially? Because we thought it would look better on the resumes," Eira replied.

"But do they really matter at this point?" Reist asked.

"I mean, no, in all honesty," Eira threw away her sandwich wrapper and took a swig from her bottle. "But it can't really hurt us having extra information, can it?"

Reist nodded. "Yeah, and a leg up in medic school, and all that." He thought back to archery and learning how to pick locks. This was his magic growing. But at least shooting an arrow and picking a lot had been fun. Working at a hospital didn't sound fun.

The first day of lessons, while Reist was grateful he found the junior college campus, and wondered which classroom he needed, Eira was already there, all but jumping in place. She had grabbed Reist by the sleeve, dragged him to their room, and insisted they sit in front the entire time. While Reist was looking at their classmates, Eira was pulling out her note taking material. She scribbled away into her notebook, ready to build on her knowledge from lifeguard training. Reist was taking in the random diagrams decorating the room.

Interning was supposed to be an easy way out of taking additional classes. Gain school credits and, according to parents and faculty, get a leg up on the others in trade school the following year. Reist hadn't cared which internship he chose, but when Eira rushed to him, suggesting they take one at the local hospital, he agreed. Her logic was sound. He couldn't see himself being a medic for Recon, but if he *did* become one, then he'd have a leg up on saving someone's life. Reist gazed at the anatomical posters and dioramas and wondered about how a person's internal organs would look after taking a rifle round. Realizing how *squishy* people are unsettled him.

Eira, however, felt the exact opposite. She turned the page in her notebook and scrawled more notes. There was too much information to take in at one time. Eira realized how little she knew about Nana's condition. The week leading up to the deadline for internship requests was hard in Eira's home. Nana was forgetting common things: where the bathroom was, the name of Eira's mother and father, and—on two occasions—that she couldn't walk. Eira had just come back from a run that afternoon to what sounded like a dying animal coming from the center of the house. It was horrible to think Nana could make such a noise, but there she was, lying on the carpet in her room. She must have been on the floor for hours. Clothes soiled and all the fury she had completely zapped with all motivation and energy.

Nana was an old woman, and this was a fact Eira had accepted a long time ago. But knowing a fact and *knowing* a truth were two different things. At some point, Eira recognized she would have to say goodbye to this incredible woman who was nothing less than a guide and a fountain of wisdom. When that day comes, it will be hard. Eira couldn't stop it. She knew this. But it didn't have to come so soon. And she'd maximize her time with Nana every day. Understanding her condition, and developing contacts at the hospital, would give Eira a fighting chance.

Surely Reist would understand this...if she ever got around to telling him her ulterior motive. Her lie about being a better medic had made sense, even she believed it. Does it count as a lie if the logic was sound? This discussion could wait for another time. She shoved it to the back of her mind.

It was a relief when the day's lessons were over. For Reist, it meant he could stand and stretch and be done with the nonsense that his brain refused to absorb. For Eira, it meant she could relax from the barrage of information and take proper stock of it all. Reist stood and waited at Eira's desk. She flexed her hand gingerly. Speed-writing every syllable made her hand cramp. After pushing her note-book and pens into her bag, she got to her feet.

The sun hung low. Bits of orange light pierced through the trees, into their faces as they stepped outside the sliding double doors. The campus traffic roundabout was bustling with more activity than they were used to. Other students from their school, and the neighboring ones, mingled in with adults coming in for new lessons and certifica-tions for their own careers. Outside, they all scattered, going home. Some went to the nearby bus stop and others had parents pulling through the deluge of vehicles. Eira's came up, her mother waving at them through the windshield. Reist's parents hadn't arrived yet. "Bye," Eira said hastily, delivering a distracted peck to his lips. She rushed over to her mother's car before he could reply.

Her mother looked at her confused, "Are his parents here yet? We could give him a ride home too if he needs it."

"No, they texted him," Eira lied. "They said they're around the corner." She gave Reist a wave and a fake smile. Getting back to Nana was the only thing on her mind.

Reist stood in a slight stupor for a moment and waved back, more out of habit than anything else. When someone waved, he waved back. It was like answering a call on his device or a knock at the door. It was an action that required a reaction. Looking around, he found a bench and sat down. Reist checked his device and saw a message from his mom saying she'd be an hour late. If he had had his bike, it would've been fine. But every other day there was a new riot, and his parents didn't want him riding through that.

"Hey, man," came a voice behind him.

Reist turned. It was Pressin from homeroom. He almost didn't recognize him. "Oh, wow, hey, man, where've you been?"

They gave each other a fist bump. "Ah, I quit archery after the festival was over. Got signed up for this a little while after. Really great for the resume, ya know?"

"So I keep hearing. How far ahead are you? I didn't see you in the class."

"Oh, I've been coming here for a couple of weeks."

"Nice. It's only my first day. Hey, uh, how do you usually get home?"

"Buses. They're pretty good on this side of town."

Reist checked the public transport times on his device. There was a bus stop a few blocks from the house and there was one coming in about ten minutes. He typed back to his mom saying not to worry, he'd hop on the bus with a friend from school. They said they would see each other at home and Reist went to the bus stop with Pressin.

There were three other people waiting there with him; a couple holding hands and an older woman Reist recognized from class. He remembered her because she had an air of single mother looking to start her second career. The bus rolled down from the tram system and stopped with a hissing shush in front of the bus stop. Reist followed Pressin on board, waved his device over the fare meter, and sat halfway down on the bus.

Reist's dad had always sat near the back, be it public transport or at the cinema. It could be a sign of a Type A personality who needed to feel in control. In his youth, Reist would mimic this like a little shadow for his dad. As a teen, Reist had stopped doing it, but now wondered. Several of the vids Reist had watched included military or police doing this.

Maybe Dad missed his calling, Reist thought. But then he remembered the rioting. The idea of his dad falling in battle seemed unlikely. The old man always carried himself in a way of control and strength. It would take a lot to bring him down. Reist pushed away those thoughts. His dad was *squishy*, too. So was Sgt. Harold Mutatio. What did it sound like when someone got shot? Not from an arrow, but a round.

In the time his thoughts erupted and settled, the couple left and a group of three took their place on the bus. They wore red bandanas—one on his forehead, and the other two loosely around their necks—they each had a patch with a symbol Reist hadn't seen before. The air on the bus changed instantly as they walked on. The idle chatter hushed, and everyone turned to look out the window.

The three of them sauntered to the back of the bus and kept their heads together in quiet, rapid muttering. Reist turned to listen closer. It wasn't any Efferan phrases he had learned from the vids. Maybe it was a dialect unique to Efferans on Corvus. Either way, it was still difficult to hear, let alone translate. *Translate*, he thought, rolling his eyes at himself. It was the first day of archery all over again. Learning at least one of the many offshoots of Efferan couldn't hurt. Most of the pirate and mercenary groups the CDF contends with have Efferan origins. But he had only picked up a couple of phrases. Nowhere near enough to 'translate.'

They spoke louder as the trip went on. The other passengers' attention hardened in their focus on anything else. The Efferans started jeering loudly at the older woman. "Ey!" shouted the one with the head bandana. "Mahmee, scaba clair este? Huh?"

The woman, sitting across and two seats forward from Reist, did not engage or look back.

"Ey, fuck you, bitch," Bandana said with a thick accent. "I'm tryna say you look good, but if you gotta be nasty to me, then maybe not."

He turned to his two friends and said something that made them cackle. The bus driver glared at them from his rear-view mirror but said nothing. Pressin gave an annoyed glance at Reist and looked forward again. Something changed in the air, like a dark sickness radiating from behind them.

"Ey, you," Bandana said, no longer jeering, but furious. "Ey, fucker. Boy in blue, I'm talking to you, hear? I know you ain't fuckin' ignoring me."

Pressin's face fell before he turn. "Me?" He asked.

The three sat back in their seats like they were just slapped. Bandana stood and threw his arms out. "You see anyone else in blue on this shit?" There wasn't. "You got a fuckin problem?"

"Nah, man," Pressin said, to sound nonchalant. "I'm cool."

The radiation of sickness changed. Bandana eased towards him, reaching for the grab handle and pulled himself up, glaring at the teen with dagger-like eyes. "Oh, you cool, ain't ya?"

"Yeah, man." Pressin kept the tone, but it was softer now.

Bandana closed the distance and stood directly over him, his two friends followed closely behind him. "Maybe I don' care if you cool, blue," he hissed. "See this?" He pointed to his red bandana. "Means 'Ribellios.' Know what that is?" Pressin shook his head. "Means 'soldier' I's a kingsman. We're all kingsmen and cool people are owed a vengeance, hear?"

Pressin stammered. Bandana appraised his two friends. Corvic-Efferan rapidly flowed from his lips for a moment and laughed again. Reist tensed as the air changed again. They weren't returning to their seats. Instead, Bandana reached into his vest. A quick flash of light reflected off clean steel. The hilt of his knife rammed into the soft skin at the base of the older lady's skull.

Pressin jumped back into the little space he had, collided into the window, and screamed. Reist stared. Everyone scattered away. Brakes screeched, forcing everyone on the bus to the forward. Reist hit his head on the seat in front of him. The three Efferans fell to the floor.

The driver slammed his pale, meaty fist through the thin casing above his head, onto the red button with white lettering, "EMERGENCY." Alarms caterwauled from the bus's ceiling and roof. The three Efferans shot back to their feet and rushed towards the bus's double doors. They threw their weight against the flimsy folding doors. One of Bandana's comrades produced a knife of his own and slashed frantically at the plexiglass surrounding the bus driver. It barely made a scratch. The Efferans finally forced the doors open and sprinted away.

Sirens grew louder every passing moment, each longer than an eon as Reist stared at the blood spilling out of the woman's head. The knot in the back of her skull jutted out, almost goading someone to strike from behind. A woman was dead, killed while on her way home. Pressin spilled onto the floor and slid himself away from the woman, mouth still agape, chanting, "Shit, shit, oh, shit."

It had all happened so quickly. That was what Reist would obsess over for a long time. There was the obvious buildup of events, aggrandizing, and posturing. Those things made sense. What didn't make sense was the wantonness of it. At least with the riot, there was a clear chain of events. Many of them may not have been visible, but the cause and effect were still clear.

There wasn't one here. Bandana didn't care about how the woman responded to him, and he didn't care if the Pressin was afraid. And nothing would've changed if Reist had spoken out. *And why didn't you?* he heard Eira's voice asking. It was part challenge to be brave and part challenge for the sake of antagonizing. Why did fighting someone bigger and stronger than her entice her so much? *Because fuck you, that's why,* her voice said. She would've done something.

The police came and Reist stammered through the statement he gave while his mom stood next to him. He didn't remember when she had gotten there. His brain focused only on bits at a time, and none of them were important. Logically, the event was over and done. Black police radios nearby squawked garbled words just as foreign as another language. Logically, there was only the next step to accomplish. These officers understood that, and this makes sense.

Nothing he could do about the poor woman and Reist had no responsibility to her or hers. But...if this had happened to him, it would be nice if someone cared. If that had been his mom, he would feel better if someone was angry about it. No, it wouldn't solve anything. There's still living afterwards. But now, it'd be nice to be angry.

Reist recognized this and shuffled it away. Logically, there'd be no need for him to do anything except what he was doing now. The statement had finished....some...time...he couldn't quite place it in his memory. His mom hugged him tight and apologized for something. It wasn't her fault. But she had a large heart, strong enough to take on anyone's woes. On the drive home, Reist's attention flew away, and his gaze faded.

Pari was the first one to tackle Reist when he came through the door. Their dad joined in, then their mom. The family held strong for a long time in the foyer, then let go. When Pari and his mom were out of earshot, his dad leaned towards him and whispered. "They got 'em. After they ran off, some cops tracked them down. There's footage of it. They lit 'em up."

Reist's stupor had faded away and what little brain power he had pictured an overhead view of the event. Uninterested in being arrested, Reist pictured Bandana producing a new knife and running towards a wall of gunfire, screaming, *"Fuck confederali! Ribellio till I die, ye fuck!"* His comrades would join him in their afterlife. Like a meat hook, Reist latched onto the realization he knew so little about Efferan mythology and funeral rites. He nodded to his dad and went to go research it.

Chapter 12

A COUPLE OF DAYS LATER, Reist and Eira timed their second attempt at the ten kilometer run. Reist kept pace with Eira the entire way except for the last stretch, insisting to sprint the last half kilometer to "finish strong." It made sense, but it didn't change the fact he could've gone faster. "Just pace yourself," she said. "If you can sprint like that, then you can go faster." They walked a lap to cool down.

Eira was ready to leave, but Reist took her hand and pulled her over to the bleachers. "My dad will come pick us up in a bit. I like the breeze here." There was a small jolt of energy when their fingertips touched. Fingers intertwined; the space charged before making contact. Reist wanted that sensation every day.

Had it been anyone else, Eira would've yanked her hand out of the sweaty grasp. But Reist disarmed her. Holding hands never made practical sense. But now, she didn't mind it. Admittedly, the breeze from the shoreline *was* rather pleasant. And so close to when they fired during the festival. Or the spot in front of them, dead center of the field, she could still see the javelins landing. The coolness mixed with the warmth of the summer sun mixed smoothly with the post-run endorphins rushing through their systems.

Eira got her breath back but couldn't relax. A new medical article about Nana's condition released that morning. The faster she ran, the sooner she could rush home to read it. "We don't have to wait," Eira replied finally. "There's a bus stop a block away." Reist cringed. Eira rolled her eyes. "Really? *You*? There're thousands of buses all over the grid. What're the chances *another* attack will happen, and what are the chances the both of us will be on that one?"

"Probably about as much of a chance there was when I was on it," Reist said.

Eira paused, all thought of Nana and the article pushed away. "Run that by me again?"

"The bus attack last week," Reist began. "I was on it."

Eira stared. Reist stared back, unsure of what else to do.

"That was four days ago," she stated.

"Yeah."

"We've seen each other..." she thought for a moment. "...two of those days."

"Yeah."

"And we message each other every day. Like, *a lot.*"

Realization bubbled to the surface. "Oh."

"'*Oh*'? *That's* all you have to say right now?" she asked.

Before Reist could reply, she slammed her fist into his shoulder once, twice, and several more times. Each punch paired with a word. "Absolute. Shit. For. Brains. Asshole!" There was one last punch. Reist couldn't block any of them. He didn't want to. This was on him. "Why wouldn't you tell me this?!" Her screech reverberated across the track and field and echoed back from the opposite bleachers.

"I don't know..."

"Oh, you fuckin-" Eira gave him another punch. "Try again!"

"I wasn't thinking about it!"

Eira paused. "Better answer, but you still sound dumb as a box of rocks. What *were* you thinking then?"

"How our afterlife differs from the Efferan one," he replied.

Eira blinked at him, all fury replaced with dumbfounded confusion. She punched him again. "You have the dumbest fucking answers." She took a deep, shuddering sigh. "We *have* to talk to each other, idiot. We're gonna be in combat together. All kinds of stressful situations. If you're shot and in shock, I'll need you to talk to me, otherwise your dumbass is going to bleed out and I won't have my backup anymore. You don't talk to me and we're both fucked, okay?"

"Okay."

"Ya know what? No." She stood up to further her point. "Are we actually doing this? Because this is two things in, like, a half hour. You don't give enough of a shit to push yourself on the run and now you don't think to tell me you saw someone die the other fuckin day? I'm out, man."

The bleachers echoed a horrible reverberation with every heavy stomp Eira took on her way down the steps. Reist watched her walk out onto the track, moving towards the parking lot. Blurry clouds pulled away from his conscious mind. Anger pushed it aside and evaporated it.

Hopping over the steps, Reist was on the rubber track before Eira took more than five steps away from him. He reached out and grabbed her by the back of the shirt and stepped towards the field. She cussed at him, but he said nothing, and threw her to the grass. She landed on her back and glared up at him with a shrugging posture. "What? What're you gonna do? You passive pussy, you gonna man up now?"

Reist's hand curled into a fist, and Eira mocked him again. Instead of hitting her, he grabbed Eira by the throat and lifted her off the ground, chucking her further into the field. She was ready for the landing this time. On her feet, she took a low defensive position and eyed him as he matched it.

Neither of them knew how to fight and the worst scuffle they had ever encountered was with the security guards. If anyone passing by looked over, their fight might've been ridiculous. But for them, it was the first of several turning points in their relationship. Reist stomped towards Eira. She gave a quick jab to his face. The distraction gave her enough time to lean in, pull his foot off the ground, and shove her shoulder into his stomach. He fell onto his back and she hammered her fists down while straddling him.

As if the punches didn't affect him, Reist took the hit and used that half moment to grab her arm and shoot an elbow to her jaw. Pain spider-webbed through her face. He bucked her off and retook the mount. He blocked out the sun as he loomed over her, straddling her waist and pinning her arms to her chest. There was an anger behind his eyes she'd never seen in him before.

"Would you like to know what it's like to watch someone die?"

She paused in her struggle, panting heavily.

"It's fucking random," he replied. "No lead up, no setup, no reason. Nothing."

Reist pressed one hand on her elbows and held lazily against her struggles. The other hand came around behind her head, and he poked at the spot below her ponytail. "Right here," he poked it again. "Right here is where some random person got a knife stabbed into her skull. She didn't do a damn thing. She just sat there, minding her own business and she still fucking died. She fucking died, and that was it. That could've been me."

Eira paused at that. She thought about how she would've found out, but kicked it down. "Don't say that."

"She reacted the *exact* way I was. She ignored it and just pretended the bastard didn't exist. Someone else spoke up, though. You remember Pressin? He was in archery with us. Has a locker next to mine. Doesn't matter. He spoke up. Not very loudly, but he still did it. How am I supposed to call myself a good person if I didn't? What does being good even matter if it doesn't keep you from getting killed? *That* is the shit I'm thinking about. So, I beg your cunting pardon if I didn't have enough brainpower to tell you I watched someone get fucking murdered."

Reist still panted erratically. He whispered, through puffs of air, "I think she was in our class, and I didn't even know her damn name."

124

Eira's breathing slowed. She stopped fighting and fluttered her fingers weakly to signal surrender. Reist nodded at the innocuous action that no one else would have thought anything of and pulled away. Eira sat up, leaning forward at the curious sight of Reist kneeling and staring at the shortcut grass.

There was a heartbeat's pause, and they made eye contact. Eira moved forward, kneeling the same way. She lifted her hand. Reist clasped it. They gave a tight, one-armed hug. "If we're gonna do this," Eira began, "I want you to talk to me. You don't have to tell me everything, but I want you to tell me enough, so I know what we're doing."

"Okay."

"Do that for me and I'll do the same for you, okay?"

"I didn't..." Reist sucked his teeth. His eyes darted around as if looking for the next word. Did he *ever* talk about his thoughts—any thoughts—before this? "I didn't realize I was holding it back," he said finally. "I couldn't see anything. I couldn't see myself or my room."

Eira leaned in and grabbed either side of his face. "See me."

"I see you."

"No, seriously. *See. Me.*" She kissed his lips. "I've got you."

His shoulders dropped and his forehead came to hers. Reist let out a deep exhale that removed the weight from his back and out into the world.

"You wanna come over for dinner?" she asked.

Reist looked up to her, confused at the sudden change of topic, "Sure."

"No," she replied. "Do me a solid and go with 'Yes' or 'No', okay?"

"Okay." Reist thought and nodded. "Right."

"Now you're getting it. Active decisions. It won't magically make you stop a stabbing, but it's something small you can work off of. Do you want to come over for dinner?"

"Do you want me there?" Reist asked.

"Don't be stupid."

"Be open about what you want."

"Boy, we're about to fight again," Eira said. "Yes, okay? Yes, I want you over to meet my family and eat our food."

"Good, because, yes, I want to be there," Reist said.

"Good. Gods."

Reist stood and offered his hand. She rolled her eyes and took it. She did that a lot, and usually because he did something. But there was a different tone to each one. Some had a softness to them that felt endearing, and others seemed irritated.

Eira was noticing other minor differences in Reist's everyday actions. It had been a month into their friendship before he showed much emotion besides shrugging. Another month and she noticed a little light flicker behind his face whenever he saw her. This memory made her take his hand in hers as they walked up the track to the parking lot. True to his word, Reist's dad pulled into the front entrance for the campus about fifteen minutes after the pair of them found a bench to sit on.

Chapter 13

REIST RANG THE DOORBELL and waited with a bottle of wine tucked into his arm. It was so much quieter on this side of town. Every night, he could hear the bugs chirping from his bedroom window. Not hearing anything felt...wrong. Silence felt wrong. Reist studied the stained glass fixed into the double doors of Eira's parents' house. Its opulence was just as distracting as the silence, but people liked it?

Shadows formed and grew larger behind the stained glass. The door opened and Reist made to introduce himself to the dark-haired woman. "Hi, my name is Reist and I'm here for—" She gave him a modest bow and opened the door for him. "Oh. Thanks." She accepted the bottle and shut the door behind him. Eira's foyer was large and nicer than Reist's. It had cleaner tiles and a couch he might have seen in a museum. The woman took the bottle through a side door without a word. "...Okay...?"

"Sorry for the wait, babe." Eira came in while Reist was staring at the crystal chandelier. They hugged and kissed, and she took him through the hall to the living area. "Mom was losing it. Just compliment her hair and she'll love you."

The living area was enormous. Paintings covering most of one wall, from floor up to a high ceiling. Another wall had wide bookshelves on either side of a massive vid screen station with large speakers. A head with wispy, graying hair turned from the couch and rose. Mr. Filodoxia outstretched his hand. "Young man." He tried to crush Reist's hand. Reist squeezed back and kept eye contact through the

JIM ROSE

handshake. Apparently satisfied, he released Reist's hand. "Adeio, eh? What does your father do?"

From one of the side rooms, a grayish blonde-haired woman stepped out; Eira's mother. She was wearing a nice, though still somewhat casual, aqua blue dress. Her charm bracelet jingled as she reached to shake Reist's hand gingerly. "Your hair looks wonderful tonight, Mrs. Filodoxia," he said. She blushed.

A motorized whirring came from the next room and Reist noticed Eira stiffen. An old woman steered her chair into the living area with a small control on the armrest. "Serva showed me the bottle you brought. Chatuea Q'inas," she said. "Excellent company. But I know a nice young man like you doesn't know a *thing* about what good wine is yet. Our girl here swears she didn't give you any hints about what to bring. So, who picked this bottle, young man?"

"My mother did, ma'am," Reist answered.

"Oh, no need for that 'ma'am' nonsense, child. I don't need to be reminded I'm old," said the woman Reist assumed was Eira's grandmother. "Although," she continued, "if you're of the same stock that bought this bottle, I'll have to have you come around more often. Your mother has excellent taste. This vintage is my favorite." She held out her hand, "Melanie Filodoxia, charmed."

"Reist Adeio, Melanie."

Though there was a slight, but noticeable change in the air, Reist was confident. The dowager Filodoxia didn't say what she wanted to be called after tossing out 'Ma'am.' And Reist had a hunch she would appreciate the play. Melanie smiled and joy gleamed behind her eye. It was the same look Eira had when he had suggested they break into the coaches' office. That seemed so long ago now, but his mind always came back to it. It felt good to see that look.

"Why don't you come sit by me?" Melanie said, steering the motorized chair through the living area. Reist followed her—Eira close behind—out their sliding glass doors and onto a wooden porch balcony. He stared at the breathtaking view of the massive lake below them, glowing amber by the setting sun. "Over here, young Hovmester," Melanie sat, patting the chair next to her.

Reist sat where she pointed, unsure about why she was calling him...whatever name that was. He sat between Melanie and Eira, who was looking at anything that *wasn't* her grandmother and boyfriend.

"Tell me, handsome, did you drive here?"

"I did not," Reist answered. "My mother dropped me off."

"Smart on two fronts, then. You're still too young to be wandering around with a bottle of alcohol. And this means we can offer you a glass," Melanie said as the housemaid came out with a tray of wine flutes.

"Yes, please," Reist said evenly. It wouldn't be the first time he'd had an alcoholic drink.

Officially, his only drink was when his dad gave him a shot of rum for his thirteenth birthday. But the other times had involved an ex-girlfriend when he had snuck out to go spend the night with her. She had snuck a bottle from her parents' stores each time he came over. This was more of a gamble, but Reist had to be an adult at some point. If he kept spending his teen years reminding himself that he's a teen, then adulthood was bound to be rough. Life wouldn't slow down for him to realize he was an adult. *So, take the initiative*, he thought.

When Reist took a glass and handed it to Melanie first. She smiled and accepted it with a nod. Reist took a second glass and handed it to Eira, who stared at him for a moment and accepted. Reist kept the third for himself. "Thank you," he said to the housemaid, who bowed and retreated inside.

"A gentleman as well," Melanie mused over her glass. After a sip, she shook her head. "Where were you when I was younger? I had to work with whatever was left."

"Oh, you didn't need me, Melanie." Reist was showing a charm Eira had never seen from him before, and even he surprised himself at what was coming out. "Strong lass like you could've left anyone in the dust and gotten farther as a result."

"This is true," Melanie said casually. "Society is an ever-changing thing, but it was such a boys' club I might have done better cutting my hair and throwing on slacks. The world might've benefited from that, I think. Continue being clever, my dear. Men are fun when they're frustrating, but only when they're challenging and not when they're idiots."

"I will continue to strive for cleverness, then." Reist sipped his wine. It had a crispy bite, but nowhere near the kick his ex's father's whisky had.

"I hope you do," Melanie said. "I'm confident my granddaughter will see you along the proper path and you'll do the same for her. If you're meant to, at least. If not, that's alright too. No need to keep on a road that isn't yours."

Reist felt a whole different vibe from the implication, like a punch to the back of his skull. It was like he wasn't sure about the image he wanted to portray. He hid the fear behind a smile as he passed to Eira.

His smile stirred something in Eira's chest. She might've called it a flutter and if she stood now, her knees might give out. Reist turned back to continue talking to Nana, but Eira studied the lines and curves of his face. His jawline at this angle demanded to be suckled, and the way his neck stretched looked strong and warm. It was a disgusting feeling. The last one was almost giddy. Eira blinked back into reality and caught Nana's gaze. She smiled at her granddaughter, having caught her admiring the lad's kinder features.

"-no, I'd say we're pretty evenly matched," Reist was saying. "I can be quicker, but I don't think that has to do with any talent. Some things just come naturally to me. Her, on the other hand." He stuck a thumb at Eira, which was what had caught her attention. "She works for it. She works *hard* and often drags me in on it." He said that last bit directly to Eira's face with a little smile that caused a small flame to erupt behind her cheeks. The bastard.

"But," he continued, "she makes me better. It'd be easy to fall back on what I'm already good at and never try to be good at anything else. It would have taken me a long time to figure that out without our girl here."

Eira stared at him again. He was speaking so highly of her. When did he feel *any* of this?

"I think you're making my baby nervous, lad," Nana said. "Handsome young men are often flattering when they want something."

Reist looked over at her with his frustrating smile. "Problem?"

"Yeah," Eira finally replied. "You're being nice. It's really weird. Quit it."

"Make me."

Eira's jaw dropped, and the small flame behind her cheek grew. Nana cackled at this. Reist looked back to her, "So that's all it took, huh?"

"Sometimes that's all it takes," she confirmed.

"I'm not going to invite you over if you're just going to be mean to me with my family," Eira said.

"Fine, you can come to my house and be besties with my family," Reist said.

"I like that better."

"Oh, and that reminds me, lad," Melanie said. "Do compliment whoever it was who baked that wonderful cake."

"Dad baked it. Mom suggested our girl take it with her."

"Dear," she said to Eira. "It is a good indication of a man if his family can cook. So even if he can't, at least an in-law can. It's good to start somewhere."

"Yes, Nana."

They spoke further before Eira's parents came to join them. Mr. Filodoxia had a glass of—what smelled like—the same brand of rum Reist's uncle favored. Eira's mother had a glass of a different brand of wine. "I'm not trying to be rude, I swear," she said. "That brand gives me migraines."

Reist waved away her apologies as she sat with the smile he'd been getting ample practice with tonight. "It's no trouble."

Their chef came out with a trolley of steaming food on wide platters. Overall, the dinner was lovely. Reist was calm and didn't feel sick to his stomach like when he had met his last girlfriend's family. Eira's father barely acknowledged him until the subject of trade schools came up. Then he was *very* curious about his scores and grades.

When they finished the main course, the chef came out with dessert. The presentation rivaled what Reist and his dad watched on cooking shows. Though the taste lacked the same level of care and attention, his dad naturally dropped into his cooking projects. They began discussing future options for Reist and Eira, and the rest of their graduating class. Mr. Filodoxia was very curious about where Eira ranked in the class. Reist didn't know. He never looked at the class rankings. But he made it clear she was better than any of their classmates.

This answer served Eira's mother just fine, but her father resigned to accept it as the only one he would get. He said little for the rest of the night. Their housemaid cleared the plates when they went into a sitting room next to the living area. This house was bigger than Reist's. In the sitting room was an isloru, a classical, stringed instrument, with a row of keys, and took up half the room. Reist had never learned how to play but used to play a biack, the upright, and deeper tuned stringed instrument. But that was before hi-ed and he was rusty. He didn't mention it when Eira's mother started playing.

She played a piece that sounded like a classical song, but Reist didn't know it. Mrs. Filodoxia looked up expectantly at Eira and waved her over. Eira resisted the urge to groan or roll her eyes. Instead, she made a face before taking a seat next to her mother. Together, they played the piece for another few minutes. Eira rushed back to her spot by Reist. He and Nana clapped. Her father slapped lightly on his chest.

"That was really cool," Reist said to her lowly.

"Shut up," she bit back quickly. No need for him to make fun of her now. But her parents *were* flaunting, so it's only fair he gets a bit of revenge. Another two hours and the energy died down. The evening was over. Reist's mom came by to pick him up. Eira walked him out to the car. "Sorry about all that," she said to him, down the pathway.

"Sorry for what? I had fun."

"You don't think they were patronizing you?"

Reist thought for a minute and shook his head. "Nope."

"They totally were, and I'm sorry about that," Eira said. "Nana wasn't. She loves you. But my parents were."

Reist shrugged, "Cool." His mom waved at Eira through the windshield, and she waved back. Reist pulled Eira in for a hug and pecked her lips. "I'll message you when I get home."

A rock dropped in Eira's stomach. When she gave short answers, it was because she was mad at someone. Now Reist was giving short answers. That fluttering feeling from earlier was a fleeting thing, dashed down by her parents' hubris and this time tomorrow or next week, Eira wouldn't have a partner any. She waved at the vehicle as it drove away and walked back inside. *This was dumb*, she told herself. If Reist dropped her because he couldn't take a joke from his social betters, that's his fault.

Eira shut the door and froze in the foyer. She just referred to herself better than Reist. Both of her parents were already changing

133

into more comfortable clothes. Eira didn't and went straight out to the balcony again, where she knew Nana would be. Nana had reclined her motorized chair some and gazed skyward. Eira pulled up the chair Reist was sitting in.

"He was a nice young man," Nana said.

"Are we his betters, Nana?"

"Why do you ask that, honey?"

"We have a bigger house, and enough money to afford a second servant. His family forfeited theirs back to the state."

"Everyone had to tighten their belts then," Nana said. "You remember."

"But we only lost the gardener."

"That's their business, dear."

"I know but-"

"Where's this coming from, honey?"

"They were flaunting tonight," Eira said.

"Your father was," Nana agreed. "He's always been like that. I tried to raise it out of him, but some boys never stop showing off their toys, no matter how old they get. Your mother? No, she just liked having someone to play for."

"I think he's mad at me."

"Let him," Nana said simply. "Emotions are fleeting, my dear, not a state of mind. Whatever he's mad about, he'll get over it. And if he doesn't, that's his problem. Not yours."

Eira pulled up her feet, tucking them underneath her dress, and leaned into Nana. The elder's arm went around the child and kept her warm.

"He's a bright young man who thinks the world of you, honey. You and your accomplishments were all he talked about while you were ogling his neck."

"I like his neck," Eira said. A shrug was her only defense.

"And he likes you." Nana pecked her on the top of the head.

A few minutes later, Eira was climbing into the shower. The hot water would wash away the nonsense she couldn't let go. The steam cleared away the infestations in her brain. When she climbed out, she was her usual self again, just in time to reply to Reist's message saying he made it home. She got dressed and messaged back.

How did they like me? He asked.

They like you, she replied before pulling up her hospital notes. There were still weeks left in the instructional side of the internship, but Eira wanted to study. And she told Reist this. He messaged back saying that was alright and he'll see her at the next class. Steeling herself, as she interpreted this as him making it clear he was mad at her, Eira redoubled her focus on her studies.

Miles away, Reist was researching instruments and classical music. He didn't know the song Eira and her mother had played, but he wanted to find it. And maybe, Eira would certainly make fun of him for considering this, he could find an instrument to complement the one she and her mother played. He could learn to play that, and they might play music together.

Before he knew it, an hour had passed, and he had found nothing that sounded remotely like the melody he had heard. What didn't help was Eira and her mother played a single instrument, and all the compositions he was hearing included entire orchestras. He'd ask next class.

"Why're you listenin to old people music?" came a little voice behind him. Pari was poking her head into his room. Reist still hadn't changed.

"I'm trying to find a song I heard tonight," he replied, turning to his sister as she stepped further into his room, eyes on the screen. When she got closer, he scooped her up into his lap and pulled up one of the computer games she liked. Reist pulled up her hand to look at the dried paint smeared up her little fingers. "Painting our friends in the garage again?"

"Yep," she said, going back to the computer game. "I gave one whiskers."

They played a few rounds before Mom came in to say it was time for bed. Reist went in for a shower. He met Eira's parents tonight. She, and their path, solidified in his mind. It was more real.

Chapter 14

AT THE NEXT INTERNSHIP class, Reist noticed something wrong. Eira was quiet during the lecture breaks and neither did Reist. She was probably working out something in her mind, the way Reist had with the bus incident, and needed the brain power. Or she didn't sleep well, so taking notes and existing was the most she could do then. Either way, their plan was solidifying, and he was going to be ready.

"We could head over to the weight room after lectures tomorrow," Reist recommended.

"Why not go today?" Eira asked.

"Today's good too. Just thought you'd want to rest."

She gave him a look like she smelled something awful and shook her head. Eira waited for Reist to speak first, to address whatever made him mad the other night. It's been a day, so anything he'd have to be mad about should be null and void. But this was different. She was going to follow a lifelong path with this man, and she realized she knew so little about him.

Originally, she had figured whatever emotional temperament he'd express, she could manage on the fly. No matter what was to happen, they'd figure it out together. Now it felt like the 'talk to me' fight the other day was already forgotten. *Just push through then*, she decided. *Two can play this.*

Class ended, and they split away from the sea of students leaving to go home, and went the other way, towards the weight room in the next building. They went to change. Reist had a list of workouts he had found last week. Eira eyed the differences in weights being added to the bar during Reist's repetitions versus hers. She knew it was stupid to compare. In a reasonable part of her mind, she recognized the obvious physical and genetic differences between them. But it was still annoying how much stronger he was. She'd have to find something else to best him in than raw strength.

Endurance might be her ticket, as this regiment aimed for muscle failure. It targeted body parts the archery team neglected. When Eira stepped into the squat rack and struggled through her set, Reist loomed over her, cheering her on. When it was Reist's turn, Eira demanded, instead of cheered. A vein pulsed out of Reist's neck as he rose through the squat. The weighted bar pressed into his shoulders.

Eira was in his ear. "Are you serious?" she asked. "Is that the weight a blood drinking Recon man is pushing? Well, let me just look that up." She had a mocking tone when she activated her device. "Well, I'll be triple teamed in an orgy," she said, trying the phrase she had read online. It felt dirty and exhilarating. "Says here the standard weight of a Recon member through an average mission is *twice what you're pushing*. Congrats, fucker, you just got left behind by your team and are gonna die from the elements."

Reist's face deepened into another shade of red as he pushed through the repetition and shoved the bar back onto the rack with a shout. He draped flaccid arms onto the bar and bowed his head, panting. Sweat dripped and pooled at his feet.

"You beat it," she said, slapping his back. "One more set and it's my turn."

A glare with all the gentleness of a brick to the teeth peered over Reist's arms, outlined by the burning red of his face. If there was ever going a face he'd have before murdering someone, this was it. And Eira yanked it out of him. Pride exploded in her chest at that. She ignored, and not for the first time, the idea of either of them taking a life one day. Several, maybe as Recon.

Reist struggled his way through the next set. Then it was Eira's turn. Reist pulled off the weights to accommodate her. They thudded heavily to the ground, sending vibrations to Eira's feet. *That's a point for him*, she thought. *That's fine*. It was a low blow and Eira tried to keep her face even but couldn't stop it from going red during her set.

"You can do more," Reist said and added plates to her bar.

Eira blinked at him, slightly nervous, but shoved it deep down. "Hell yeah, I can." She climbed under the bar and began her set.

"Stop," he said. Eira paused mid lift on her second repetition. "You can do more." Reist pushed the bar back into place and added another plate.

"Uh, babe? I think that's enough."

Reist stared at her. "Something the matter?"

"I don't think I can do that much." She hated the words that came out. But it was the truth, and she hated it more for that reason.

"So that'll be some diet blood for you, then? Or do you want me to water down the blood I drink? I can always pass it along to you momma-bird style, too."

"Fuck you."

"Shut up and get under the bar," he said.

Eira said nothing. She pressed her lips together and went under the bar and started her last set. Within the first two repetitions, she knew it was too heavy. It had to be. Reist's glare was pressing down on her and she grunted through the next one.

"Get it, Recon," Reist muttered. "You think they'll give you the time of day if you can't push your own damn weight?"

Another rep.

"You'll have to carry my ass across a battlefield or else I'll die. You gonna leave me behind like that?" Reist asked.

Another rep.

He started slapping her face. *"Are you going to leave me behind? Are you?!"*

Another rep. They were getting stares from the other people in the weight room; people studying to be trainers. Another struggling rep. Eira's legs were wobbly. "NO!" she screamed.

Reist rushed behind her and grabbed the bar at the exact moment her legs gave out. His legs went wide, the bar resting in the crux of his elbows. He passed around her crumpled form and placed the bar back on the rack. He knelt next to her. She stared at the ground, realizing her failure. He lifted her chin, and the angry gaze he had a few minutes prior was long gone. With a soft voice that felt like home, he said, "Fuck yeah, babe."

They pressed their foreheads together for a moment, and he helped her up. Whatever he was mad about before washed away and lost to history. Eira went back to the bar. She still needed to finish her set. They didn't take any weight off. They decided to stay all day, if need be, but they'd finish.

IN THE NEXT LECTURE, Eira had a new light coming from her Reist didn't see the last time. He kept sneaking glances at her throughout class, though she was as oblivious as ever. She focused on note taking. Later, in the library, they compared notes.

"How you've made it this far academically," Eira said, glancing a disapproving eye over his miniscule markings, "I will never understand. I think it is a sure sign of the dumbest luck I've ever come across. I mean, really, asshole, the least you could do is rub some of that luck off onto me."

Reist raised his eyebrows at the comment.

"Shut up," she said, pointing into his face. "That came out wrong." *Or did it?* She wondered. There was a quiet *ping* and Reist booted up his device. "Really?" Eira rolled her eyes. "Library? Come on, man."

Reist's eyes squinted whenever he was concentrating on something. From what Eira could understand, he mapped his thoughts the way a blind man followed a path in a forest. When he found a thread, he followed it. Sometimes he knew exactly where he was and other times he didn't care. In the end, he always got to where he was going. She found it frustrating but figured it could be useful in the future for Recon work.

The blue holographic glow softened. Reist scanned over their disheveled pile of papers and pushed some around. His eyes lit up when he pried one from the others. Holding the paper to his device, he stared back and forth. "Look at this," he said, angling the paper and device to Eira.

On Reist's device was a news article about the latest Efferan riot. Next to the usual threatening eye they'd seen a dozen times was another symbol that matched the rough sketch Eira had copied off the lecture board the previous day. It was a ten-pointed star. Doctors scribbled it onto a chart if the patient was resuscitated by the second or third try. The article didn't talk about the star because it was one of many other random symbols. The writer went into detail about the statistics of these symbols and how they were popping up all over Urbis. But no one could discern what they all meant.

"Okay," Eira said. "Weird."

"Ten points," Reist agreed. "It's a bit excessive for a tagger to put up unless it meant something. And would doctors *really* need to doodle up a star if their patient is alive? There're more productive ways of writing that down."

"I don't know," Eira countered. "Scribbling a quick picture is easier than saying 'guy's breathing.'"

Reist shrugged, but then sat up straighter. His eyes scanned along the aisles of shelved books. "I'm gonna go look it up."

Eira stared at him, fighting the urge to go cross-eyed as she felt what had to have been an aneurysm erupting behind her temple at the brainless spontaneity. She conceded, "Yeah, cool."

In the year or two prior to meeting Eira, and ultimately making the first step on the path to his true fate, Reist had spent time after school in the library. It was quiet. And there was always a book he could stumble on and get absorbed in. As hi-ed became busier, he stopped except for when he and Eira worked on their project not too long ago.

There was still that familiar feeling on Reist's fingertips as they danced across the books' spines until he found what he was looking for. *Intergalactic History and Cultures*. He pulled it out and flipped through the section on Efferan mythologies. And there it was, Monomyth.' The story followed an ancient hero, whose name was lost to time, and came back from the dead. He conquered the mortal chains of death and ascended to what is now called a demi-god. Scholars theorized this being went on to be the god of war and death for Efferus, the same one all the kingdoms called on when they fought each other.

One war led to another, and the cycle of violence pushed further and further until the kingdoms nearly destroyed their planet. Most of it is still habitable, but large chunks orbited the planet among their scores of moons. Many of those were blown to pieces throughout the years. They only have thirty now, but it was believed they had as many as sixty before they developed nuclear weapons.

The symbol, though, the ten-pointed star, was carved into subjects who would attempt to recreate the war god's path to ascension. There needed to be a sacrifice of blood, usually innocent blood, before the subject allowed himself to die. The more violent, the better. According to all historical records, no one had ever been successful.

Reist brought the book to their table to show Eira. Her eyes squinted as they adjusted from reading a medical text to a historical and anthropological one. Though she originally seemed annoyed, there was a spark of excitement when she grabbed the book out of Reist's hand and read the same paragraph two more times. "Oh, that is brutal," she whispered. She read the pages hungrily, a toothy grin rising on her face. She flipped through the pages further and looked to Reist. "Where'd you find this?"

He shrugged. "Just random stuff I find in here."

She went back to the book. "So cool. Wait." She slammed the book shut. "Nope, nope, nope. We're here to study."

"This counts as studying." Reist pointed to the symbols.

"Totally doesn't count."

"I disagree. Peripheral knowledge is enhanced knowledge."

"Shut up and put the book back, dummy." Eira allowed a smirk but rolled her eyes.

"Yes, dear."

Hoisting the text from the table, Reist went back down the aisle and returned the book. He came back to the table, and Eira motioned for him to stand by her with her finger. When he got closer, she elbowed him in the crotch. As he doubled over with a coughing exhale, she grabbed a fistful of the front of his shirt and steered his ear close to her mouth.

"I'm not your fucking wife." Her breath was hot against his ear. "Don't call me 'dear.'" She planted a soft peck on his temple and let go of his shirt. He leaned back, standing straight again, and didn't move. She heard his breathing slow as he fought to calm from the blow she leveled his way. But he didn't seem afraid of it. He hadn't stepped from that spot.

When he did, he came directly behind her and leaned in to hug her. He planted a soft peck on the top of her head and wrapped his arms around her chest. She felt his chin press onto her head. He was scanning the room for something. His arms moved up from her chest to her throat. Not swiftly or quickly; it was a calm and quiet action.

There wasn't any room to move, to evade. He was directly behind her, and she couldn't get out of the hold. Even if she could slide down her seat. His bicep and forearm closed tight around her throat. The opposite arm pressed into the back of her neck and that hand planted on the top of her head. He soothingly scratched her scalp while cutting off her air supply. She hated having her hair touched and had told him this several times, but he didn't care. He liked playing with her hair and would often reach out and touch her for no other reason but because he wanted to. It was like a silent claim of ownership that only she heard and noticed only by anyone truly paying attention.

There was no overt strangling. Reist slowly, and simply, flexed his arm while closing that gap between bicep and forearm. Eira brought her hands up to try and slip between his arm and her throat, but couldn't. From any angle, fighting against him—muscle for muscle—she'd lose. Nails dug into Reist's skin. It was a sharp pain, but it was manageable. In fact, he turned off his conscious mind and let a more logical part of his imagination study the sensation. What was it about this pain that made it 'sharp'? Naturally the nails and their piercing through the nerves. Reist found himself wishing Eira would cause more pain. He wanted to see how much he could endure before giving in.

Eira was testing her own endurance. Reist's slow squeezing said he was in power. *I can do this all day,* the casualness seemed to say. Eira twisted her head to the side, then to the next, trying to find some pocket to breathe. Panic seeped into her brain, flooding the senses. Eira tapped twice on Reist's elbows. He instantly let go and she gasped in the cool air. Cold beads of sweat trickled down her forehead.

A slight pinch and gentle rub down Eira's earlobe sent a shudder through her arms and legs. She went limp for a moment as Reist whispered into her other ear, "Well done, dear."

The kiss to her opposite cheek was just as gentle. Eira stared at the book in front of her. The words mingled together into a hazy, fuzzy jumble. Reist took his seat again and pulled out a page of her notes to look through. It was like the last few moments didn't happen. *We're done now, pet,* these actions seemed to say. *This round is over. Get me next time.* This attitude was confirmed further when Reist offered her no reaction or noise when she kicked his shin under the table, muttering to him, "Asshole."

THIS TIME, REIST'S mom picked him up and asked about how their day was and what interesting things they had learned. When Reist was younger, he thought it annoying. When he messaged Eira about when he got home, she called him an idiot.

She's helping you retain what you learned, she told him. *And it helps **you** develop your self-esteem because 'Hey, you're better than you used to be because now you know *this*.' You're an idiot and you don't deserve your family.* In response to this, Reist sent her a photo of him showing a rude hand gesture. She returned it with an unimpressed look on her face.

There was a tiny knock at the door. Not really a knock, it was more like a tap. Pari didn't like knocking as she wanted to be as small as possible and not bother anyone, especially not for her big brother.

With a smile, Reist ushered her into his room, "What's up, little wing?"

"Are you busy?" she asked.

"Not very," he replied. "What ya thinking?"

She shuffled her feet and asked, "Alien hunter?"

He pretended to seriously consider this, running through a warehouse of thoughts to find all the reasons to say no to this tiny and pure request. Pari gazed at him expectantly. He was closer to a grownup than a big kid and didn't always have time for her and their games. "Let's go hunt some aliens," he said in a low and gravelly voice, very much like the action heroes in Dad's low budget vids.

Despite the mountain of homework he had left, Reist could only focus on the excitement on Pari's face and her joyful skip. His grades were good enough to get into the Confederate Defense Force. One night wouldn't ruin that.

In the garage, Reist tapped at the mannequins, making sure the paint on their 'aliens' had dried. The designs were based off the fishy and lizard-like descriptions in Reist's favorite book series *The Faceless God*. But with the whiskers Pari had painted, these horrid beasts seemed harmless.

They loaded up a small cart with their plastic enemies and toy blasters and tied to the back of Reist's bicycle. Pari rang her bell before soaring out of their driveway. This was one of their dad's rules. They rode to their favorite spot, a forested hillside in the middle of the neighborhood. Reist carried the dummies up through the trees and told Pari to wait while he set them up. He hid one in a bush, a couple behind some trees, another carefully hidden in a ditch. *Eira might get something out of this,* he thought.

The dead leaves rustled and crunched under Reist's feet as he shuffled back downhill to Pari. She already had the toy holster strapped to her waist. Reist took up his and tied it on. He kneeled in front of his sister and slipped back into the gruff character he always used during their games. "Now, listen here, hunter," he grunted out. Pari covered her mouth to keep back in the giggles. "Up over there, yonder are some bad folks. They came crashing here lookin' for a fight. Well, I say we give it to 'em. What'd you say?"

Pari yanked out her toy blaster pistol and aimed it at the air. It lit up with fake *pews*, mingled with plats, electric noises, and a rainbow of lights. "Let's get 'em!" she yelled.

Staying close behind her, Reist let Pari puff her way forward, up the incline. This was about her fun. Let her be the hero. "Oi, hunter!"

he called out to her, his shoulder pressed against a tree. "Take cover! They might get the drop on ye!"

Pari dropped behind a bush and pointed her toy pistol up at the mannequin. Reist thought back to the infantry and Recon vids he had been watching and rewatching, ad nauseam. This was good practice. "Hunter!" he called out, "Cover me! I'm moving up!"

"Okay!" she shouted back between *pews*.

Reist flew through the trees to a spot about one hundred meters up from her. He took a knee behind this new cover and fired his toy blaster. Pari called for him to cover her as she moved. "Covering!" he called back, firing in as much of a dramatic fashion as he could muster. She was quick, learning through mimicry, just like him.

"I see two more!" she cried from her newfound cover. "Two are hiding there!"

"Cover me!" He shouted, "I'm gonna flank 'em!" Reist had seen flanking mentioned in the action vids and historical action pieces; time to practice it.

When Pari's weapon exploded in its kaleidoscopic anarchy, he ran again. Reist banked wide around one of his 'aliens' and dove forward. He tackled the dummy into a pile of leaves. While rolling with the inanimate enemy on the ground, he pulled it on top of him. "Hunter!" he cried, "It's overpowering me!" Reist pulled one of the fake hands to his throat and made choking sounds. "Take the shot!"

Pari aimed her toy at the mannequin and shot rapidly, moving out from her cover and running towards it and Reist. She kicked it off and fired, point blank in its face. Without giving him a chance to appreciate the level of natural efficiency and ruthlessness, Pari moved to the closest source of cover. "Come on!" she screamed, "Let's get 'em!"

They successfully cleared the alien stronghold shortly after, and once more after that, for good measure. The sun was getting low, and they rode their bikes home. Pari put away the aliens and the blasters and Reist hung up their bikes on the wall racks. Then he went into one of their dad's tool kits for an extra set of batteries and recharged their toy blasters.

Overall, Pari showed a better taking to the combat situation than he did. Just like him, she learned by watching and doing. If he went into Recon, or any combat duty, really, how likely would she follow?

The answer came to him instantly. She would not hesitate. It didn't matter how quickly she took to the craft. *Can I really call it that? A 'craft' like fighting is an art?* Reist couldn't let her near a battlefield. That would demand he turn away from the Recon path, however. When he got back to his room, he messaged Eira.

Chapter 15

AS SOON AS MRS. ADEIO dropped her off, Eira stepped in through the front doors and felt something was wrong. "Hello?" she had called out. "I'm home!"

A weak voice had strained through the halls, "Honey....I need help..." The rest of the house—her mother's tacky paintings, or abhorrent wallpaper and ugly, uneven molding—had washed away in Eira's vision as she flew to Nana's room.

It had never got easier seeing Nana on the floor. So frequently, she had been coherent and brilliant. Then sometimes she'd forget who Eira was and forgot she hadn't been able to walk since Eira was in pri-ed. The old woman's legs had atrophied, and the bones had nearly hollowed out from the aggressiveness of her cancer.

The carpet under Nana was soggy, and there was blood coming from her temple. Eira saw a sliver of wrinkled flesh hanging loosely on the end of the bed frame. Nana's face was pale, and her eyes shot rapidly from side to side. "Kari, dear." Her voice was raspy and croaked. Nana thought Eira was her aunt, her dad's sister. How long had she been screaming for help? "I think something's wrong with my legs."

Eira's device blinked on. She didn't remember calling an ambulance. But they didn't come in the door next. That was Serva. Grocery bags hoisted to the kitchen counter. She came at Eira's shouting and the damn woman stood dumbfounded by the scene. Eira directed her to grab another set of Nana's dresses and underthings; something she wouldn't miss if the doctors needed to cut it away. Nana didn't deserve an ounce of shame, not from the medics or anyone.

They had her changed in time before the medics came. Nana muttered quietly as she was hoisted up into the transport. Eira hopped in to ride along, telling Serva to notify her parents and meet them at the hospital. The medics asked for basic information: age, medications, allergies, and illnesses. She listed them off, her words hollow and far away. It would be at least another hour before the shock faded away. Nana needed her. That was all that mattered.

At the hospital, Eira rushed along with the cart but the orderlies stopped her. She wasn't hospital staff. It didn't matter she was an interning student. Instead, led her to the waiting room where a hospital representative asked her the same questions the medics had asked. Eira verified Nana's identity and waited. The chattering in the waiting room assaulted Eira's senses. The sliding doors beeped, and trolleys creaked. Bright colored cartoons danced on the vid screen. Children moaned to their parents about the wait. Other people, waiting to be admitted, moaned about aches all over.

She barely noticed when her parents arrived with Serva. Her mother rushed over, clasping her clammy hands around Eira's, and asked where Nana was. Eira's mother's gaze darted all over the room, as if Nana was hiding somewhere. Eira's father, however, was more composed. His gaze followed a more linear path. Not seeing his mother anywhere, he went to the nurses' station. He gave his name, and they told him Nana was still being seen by a doctor and wouldn't be able to accept visitors yet.

His shaking hands reverberated up his body. But he clenched his hands into fists, nodded thanks, and came back to his wife and daughter. He took a seat. Eira's mother glared at him, confused. "Well?" she asked. "What did they say?"

"Sit down, Beuta," he muttered. "We'll see her soon."

Eira sat to his right and her mother to his left. Her mother grabbed his hand and could not sit still. She fidgeted in her seat, convinced the answer to all their woes hidden somewhere amongst the sea of people around them. Shock slipped away, and annoyance scratched manically up in its place. Eira gripped the arm of her chair to keep from smacking her mother into stillness. Serva sat opposite of them and Eira glared at the silent housemaid.

Memories came back. Serva was out grocery shopping. Nana would make her run errands to get some time to herself. But this also wasn't Nana's first fall. Being the one that cleaned up afterwards, Serva should've been the most aware of Nana's condition. Eira wanted to throttle Serva for leaving Nana alone and for having the audacity to be sitting here with them, waiting. Eira expected the housemaid to make some mighty feat towards bettering the situation. Just do *something*, damn it, instead of waiting, instead of nothing.

"Mom," Eira said. "Stop. Moving."

"I can't help it. I'm nervous."

"We're all nervous," Eira said.

After another century, a nurse came out. They all jumped up and followed the nurse back, riding on her heels every step of the way. The short of it was, as the nurse explained, Nana was okay, but the doctor wanted her to stay here for a little while for observation. "She'll have more information," the nurse said. She held the door open for them and Eira led the way into Nana's room.

It was a small room. It took only a few steps to get from the doorway to the window on the far wall. The head of Nana's bed was against the left wall and there was only a couple of steps' distance between the foot of the bed and the right-side wall. To the immediate left of the doorway was a small bathroom. There were blue tiles with a side table in the far-left corner. It had a fake plant. A vid screen hung from the ceiling on the right side of the room, and other screens showing Nana's vitals were on the left, hanging along the wall separating Nana from the toilet.

The doctor looked at a chart. She was a head taller than Eira, with dark skin and brown eyes. Her hair was braided, pulled back, and tucked into the back of her white coat. The doctor returned the chart to the plastic tray hung at the foot of Nana's bed. "Mr. and Mrs. Filodoxia?" she asked.

"Yes," Eira's father said. He strode past the doctor and stood by the fake plant and held Nana's hand. "You okay, mom?"

Nana nodded, "I'm just fine, kid." She looked at Eira and reached her free hand out. It was thin, pale, but not as much as before. The IV was stuck above her middle knuckle, plumping her skin just enough so her veins weren't as noticeable.

Eira closed the distance and took Nana's hand. She had a bandage over her temple where she was bleeding before. "I'm sorry," Nana said, in a low whisper, and looking directly into Eira's eyes. The eyes held so much power. She rubbed her thumb over Eira's fingers. "I'm so sorry you have to keep seeing that."

"Nana, it's okay," Eira said. "We fall down sometimes."

Her grandmother beamed at her, but it was weaker than usual. Whenever Eira found a chance to quote *From Far Away*, it bolstered a bond between the two of them. This time, it wasn't as strong. The light behind Nana's eyes was dim today. Eira looked at the bandage on Nana's temple again. She kissed her grandmother's hand and turned to the vitals on the screens behind her.

The doctor was going over her findings for Nana to Eira's mother and father. Eira listened while studying the screens. The basics were there: pulse, body temperature, mental activity. They lined up with what the doctor was saying, though Eira noticed she was dumbing it down for them. Eira was barely a nursing intern. At best, Eira knew how to stop bleeding or pop a bone back into place. Even that second one was she was worried she'd mess up.

While the doctor continued her metaphors about Nana's condition, Eira stepped towards the foot of the bed, never letting go of Nana's hand. She picked up the chart and compared what she saw on there with what was on the vital screens. An icon at the bottom of the page sent a strike straight into Eira's ribcage. The ten-pointed star. Nana was clinically dead but was resuscitated. Eira paled and returned the chart to its tray.

"-and that's all there is," the doctor finished. "There's a few more tests I want to run her through, see what we can do about better quality of life."

While Eira, her parents, and fucking Serva were outside waiting, Nana was in here. Dead. The chart didn't say how long she was dead. It was less than ten minutes, otherwise they would've stopped. Nana had been dead. She's alive now, though.

But she had been dead. Eira studied the patch on the side of the IV bag. It read nothing out of the ordinary. Except for the last line, in red lettering. It said to give this fluid only to someone who has bio-necroline in their system.

They couldn't use the paddles on Nana. She was too fragile and feeble. Any jolt of electricity would have burned through her thin and aging skin and cooked her organs. They couldn't chest-press her because they would break her rib cage in the first press. They couldn't use adrenaline because then her heart would explode. Bio-necroline was the least aggressive way to rejuvenate the system. But this meant now that it was in Nana's system, it was less likely to work next time, if at all. Eira waited for the doctor to mention this. He didn't. So, she left it alone. No need to worry her parents further. Maybe was waiting to drop this bomb after the tests finished.

Eira's device buzzed.

"I'll leave you guys be for a bit," the doctor said. "If you need anything at all, there's an emergency button right there on the wall." She walked out.

Eira's parents peppered Nana with questions and affection. Eira pulled out her device to check the message. Reist was asking if he could come over to talk. *Sure, fucker,* she wanted to say. *If you want to break up with me, now is as good a day as any.*

I'm at the hospital, she messaged.

He replied instantly. *What? Are you okay?*

It's Nana.

I'm on my way.

She rolled her eyes and shut off her device. He didn't need to come, but...she wasn't going to deter him. "I'm sorry, are we boring you?" her mother said.

"Reist is coming," Eira replied.

"This is a family matter," her father grunted through gritted teeth. "Tell him 'Thank you', but we don't need him here."

"I want him here," Nana said. "I rather like the boy and I think it's sweet he's coming to see me."

"I want him here too." Eira stood her ground.

Her father looked from both Eira to his own mother and looked away, with a sour face. "Fine."

THE TIRES OF REIST'S bicycle slashed through a puddle and squealed to a halt in front of Eira. She sat on a bench outside the sliding double doors of the hospital's front entrance. His worried eyes ran up and down Eira, looking for some sort of clue past what she had told him over the call. Nana was in the hospital. That was it.

"Hey," he puffed, catching his breath.

"Hey," Eira said, standing up. "Can we go for a walk? I want to get away from here for a little bit."

"Yeah, of course." Reist locked his bike to a stand and set up the wind catcher behind his seat. He stuck his thumb back to the hospital. "Are we not...?"

"We will. I just needed out of there," Eira said. Reist nodded, and they started walking.

They went up to the main road, leaving the wailing sirens and screeching ambulances behind them. The air grew lighter, as if all the problems were being held somewhere. Eira could relax, albeit slightly, and remove some emotional weight. Even if it were only a few minutes, it was enough.

As they walked, Eira recounted the last hour and a half to him, from the time his mom dropped her off to the moment he rolled up on his bike. She was cruel about the family housemaid and sighed. "I don't know when I'll be ready for Recon. If I'll ever be. This has gotta be the beginning of the end for her. Just one more fall might be all it takes."

Eira pressed her face into Reist's chest. His arms wrapped around her, and they rocked back and forth. Reist looked over the top of her head. Based on the turns they were making during this walk, one more left should take them back to the hospital. Reist recognized the hospital as the same one his own grandma had passed away in a few years ago. Grandpa passed away when he was a child. There were strained and fuzzy memories of birthdays and other Founders' Day dinners at her house, but those were the only times he saw her. He had not gone to the funeral either. There was a school trip he had wanted to go on.

People leave in one manner or another. Be it friends growing apart, family breaking off to start their own families, or the inevitable call of death, people will leave. Some nights Reist wondered how much longer it would be until Eira messaged him less and less until he wouldn't hear from her at all. It wouldn't be anything personal. If she wanted to talk to or spend time with him, she would. The same went for his grandmother's passing—and his other grandfather's passing years prior to that—someone's death wasn't personal either.

Reist could never make sense of why his dad was furious at Granddad's death. During the burial, Reist's dad shouted himself hoarse at the gravestone. They couldn't afford the full service of having Granddad's body shot into the nearest star. Though, Reist thought that might be a cool way to go. It would be another year from now before Granddad's coffin would make contact. But loss was all relative to who you were speaking to. Reist couldn't make sense of an aging relative's death and its effect, but it was bothering Eira. And that was all he needed to know. Gods help him if he could figure out what to say to make it all better.

Sometimes all you can say is nothing, was what his mom had said after they buried Granddad. His dad was still upset and Reist was holding newborn Pari on the back porch. She didn't like the yelling, but Reist could get her to settle. Their mom had come out to join them and Reist wanted to ask why his dad was upset, but thought better of it. She said he had a lot of feelings he doesn't let out enough.

Reist could relate to that, but not today. Today was Eira's. Tomorrow could be hers too, as long as she needed. He ran through a mental inventory of his closet. He'd have to make sure his formal wear still fit. There's no telling when the funeral would be, not yet at least, and he should make himself available then too.

"How'd you know?" Eira asked, dissolving Reist's mental sprints.

"Know what?"

"That something was up."

"I didn't," he said. "I thought of something and wanted to talk it through with you."

"What is it?"

"It can wait," he said.

They were still hugging each other. Eira shrugged off his arms, but kept her chest pressed against him. Though with their height difference, her chest was closer to the top of his stomach. She angled her head up completely, placing her chin against his sternum. She took both his hands in hers. "With everything happening in the last hour," she said, "I would happily accept a distraction."

Rubbing his thumbs over her hand came so naturally. They were so small in his. Reist nodded, "Okay...It's about Pari."

Eira straightened up, concern flooding her gaze. "Is she okay?"

"Yeah, gods, yeah, she's okay," Reist said. He told her about the image of Pari on some battlefield somewhere, all to chase after the same career choice her big brother made.

He thought back to that night, holding her when she was a couple of months old. So small, and gazing up at her big brother, laughing at the faces he'd make to distract her from their dad's mournful howls and shouts. How could something so small carry a rifle? Slapping Eira to press the same weight as a Recon's pack and threatening to force feed her blood, that made sense. But not for Pari.

During Reist's turn to talk, Eira took a step back but still held hands. Reist wanted to step forward and keep them close, but if she stepped back, then she had a reason. People rationalize differently. "That makes sense," Eira said, with a thousand-meter stare. She blinked and was back with Reist again. "Yeah, that makes sense. What do you want to do about it?"

"Let's sleep on this," Reist said. "A lot of stuff got chucked at us today. We'll need some time to process it."

Eira nodded, not like she agreed, but softly and rapidly. She appeared to be trying to rush the mental processing along, but was getting nowhere. "Are we still working out?" she asked.

"Oh, fuck yeah," Reist replied. The endorphins were too good to pass up. Becoming stronger was too good to abandon. He could do it on his own. The motivation from Eira was too good to walk away from.

"Okay," Eira shut her eyes for a moment and her shoulders dropped slightly, like a weight slipped off her back. "Good, because I'm ready for the next session."

A few beeps and presses on Reist's personal device, and the fitness regimen he was tracking their progress on, came up. "Looks like next time is rucking," he said.

"The hell's rucking?"

"Those huge packs in the videos?" Reist said. "Those are rucks. We'll carry them on our backs and walk a pretty long distance."

Eira squinted at him suspiciously. "We're just...walking? I don't trust that."

"Me neither..." Reist said.

They both paused, staring at each other with blank expressions. Little by little, the facade fell away, and they were grinning and laughing. They agreed that whatever it was, it was going to suck.

RUCKING, IN EIRA'S unprofessional—though still completely and undeniably unique—opinion, sucked. The straps sliced into her shoulders at the start of it, and a few kilometers in, they felt like the weight was re-aligning the bone between her shoulder and neck.

Reist was beside her, puffing away, hunched over, and keeping his eye on a far-off destination they were pushing through towards. This singular determination offered motivation and fuel for her to keep going. If he was struggling with the same weight she was lugging, then it'd be *that* much sweeter if he gave up before her.

That morning, they met at a spot equidistant between both their houses. Reist came up with a route for them to follow. Eira pointed out how stupid it was to take all those twists and turns their first time and altered it, so it was a straight line. "There and back," she had said that morning. "See? Easier that way."

Relief flooded Eira as Reist slapped lightly on a street sign and turned back the way they came. "Halfway point," he said.

The relief subsided like matter into a black hole as she turned as well and saw how far they had come and how far they had to go. "Kill me," she said.

"I love it when you're kinky," Reist replied.

"This sucks so hard, man," Eira hissed.

"Like a rock through a reed," Reist grunted, and thrust his hips backward to readjust the ruck. "But," he grunted, "this is good. Means we know better what we're getting ourselves into."

"We're getting ourselves into a world of shit," she said.

"Plagued by diarrhea hurricanes."

"You're disgusting," she grimaced.

"Am I inaccurate?"

"No, just disgusting."

The rest of the journey was not as silent as the first half. They griped and complained all the way through, which helped a little. Rucking kept Eira from thinking of Nana. Finally, they arrived back at their starting point, which was a bush Reist had pointed to. They finished the ruck, but neither was ready to drop their packs. "If I take this off now, I'll still have to carry it home," Eira said.

"Yeah, I was thinking the same."

"Cool, see ya tom-" Eira made to move in the direction of her house, and Reist made to follow. "-what're you doing?"

"I'm walking you home."

"Yeah, no you're not," Eira said.

"Yeah, I am."

"This isn't a date, dumbass," she said. "Go home."

"I will, after I walk you home."

"What? So you can brag about struggling farther than me? Nah, we're ending this where we started and we're heading straight home."

Reist pressed the issue. Eira threatened to shove him on his back every step of the way. She made good on this threat the moment Reist stepped closer. Using all her might, Eira rammed her shoulder into his gut and shoved him back. "What did we learn?" she asked.

"Fair enough," he said from the ground, flat on his back. "At least help me up?"

"I ain't lifting your heavy ass up. You brought this on yourself."

She started back home, though slowly, turning slightly to make sure Reist stood up. Awkwardly, he did, but then rushed after her. Of course, he had another burst of energy left in his stupid body. Eira went to push him again, but he was faster.

The little yelp she made on the way down, Reist would later describe as "cute" and she would reply to this description with a punch to the arm. Eira coughed on the landing. Reist turned in the direction of his house and said he'd see her in class tomorrow. "You're an asshole!" she called from the ground, taking a moment to—out of spite more than anything else—to admire the cloud formations this afternoon.

"What did we learn?" he called back. Both her hands shot up in the air, carrying rude hand gestures. They were meant for Reist, obviously, but Eira wasn't too picky.

Standing up on her own was tricky, but it wasn't difficult. A girl might be upset her boyfriend didn't stick around to make sure she got back to her feet. But Reist wouldn't insult her and pretend she couldn't get up on her own. And Eira couldn't blame him. If he was nearby, she would've knocked him over again. They would've been at it all night, knocking each other down.

With short steps, Eira eventually made it back home. If her strides were too long, she'd risked messing up her balance and fall over on her own. She dropped the ruck in the garage. It made a thudding *clunk!* when it hit the ground.

The house was quieter with Nana in the hospital. Her father lounged on the couch, watching the news. Her mother was in the side room, muttering over stacks of documents. Serva was fired, and they needed to hire a new housemaid if they wanted to maintain the arbitrary and invisible status they had. It was pointless. They still had their chef Cuquas and his cool confidence at everything happening fascinated Eira more and more.

Adversity, if used properly, could chip away at the marble column of a person's soul. And, if they're lucky, could become a hyper detailed masterpiece by the end of their worst trials. Eira was eager for the next series of chips and hammering that would take her one step closer to who she was supposed to be. That version of her wouldn't be crying randomly in class or waking up in a cold sweat because any minute, or any day now, her grandmother would be dead.

After her shower, Eira went to her room to study. They would begin their practical phase of education tomorrow, which meant making rounds through the hospital. More hands-on work with Nana's health felt like a light at the end of a dark street. It was a goal. Goals made sense. Mortality was too much to ponder on.

In her notes, the ten-pointed star sat in the margins. It magnetized her gaze whenever she studied, and tonight was no different. Eira put the papers down and pulled her tablet onto her lap. Researching the origins of the star flexed a separate side of her brain, giving the part focused on studies for some time to relax and recuperate. One article led to another and two hours had passed before Eira noticed the time. She copied a link and sent it to Reist with the message: *Let's try this* at the bottom.

WHEN REIST GOT HOME from the ruck, he was smiling. He dropped the rucksack in a corner of the garage, next to the mannequins, and took a shower. After dinner, stayed at the table with both legs propped up on chairs and ice packs tied to his shins. "You'll be hurting tomorrow," his dad said.

Papers and flashcards spread along half the table with his tablet propped up and open to his weakest topic: anatomy. The organs were easy enough, but why did the skull alone need to have so many names sectioned off? Some of the other bones were easy to remember, but the veins and muscles, not so much. The words blurred together and

Reist's brain was running low on fuel. He rubbed his face, trying to stir up some of the old mental reserves. Nothing was coming up.

A slight scraping sound caught his attention and Reist pulled his hands from his face. Pari was pulling up the chair opposite him, carrying her own homework with her. She spread her papers similar to his. Checking her work and simplifying Corvic history was a welcomed distraction and break. Basic math made sense, and history was easy to retain.

Reist's device chirped. It was from Eira. *Let's try this*, it read. He swiped it away when he saw it and would open it up later after his mom ushered Pari off to bed and recommended Reist do the same.

Climbing into bed, Reist opened the link Eira had sent him. It was a history article documenting, based on several accounts, the steps in the Efferan resurrection myth. It began with a struggle, traditionally, a fight to the death. The more blood spilled, the more effective the magic would be. When the conflict (it specifically called it a "conflict" as it could be anything from a single man fighting a legion, to a one-on-one brawl) was completed, a loved one or 'combat brother' would resuscitate the fallen warrior. The combat brother would cut his palm and that of the fallen warrior and offer the blood to the war god. If the god was appeased, or if the blood was pure, then the spell would work and the fallen would rise from the dead and continue to rise above mortality altogether.

Specifically, how blood was deemed pure was, in the article, packed with speculation. Many argued it was a genetic statement. The war god was more likely to reach out to one of royal blood, as the royals were descended from the offspring of the war god's first order of priests. Other, more spiritually minded, people argued the rage, or passion, needed to be pure. The war god's greatest gift, according to the Efferan early scriptures, was adrenaline. In times of high stress, the strength and endurance of mere mortals multiplied.

If the passion was pure, the spiritualists argue, then it was returning a gift back to the war god. Not returning the gift as is, but returning it improved. The way a child created art was based off the rough
materials a parent supplies. Show the war god you understood the
value of his gift, and he will adopt you as his own. There needed to be
an action vid series of this. If there was, it'd be Reist's new obsession.
But his eyes went back to *Let's try this*. He replied, *When and where?*

The device chirped back later, but Reist was drifting to sleep by
then. He'd read her response in the morning. It said, *My place, after
rounds?*

Chapter 16

THE USUAL MORNING BUSTLE successfully hid Reist from Eira's attention until he sat in his seat next to hers. "Mornin," he said.

"Morning. Get my message?" she asked.

"Yep. I'm down," he replied, though he still had several questions about what "*this*" exactly was.

"Okay," she said. Her body language was subtle but spoke volumes when Reist learned it. The slight rise in pitch in Eira's voice, the small curve on the side of her mouth, and her quickly facing to the front. To everyone else, she didn't seem to care. But to Reist, she might as well have been skipping and hollering.

The instructor came, gave one last lecture about safety around the hospital, and ushered them all out of the class and into the main building. As always, Eira was at the front of the procession and Reist on her left. These side corridors housed on-call rooms, darkened with bunk beds. They passed the locker rooms and the staff lounge. It would be another few disorienting turns before either Eira or Reist could identify where they were. The instructor pushed open a set of double doors and the recognizable nurses' station doubling as a front desk came into view.

Just a few paces from here, as the instructor introduced the on-duty nurse. She was the same one Eira had met on that awful day a few weeks ago. Since then, Nana had moved from under emergency observation to a more relaxed status. She wasn't released to go home yet, but visiting times had expanded. Eira took advantage of this as often as she could and always started each visit, looking at Nana's chart.

The rest of the hospital tour was uneventful. Reist often wandered these halls since Eira's grandmother had been admitted. Sure, he knew both Eira and Melanie were happy to have him too, but it still had felt wrong. He wasn't part of their family and didn't want to intrude. So, Reist explored the hospital. The internship would make him familiar with the entire building before long and he wasn't far in case Eira needed him.

Students split up and had tasks assigned to them; mostly administrative, busy work. There was no time to sit and think because as soon as they finished one job, another one pulled Reist and Eira in a different direction. The most beautiful thing Reist had heard up to that point was when someone said, "Alright, kid. You're released."

He didn't stay to see who said it. So many nurses, doctors, and technicians moved in and out of sight that all of their faces and names blurred together. He left the floor, climbing the stairwell, and messaged Eira. *Hey, we got released.* A moment later, Eira replied with Melanie's room number. She had moved again. It was three floors up the stairs and down to the opposite wing of the main building. Reist weaved and ducked through the bustling bodies, wincing with each step. His dad had been right. His shins felt like they had daggers stabbing deep. The room came into view.

"Knock, knock," he said.

"There he is." Melanie grinned at him. Her bed was in a reclined position, pillows propped her up, and her eyes were mostly shut. "Having such a handsome gentleman caller does these old bones good, knowing I still got it."

"Sexy piece of ass like you," Reist said. He stepped in, coming to stand next to Eira, and putting a hand on top of hers. She was always holding Melanie's hand when she came to visit, and never deterred Reist from adding his hand to the small pile. "I just can never keep away." He winked.

"Young man, I have met many people over the course of my life, and I can only count on one hand the slutty men who had dangerous winks," Melanie said. "And you're one of them."

"I am who I am, and I'll never apologize for it," Reist said.

"Babe, please don't call my Nana a 'sexy piece of ass,'" Eira said.

"Prude," Reist replied.

She glared at him for a moment and kicked him in the leg. He grunted deeper than usual. Her perfectly aimed strike hit the part of his shin that was hurting the most. He sucked his teeth and returned her glare, mouthing a swearing threat her way. Eira puckered her lips and kissed the air.

"Oh, get a room, you two," Melanie said. "You're far too young for me to contribute."

"*Aaaand* we're done here," Eira said, yanking her hand from the small stack. "Let's go, asshole. We have that assignment we need to do."

"Coming, dear," he said. Reist gave Melanie's hand another squeeze. "I promise not to neglect you."

She smiled and shook her head at him. "Away with you, young man. I know a heartbreaker when I see one."

"SO," REIST SAID, DROPPING his bag in the corner behind Eira's bedroom door. "What is it exactly we're trying?" That morning Reist's mom shared a ride with his dad to work, leaving Reist the car. When he and Eira finished visiting Melanie, he drove them to her house and parked on the curb.

The *thump* of Eira's bag when she dropped it on her bed gave it a heavier sound than he expected. It was bulkier. It had sounded weightier when she had tossed it in the backseat, but he had thought nothing of it. Reist had assumed she had packed extra textbooks. She did that all the time. In fact, that was the reason they had gone to the library. There was a topic Eira didn't understand and Reist wasn't helping. She had dragged him with her to spend hours researching the nomenclature and history behind a specific disease he still couldn't pronounce. It was not an extra textbook, or several, that was weighing down Eira's bag. It was a defibrillator kit. Reist stared.

"What."

"Okay, so here's the paddles," Eira muttered to herself. In the kit was a densely folded packet with diagrams and detailed instructions. Inside, next to the paddles, was a thin, plastic mouth sleeve for mouth-to-mouth resuscitation. "But where's...okay, here it is." She held up a vial to her eye and inspected the minuscule lines ticked from the base to the cap. With a nod, Eira replaced the vial in the foam pocket in the corner of the case. "We still need a knife." She scanned the case.

"The fuck?" Reist finally finished.

"Hm?"

"What. The. Fuck?" Reist repeated.

"The ritual, dumbass. Try to keep up. Do you have your pocketknife with you?" Maintaining the confused, stunned look on his face, Reist's arm moved on its own. It reached into his right pocket and pulled out the blade, still folded in. "Perfect," Eira said. She held out her hand and Reist surrendered it.

The blade flashed briefly, reflecting the light coming in through Eira's thick violet curtains. It gave a satisfying click, and the coolness of the metal sent a slight chill to Eira's core from her arm, starting at the finger that slid over the sharpened edge. A small jolt of slicing pain and a single bead of blood formed on the topmost digit of Eira's forefinger.

"Perfect," she said, and sucked her fingertip clean. "We're in business."

"What," Reist began, rubbing the bridge of his nose, "the *fuck*."

Rolling her eyes, Eira lowered the blade. "Did you even read the link I sent, dumbass?" She asked.

"Yeah," he said. "And I get it. I'm not asking what we're doing. I kinda pieced it the fuck together. What I'm more curious about is what the fuck is going through that head of yours?"

"You going to follow me to the Ebony Gates, or what? Or was joining me in combat just a bunch of shit talking to get in my pants?"

"We haven't even had sex yet, first off," Reist said. He held out a finger as if to count. Eira interrupted him.

"Is that a problem?" She asked.

"What? No."

"Then why bother listing it?" She asked.

"Why accuse me of wanting to get into your pants if we haven't had sex?"

"I want to be Recon, but I haven't gone through the training yet. Not having done something doesn't mean you don't want it. In fact, wanting is the first step in accomplishing something. So how horny are we?" She waved the blade in front of her again and said, in a sing-song tone, "We can do some *bloood plaaaaay.*"

Moments ticked by in silence. Reist stared at her. His face was mostly blank, but Eira could spy the slightest bit of anger rising through the tectonic shifts of expression. Eira matched him. Normally, he could decide how to react based on how she was acting. But it was impossible not to get caught up in her excitement. Joining her, sharing this was a high Reist had never experienced before meeting Eira.

A deep sigh from Reist broke this still frame of their lives. He stepped forward and picked up the sheet from the defibrillator kit. It doubled as an instruction manual and inventory sheet. One by one, Reist went down the list of items, pointing at the paper and then to the corresponding device. He even picked up the paddles and compared the serial number on them with the sheet. They purred when he swept a thumb over the power switch.

The humming of the paddles morphed into a familiar song as Reist inspected them. Eira stared. This clueless bump-on-the-log, who barely took any notes, performed a seamless function check they had only spent an hour learning. Even she could only remember the vague steps and would have needed to refer to the notes. It would have taken twice as long as it took Reist. How good was his memory?

Reist returned the paddles to their foam cut out and continued through the inventory sheet. He went through it all again once more and turned to Eira. "How are you going to kill me?" he asked.

The question hit her like a kick to the stomach. It echoed up her chest, evaporating everything in its path before she regained her composure. "After you kill me," she replied. "By then, I'll know it works."

Reist blinked. "You fucking moron," he said. "People have been trying to recreate this for millennia, *all failing*, I might add, and you think we can figure it out here?"

"How many of them had what we have?" Eira asked. She reached past Reist, letting the moment ferment with tension and passion as she maintained eye contact. He wasn't good with emotions, but he was a romantic. She could use that to get him to agree to all of this, if she just kept her steps careful and true.

The small vial glowed teal and metallic as the gray, liquid contents sloshed around slightly between Eira's thumb and freshly cut forefinger. "How many of them had this? Bio-necroline is still experimental, but that doesn't stop hospitals all over Corvus from stocking them. It's got a ninety-three percent success rate in resuscitation. And—"

"And if you're the seven percent?" Reist asked. "I'm left in your house with a dead body that has my DNA all over the room and a few nosy neighbors would attest to my being here, too."

"Babe...come on," she said. The next steps of her path, mapped out in her mind, were falling away before she could aim for the nearest one. "It worked for Nana. Us talking to her less than an hour ago was because of this little magic liquid in her system."

"What?" A few missing puzzle pieces fell into place in Reist's mind.

"She was legally dead for about seven and a half minutes," Eira said. "After I got her to the hospital, she died in the emergency room. They couldn't use the paddles, they couldn't use the chest press, so they used some of this," she explained, shaking the vial again.

There was a rising softness in Reist's gaze as realization formed a base for Eira's next steps, even if slightly. "Why didn't you tell me this?" he asked, voice hushed.

She let out a noise that was half cackle, half guffaw. "Yeah? Why *would* I? Why *should* I admit one of the most important people in my life is going to die? Why would I admit that to anyone when I can barely admit it to myself?

"Why the hell would I even bring it up with you when you don't tell me you watched one of our classmates die?" She continued. "Why would I bring it up with you when you don't even know her, my Nana? Do you even remember the name of her disease? I've mentioned it enough. I drove myself crazy researching it the first time we went to the library. Or could you be bothered to even remember that much?" Eira lifted the knife up and studied it. She balanced it between her fingers, as if contemplating the blade itself.

"We're interning here so you can understand her illness," Reist said.

This yanked Eira's attention from the blade. "To under...no fucking duh! Gods! What is with you? I can never tell if you're the dumbest sack of meat I've ever seen or a bloody damn genius. I mean, are you really just *now* piecing this together?" She sighed. "Maybe this was a mistake." Eira closed the knife.

Reist wrapped his hands around hers, pressing the knife harder in her grip. "Think about that for a moment," he whispered. "Without knowing why, or even caring why, I followed you. No questions. No hesitation. I was with you. I have been sitting here, and we started down this path.

"You, on the other hand," he continued, "need to talk to me. I can only follow if you don't give me the full picture. I can't be a partner if you don't give me the full picture. We haven't been doing this long enough to read each other's minds yet. Had you told me, I could have helped you search. I doubt I could have found anything, but I would have helped because I love you and your family, you idiot." The grip Reist had on Eira's hand loosened enough for him to take the blade out of her palm. The blade clicked open and Reist held open his palm.

"I'm sorry..." Eira said. She lost sight of where she would go from here. Reist was leading now.

"Shush, darling," he whispered and sliced the blade diagonally across his right palm, "and give me your hand."

Without hesitation or speaking, Eira gave him her right hand. There was a thin line of his blood stretching from tip to hilt. It sat wet on her skin, and she bit her lips shut as he slashed across her hand. Their bloody palms clasped together tight. Reist leaned over to place the knife on her dresser and kissed her.

The defibrillator kit was discarded to the floor. Eira kicked her bedroom door shut, and they undressed each other. Neither were virgins, neither were experienced, and none of that mattered. Blood was smeared and licked off each other.

About the minor preferences either of them had, a single phrase of encouragement or direction was enough for their differing frequencies to link and combine. Before inserting himself, Reist licked the bloody line off his palm and Eira copied him. When he filled her, their tongues met, and palms clasped tightly once more. He was controlled in his thrusts, and she matched his movements.

At the moment of climax, their eyes were locked, linking the final chain of their coupling. Bloody palms cupped each other's faces as their breathing slowed and settled. Sharing a deep, calming sigh, they expressed their love for each other again and kissed. They stayed still for some time. Eira refused to let him exit her, and Reist couldn't stop studying every curve and corner of her face. He committed to memory every detail of her iris, and the feel of her skin.

The pillow was cool to the touch when Eira pulled it out from behind her head and placed it over her face. Her muffled sigh was content, but shuddering. She placed her hands on Reist's wrists and steered his hands to either side of the pillow. Her thumbs grazed over the short fuzz on his forearm in reassurance. Shaking his head, Reist pulled the pillow away, and it fell to the floor. "No," he said.

"Baby," she said, disappointment falling over her eyes like a veil. Reist's gaze was immovable and steady. "Alright," she nodded and pulled him into an embrace. Her arms wrapped around him, and she traced light shapes with her fingertips across his back. One of them was the ten-pointed star.

Chapter 17

EVERYONE IN REIST AND Eira's class was designated as "intern." Unlike the doctors and nurses, they didn't have name tags. This meant that the first few weeks on the hospital floor were confusing whenever someone shouted, 'Intern!' On the third or fourth day, everyone understood it wasn't one person. 'Intern' meant anyone who was closest. This time it was Reist. A nurse handed him a folder. "Fourth floor," she said. "Urinalysis." He nodded and slid through the bustling group of people crisscrossing in his path, folder in hand.

As he left, Eira's gaze instantly went over his back, lingering on his shoulders and down to his backside until he was out of sight. Shaking her head, she brought her attention back to the forms she was filing out. The nurse who handed Reist the folder, Nurse Roberts, caught Eira's gaze. She saw Eira admiring Reist on the way out and shared a knowing look with her.

Embarrassment spiked down Eira's spine. To fight the nervousness behind her eyes or the reddening in her cheeks, Eira asked, "Help you, ma'am? Need anything?"

"Not at all," Nurse Roberts chuckled. "Nothing at all." She made to step away, but stopped herself. "It may not be my business-"

Won't stop you from asking.

"-but does he...I don't know, talk?" Nurse Roberts asked.

"Yes?" Eira answered, almost relieved she knew something the nurse didn't. It took all the pressure away from her embarrassment.

"Okay," she replied. "I've just never heard him talk before. I thought he might be...well-"

"Thought he might be what?" Anger bubbled up behind her face, but Eira smothered it; better to act polite and innocent rather than rush to a confrontation.

"Slow," Nurse Roberts stated, locking eyes with Eira. It was almost like she knew the play Eira was making and demanded they not play any games. "If he's slow, I want to be informed. There're people's lives we're meddling with in here."

"If he was slow, how would he even have made it in this program?" Eira countered. "I promise, he's one of the smartest people I know."

"WHERE THE FUCK AM I?" Reist muttered under his breath.

Room numbers were in the four hundreds, and Reist double checked the door leading from the stairwell. He was *definitely* on the fourth floor. Though he had never run a folder to urinalysis before. It shared the floor with the labs, and he had *definitely* run folders to and from there. In front of him, people busied themselves. Multicolored scrubs rushed up and down the halls. Others ran in and out of patient rooms, to waiting areas, and the nurses' stations. One nametagless body came rushing past him. Reist reached for the other intern.

"Hey, man," he hushed to the skinny blonde boy. "I'm trying to find urinalysis?"

"That way," the boy said, pointing around the corner to Reist's far right. He rushed off before Reist could say thank you.

Reist rushed over to the direction and found a side corridor. Down the hallway, about a dozen steps, was the sign reading 'Urinalysis Lab.' Below the sign was a sign giving patient instructions, and a vase filled with marbles and fake flowers on the tips of pens. The woman behind the desk looked up at Reist expectantly and clearly annoyed to be taken away from her book. "Yes?" she sighed when he didn't say anything.

"From downstairs," Reist handed over the folder.

The woman accepted the folder. She opened it and glanced over its contents with rapidly scanning eyes. Her glare returned, peeking out from under her eyebrows, "Bye...?"

With an awkward smile, Reist stumbled backward, out of sight from the desk. Slipping out of the side hallway and back into the main chaos of the fourth floor, Reist took a second to breathe. Each day was a mess of busy work and rushing around. It was great because it made the hours fly by. But this was a unique moment where he could stop and evaluate himself.

Inside Reist's mind, he couldn't find an opinion about working here. He and Eira still hadn't sat down to discuss the Recon route, or any enlistment, really. It *sounded* like she wanted to hold off until after her grandmother passed. It was a pretty grim situation, but it made sense. Eira didn't want to be anywhere but by Melanie's side when she passed away. Reist could sort of relate to that, or at least respect it. He wasn't there for any of his grandparents' passings.

The question remained: were they still set on the Recon option? They were still training as if they were. What if Melanie died and Eira turned to him immediately afterwards to say, 'Let's go. Let's do this'? There was still Pari. Whenever Reist came home, he went straight to sleep after a shower. It was going to be a hard conversation to have with his little sister.

THE FLOOR, WALLS, AND ceilings shook as the low growling rumble tremored up the building. Reist steadied himself on the nurses' station. White lights flashed along the tops of the walls, reflecting ominously off the ceilings. Alarms wailed like robotic screeching, mixing with alert messages over the PA system. "Evacuate," the robot chanted over the speakers. "Evacuate," it repeated, buffeting over the screams and cries of the people on the floor. "Evacuate."

The fragmented scratching of broken glass against linoleum floors mingled in with the noises. On the far side of the floor, opposite where Reist stood, the windows from the waiting areas and patients' rooms blew in. Nurses rushed to their patients. They called Reist as he rushed past. "Intern! Intern!" He ignored them. Eira was downstairs. And there was a massive window by where he had left her.

THE EXPLOSION WAS NEAR enough to Eira that she only heard the high-pitched ringing in her right ear. The shock of it distracted her from the three shards of broken glass that punctured the side of her face and head. Had she not been filing behind the counter, they would have gone into her eyes. Nurse Roberts was not so lucky.

The nurse had crumpled onto the floor, hand clasped to the front of her throat, struggling to keep the pressure as blood flooded through her fingers and down her front. Eira rushed, on her hands and knees, over to Nurse Roberts. Eira yanked her scrubs top off and pressed it where the flood was gushing out, shooting towards Eira's white undershirt. Nurse Roberts grimaced as she brought her hands to Eira's and pressed down as well. Eira cried out for help, but another nurse was already crawling over from around the corner of the desk.

This nurse, Jacobi, was also hit. Bloody slashes crisscrossed over his cheek, temple, and chin. He took Nurse Roberts's hand and pointed Eira to the nearest med kit. It dangled from its post on the wall. She yanked it down and opened it. Nurse Jacobi was talking to Nurse Roberts, but his words couldn't pierce through the ringing in Eira's ear. He called to Eira as she stood and rushed towards the double doors to the stairwell. "Intern! Get back here!" Nana's room was on this wing, one floor above on third.

THEY BOTH KICKED THROUGH the door to the stairwell at the same time. Reist was rushing down and Eira was rushing up. They made eye contact, and Eira reached out a hand. He grabbed it, Eira sliced through the evacuating people, passing over the bleeding and the dying, towards Nana's room. A popping noise forced them to a crouching position. Reist yanked her away from their path and into a nearby room.

Proudly strolling into view, from the opposite hallway, was a man clad in black and red. His boots crunched the broken glass under heel, a knife and pistol hung from his waistband, and a bulky vest protruded out from under a long, leather jacket. The red bandana obscured his face, with the Efferan eye painted over it. He fired the rifle into the ceiling and shouted at the patients and faculty, cowering away from him.

"Stay down," Reist whispered in her left ear.

Eira's gaze locked onto the rifle. Reist shoved her and pointed. She focused on the path leading from where they were, to where Nana's room was. The attacker was in their way, but if they could wait until he passed, or somehow distract him...The attacker leveled his weapon onto the nurses' station and opened fire. His victims were out of sight, but their final screams pierced through Eira's half hearing, and into Reist's soul. He cloaked his body further over her.

The Efferan shouted other things, but it was in their rough vernacular and spat out too rapidly for Reist to understand. Peeking from out of the bottom corner of the doorframe, Eira saw the Efferan turn towards them. She pulled back in time for the space a meter above their heads to explode. Bullets punched through the wall, across the room, and through the window on the opposite side of the door.

The rifle barrel poked through the doorway and erupted. More cries came from behind Reist and Eira. They hadn't even seen the patient when they rushed into his room. The bedridden man reached out and said, "Wait!" before blood exploded out of his belly, chest, and face. A hand slapped over Eira's mouth, muffling her scream. Reist held her close, trying to stay quiet. The barrel of the weapon vanished, and more gunfire came in the room nearby, echoed by the screams of the dying.

Wiggling and flailing, Eira broke away from Reist's hold. She muttered a single word, "Nana," and rushed out into the hall. Reist was close behind. He gazed down the hall and saw the gunman firing into the room further down the hall. The Efferan peeled away and continued. The door to Nana's room seemed heavier now. Reist quickly closed it, leaving only the tiniest gap before easing it completely shut. Eira's voice was barely a whisper. "No...no, no, no."

Turning, Reist took in the room. The initial blast downstairs had blown the window inward. Massive shards of broken glass littered the floor, darkened and cloudy. Some shards had pierced the hospital equipment Melanie was hooked to. Some shards were in bed with her, a few stuck out of her arm.

Blood pooled in the old woman's chest, spilling down to her lap. Her eyes were vacant, mouth agape, and her body still. She wasn't breathing. The machines made no noise. Pulling the dead woman's face towards hers, Eira searched the glossy gaze. There was nothing there. She fell to her knees. Reist rushed behind her. Eira crumbled to the floor, face hiding behind both hands. She shook silently, tears flowing through her fingers, rocking back and forth, and chanting "No," like a call to absent gods to correct their mistake. Nana was not your intended heavenly divines. Take someone else instead.

Turning to face Reist, she shoved her face into his chest and grabbed at whatever she could reach. Her screams muffled into his chest. Reist said nothing. He listened for where the latest gunshots were, and if there were another set of boots coming to the sound of Eira's sobbing. There were other people on this floor, still alive. Other patients' families rushed to their loved ones' sides after the gunfire stopped. Reist stayed with Eira.

The rough blueprints of the building Reist had in his mind rushed through as he tried to figure out where Eira would be safe. Any place that could act as a hardened shelter was too far from here and would take them out from behind this locked door. But Reist didn't want to keep Eira here, with the body, any longer than she needed to be. But she couldn't move. All brain power was processing an impossibly large equation she didn't want to approach or address or acknowledge.

The laugh Eira had heard all her life was gone. The twinkle and wink synonymous with Nana extinguished. All ties linking her to the mortal world slashed. Now there was only Reist. She sobbed into his chest. Maybe, just maybe, if she cried enough, it would bring her back. If Eira mourned just enough, then maybe the dream would fade away. Eira might wake up at home and realize Nana was never even in the hospital. She would have *years* to go yet.

But Eira opened her bloodshot eyes, and the ruined hospital room was still there. Reist's head turning every which way, looking for some solution that remained either hidden or nonexistent. Turning over her shoulder, Nana's corpse was staring down at them. "Fuck," she said, turning her head back into Reist's chest. "Damn it. Damn it."

Reaching over to the bed, Reist slid himself and Eira closer to the glaring body. He pinched a corner of the blanket and awkwardly tossed it upward. It mostly covered Nana, some of her hair stuck out from the top.

Fingers curled into fists, bunching bits of Reist's shirt into her palm, Eira held on hard as the world changed course suddenly and drastically. Reality was irrevocably changed. The skies would be less

181

bright from here on out. Eira held on tighter, Reist being the only sturdy thing nearby. He gave no words of encouragement, no lies to lull her into emotional security. He recognized the damage and was simply there.

More gunfire came from far away, somewhere below them. It was rapid and sporadic, not the controlled single shots from before. And sounded different. The police had arrived and started shooting. Reist and Eira knelt in the soul shattering dark as the gunfire slowed and quieted. They gripped each other tighter when another explosion shook the walls around them.

PRIOR TO THE HOSPITAL attack, there were approximately three major Efferan gangs active across Corvus. There were another dozen smaller gangs running in between them, hiring themselves out to whichever one was higher on the ladder that season. One of these smaller gangs, called the Pied-Pico, attacked the hospital. They had adopted the ten-pointed star as their central sigil and chanted throughout their attack, "Eit Vivero" which was translated into "I live again."

After the hospital attack, each major gang publicly denied having any involvement in Pied-Pico's actions. This didn't mean they discouraged the attack. The Pied-Pico's attack became a rallying cry. All their members were involved, and all killed during the gun battle with the police. 'Onniscite' was Efferans on Corvus called themselves. Each major gang came together into one and absorbed the minor ones. They were a united front now, reaching out for homage from the kingdoms in the home world. The Screaming King, after having been forgotten in the constantly rotating news cycle, was the first to make his position known to support Onniscite.

Melanie Filodoxia was one of dozens who died in the attack. The gunman Reist had seen was one of three sent inside to murder who they could. The primary focus: chaos. If the higher-ranking natives of Corvus were allowed their ivory towers, then raze them to the ground. Destroy every brick in sight. Melanie was the cornerstone of Eira's personal tower.

The last Efferan to die had pulled one last explosive out of his jacket. Hoping to take as many of the police with him, each of them—according to Efferan faith—would be a servant in the dead realms for all time. This hope vanished when a round went up his chin, through his skull, and into the hospital wall behind him. The explosive in his hand, armed and live, fell from his limp hand and blew up half of the waiting room lobby on the first floor.

THERE WERE MANY FUNERALS that month, and Melanie Filodoxia's was held during the middle of it all. Eira wanted it done as quickly as possible. It was easier that way. Say goodbye, bite the hurt back, and hopefully be able to have some semblance of closure.

Some of the wealthier families held their funerals by the bay, close to the airstrip. They collected their dead into a single vessel that would travel to the nearest star, traveling through space for the better part of a year, before being engulfed. Eira preferred this idea. This meant if she ever wanted to speak to Nana, she only needed to look up. When winter came, she would feel the warmth of the star during a run or hike. No matter where in the cluster she was, Nana would be there.

But this isn't what Nana had wanted. In her will, she had asked for one of the older funeral services instead, one she had witnessed for her great grandfather. They had laid him out in a wooden rowboat and an archer had fired a flaming arrow while it sailed away. The date on Nana's last will and testament was shortly after Eira began the archery team. She had asked if, and only if Eira was willing, she could help usher her corpse into the ocean below.

Abandoning the internships, Reist and Eira returned to their archery coach to ask permission to use the equipment. Shooting is a perishable skill and Eira had three weeks before Nana's funeral. She'd get this right. She hadn't made it to Nana's room in time, but she would honor this.

Back on the field again, with the cool and salty breeze of the nearby river to keep them company, Reist stood by Eira as she fired. He watched her form, but there was nothing to correct. Their coach stood by with a lighter and fire extinguisher. Eira shot her arrows without the flames first, and with them after, all at varying distances.

The breeze from the river, though annoying when they were on the team, helped now. Eira could practice with a heavy breeze to better train and read the wind. It was essential for Eira not to miss. First shot, first landing. The flaming arrows were heavier and required better calculation. For hours, every afternoon into the evening for three weeks, Eira fired and Reist stood by. Neither spoke a word.

Chapter 18

THE FUNERAL PROCESSION wore black with a single line of white. For the men, it was a white tie over all a black suit and jacket. For the women, the line went down the seam of the dress, breaking off over a bare leg, and down the black shoes.

Melanie Filodoxia's funeral litter was carried by Eira's father and uncle, as well as Eira's cousin, with Reist carrying the back left corner. Eira wanted to help carry, but tradition dictated she follow behind, her archery bow strapped to her back. She kept step with the pallbearers and rode with the funeral director to the dock. A black boat waited there, looked over by Nana's attorney. They had painted the rear of the boat with a symbol of the faith Nana's great grandfather kept to, though was mostly out of fashion now. Swirling concentric rings encircling two crossed lines. Eira didn't recognize it and rifled through her memory for stories Nana might have told her about this man. She remembered her referring to him as 'PopPop.'

The man riding with the transport driver was the district notary. He met with the police officer escorting the procession and stamped the paperwork to fire a flaming arrow. Eira initialed and gave a retinal scan on the notary's device. The pallbearers lowered Nana into the rowboat, laying her litter onto a bed of dry kindling.

Being their duty as sons of the departed, Eira's father and uncle pushed Nana's corpse away. Eira nocked the arrow, and the notary lit it. She lifted the bow and aimed. Reist was not by her side, but she could still make out his form in her peripheral. She focused and fired.

A small ball of fire arced through the air and landed with a satisfying *thud* into Melanie Filodoxia's rowboat. The flame grew. A crackling sound carried over the water, washed over to the mourners, enveloped Eira with a profound emptiness.

It was a relief the arrow landed successfully on the first try. All the time spent refreshing and refining her skill was worth it in that instant. Eira's flame sent Nana into the dark. The boat burned, her grandmother razed and sank to the ocean floor. How many skeletons lay at the bottom of the Corvic Waters? It was a single continent on an oceanic planet. There was room to drop bodies. Nana *would* have company, but where did that leave Eira?

As if to answer her question, Reist's hand rested on her shoulder. She took his hand, carrying the bow in the other, and they all returned to their vehicles to leave.

IT TOOK SOME COAXING to pull Eira back into the gym. Reist had gone on his own during the week Eira spent in mourning. He'd come by before and invited her, but she declined. On the third day of the second week, he didn't accept her answer. Eira clung to the mattress as Reist dragged her out by her ankles, taking the sheets with her.

"Get up," he said. He leaned over her prone form, sticking a thumb towards the door. "We got some bad guys and aliens that are waiting for us to kill them. We can't miss those appointments."

"No," she said. Eira locked her fists to her side and made her body as flat as a board on the floor.

"Ugh, gods," Reist said, pinching the bridge of his nose. "I will dress you myself and drag you there by your hair if I have to." The only response he got was a glare with a slight and challenging nod. *Do it then*, it seemed to say.

Reist glared back in stern silence. He stepped away, and Eira could hear him yanking open her dresser drawers. The soft fabric of her shorts, socks, underwear, and shirt landed on her face, thrown at an awkward arc over her bed. Keeping to her determination, Eira didn't move, not even to pull the clothes off her face.

True to his word, Reist dressed her. Roughly, he pushed her onto her face and yanked her pajamas off. Her underwear was halfway up her ass, but when she told him, he shrugged. "That's nice," he said flatly, and continued with the rest of her clothes. He nearly strangled her putting on the sports bra and she tried to kick him when he put on her socks and shoes. This was the last straw. Staying completely immobile wasn't enough to force a full response from him. She tried kicking him, but he retaliated by hitting her thigh and slapping her face.

The smack took her by surprise, and for a moment, the rest of the world stopped existing. Heat rose in Eira's cheek, and her eyes glossed over. What brought her back to reality was Reist's accusing finger in her face. "Don't kick me."

"Sorry," she said in a little voice.

He finished tying her shoes and led her out the door. Today was another day Reist's mom left him the vehicle. Guilt bubbled and surged in his lower stomach. He didn't need to hit Eira. She *was* trying to kick him, but she wouldn't really hit him, would she? Of course she would, and she'd make it his fault for getting hit.

Regardless, Reist stopped in Eira's kitchen and grabbed her usual bottle from one of the upper cupboards and filled it with water. She said nothing when he handed it to her, but her eyes *were* focusing on his gaze more than usual. He wasn't sure how to take that. Once outside, he went to the passenger door and opened it for her.

The first few minutes of the car ride were in a silent stillness that smothered them both. Reist turned his head and opened his mouth. No words came out. What would he even say? He didn't need to say anything, really. Eira turned towards him and hugged his arm. She curled her feet under her in the seat and rested her head on his shoulder.

Maybe it was a sign that no apologies were necessary. Eira wouldn't be able to voice her feelings for many years, but this was the first time she had been yanked back to reality. The backhand reminded her she was alive. The shock of Nana's death (*murder*) was, hopefully, the worst thing she would ever have to endure. On the battlefield, she wouldn't have time to mope. Reist showed he was unmoved and would get her away from danger if she ever broke down like this. And he was proving he'd be there while she pieced herself together.

THE USUAL MOTIVATIONS weren't working today. Reist behind Eira while she squatted the same weight as their last session, but her form lacked the usual determination. Whatever effect the backhand had on her was fading away. She racked the bar and stepped away for Reist to adjust the weight for himself.

Any of their motivational talks wouldn't do the trick, and so Reist didn't try. It would've been easy to throw a smile her way or make an offhand comment about killing aliens, but those weren't working today and might not for a while. Her frequency was off and Reist felt around for which bandwidth her brain was working on, with no success.

"Hey, listen," she said when they finished their sets. "I'm just being a downer today. Keep doing you, okay? I'll catch up when I'm up to it."

"I am. I just want you around during it," he said.

"And I want to be around too. I just need time, okay?"

"I hear you," he said. "Don't stay away too long?"

"I won't. Really," she said.

"Graduation is a couple months away and I bet you're getting just as many calls for interviews as I am," he said. The messages had been coming by the handful every day, and Reist's dad had voiced his opinion whenever it came up with an alternative route to explore each time. He had nodded along with whatever his dad had recommended, but didn't mention enlistment. That was his and Eira's plan, after all. Or that's what the plan had been. Reist couldn't tell if she still wanted this.

"We have to make some kind of move," he said. Reist needed an answer. If she was game to keep up their original plan, then they needed to move now. If she wasn't, then he needed to make sure backup jobs were ready. They wouldn't be nearly as exciting, but it was better than living at home his whole life.

"Yeah, I hear you," Eira said. She *had* been receiving calls for job interviews, and it wasn't any less frustrating. It was like being in a carryman's race and being the only one starting off with a 100kg ruck. While everyone else pushed through their checkpoints, Eira felt the weight getting heavier with judgmental stares and hushed questions, wondering why she kept falling behind.

The answer was simple: ditch the ruck. But it wasn't a ruck. It was Nana. Lose that and it would be like she never existed. Eira's mother hadn't spoken of the empty room in their house. The most her father had said on the matter was, "It is what it is," before lifting another glass of bourbon. He had been drinking more.

"How about this," Reist began. "Send me your copy of the documents and I'll turn it in for the both of us. When I hear back, I'll tell you when and where and we can meet up together."

Every word and syllable Reist ejected from his gaping maw was another dozen kilograms pressing on Eira. *Quit asking me questions and just tell me what to do, for fuck's sake. Hit me again or hug me or...something.* "Yeah," Eira said, any pretense of calm she may have carried falling away completely. "Yeah, do that for me."

"Hey," Reist said softly, putting an arm on her shoulder. "It'll be alright."

That was it. The last gram to break her.

"You know what? No, it's not gonna be alright." She swiped his hand away. "It's not going to be alright because one of the greatest people to ever walk the planet is now ashes at the bottom of the *fucking* ocean and no one seems to care besides me! Her own damn son just drinks to the point I think he's trying to join her and *fuck me*. That sounds absolutely blissful right about now. I'm sorry I don't have time for this shit right now," she continued. "But it is *not* alright and will never be alright again. But it is what it is and here the fuck we are."

Reist blinked and held up both hands. "Hey, sorry," he whispered. He needed to tread lightly here. Eira wasn't the type to be spoken down to. She didn't want to be gently handled during their workouts or patronized on the run. She set her own pace and wanted him to do the same. This path was a way for her to keep herself in check by having a goal to aspire towards.

Both sets of Reist's grandparents were gone. The last one had passed a year ago. This could be useful. He'll be almost half a lap ahead of her, metaphorically, but it will give her a goal like anything else. "Look," he said. Start off strong and no-nonsense and she'll respond better to that. "People die sometimes, and-"

Fire erupted in Eira's eyes and exploded out of her mouth. "What the shit?! 'People die sometimes'? Are you out of your *fucking* mind? She was murdered while we fuckin hid and cowered. This isn't some disease or old age that took her too soon. She had that, and she fought like a fuckin warrior against that for as long as I've been alive. And she was cut the fuck down. I want that son of a bitch alive now so I can slash his gods-damn face off and wear it during Founders Day Festival. But he's not here," she continued. "And she's gone. And don't you dare talk down to me. This is my pain, you selfish prick. This is my family. And....just...."

Eira glared at him with a kaleidoscope of emotions threatening to burst through her eyes. Hatred, betrayal, pain, disappointment, pleading; all of it came together and extinguished. Eira's shoulders dropped. "I'm out. I can't do this." And she walked out of the gym and walked home.

Chapter 19

EIRA DIDN'T TAKE REIST'S calls and ignored his messages. She hadn't even shown up to class. They were in the middle of finals' review and Reist had used this as an innocent excuse to go to her house and deliver notes. No one ever answered the door, and he left the notes on the front step.

It was a week with no contact and Reist was in his room. There was a knock at the front door and his mom answered. Another minute later and Mrs. Adeio's friendly tone came closer to Reist's little corner of the house. "Honey?" she asked. "Look who came to see you!"

Turning, Reist bore witness to a wide, beaming smile from Eira. "Hello, dear," she said. *So today's the day I die*, he thought. Eira stepped into his room and planted a quick kiss on his cheek.

"I'll bring in some dinner to help you two study," Reist's mom said before closing the door.

As soon as the door shut, the spot Eira kissed was met with a hard slap. The impact left Reist's head throbbing, burning, and tingling. He didn't move and waited for the next strike, but it didn't come. "That was a really fucked up thing you did," Eira said.

"I know, and I'm-"

"No," she interrupted. "You don't know. You just know I'm pissed and you're sorry for that. You don't *understand* that what you did was fucked up. I can hate you for that, but I also can't hate you because you were right."

Reist tensed at this. Eira sat on the edge of the bed.

"People die," she said. "It's nothing new, and it's not going away anytime soon and some of those people will die because of us." She looked up and met his gaze. "You still want Recon?"

"I do if you do."

"I do if you do, too," she replied. "We may be given some bad orders to follow. Let's set some rules now. Just for us."

"Okay," he said.

"No kids, no old people," she said. "I mean, if they're shooting at us and it's the heat of the moment, there's only so much we can do. But if we can help it...I don't want to kill someone else's Nana."

"I'm sorry she's gone," Reist said. "I liked her."

An invisible weight fell off Eira's shoulders. The sensation was overwhelming. She shut her eyes and whispered, "Thank you."

It was a risk. It may blow up in his face, but Reist opened his arms. Eira nodded and stood to go sit in his lap. His arms went around her and Eira rested her head on his shoulder and pulled her knees up to her chin. "You're still an asshole," she whispered.

THE NEXT TIME SHE CAME over, it was the middle of the night.

One thing Eira noticed about Reist's house was his parents and sister always went to bed on time. Definitive working class with a dependable sleeping schedule. Reist was the outlier. He liked to stay up past those hours because he wasn't tired yet. And the quiet of the early morning was soothing for him.

Eira took advantage of the Adeio household's evening routine. Reist let her in through the backyard and into his bedroom window. She tossed him a bag and lugged herself in. Inside the bag were several candles, packets she had printed out regarding 'the Reviving Ritual,' as they had called it, and the defibrillator kit. She never returned it. It didn't seem like the hospital noticed it was gone after the attack. Confusion chipped away with realization as Reist took stock of everything. Eira was vague about what her plan was. Again.

"We're doing this again?" he asked.

"Yep," she said. She eased the window shut behind her and pulled out her notes from the bag. "And we're doing it right this time. No distractions. We've already had sex a couple times, so when we do it tonight, it'll be for the ritual and not because we got horny."

"First off," Reist said, pointing to himself, "always horny. Second, I'm not killing you. How in all the hells am I supposed to explain a dead girl in my room?"

Eira looked up from the notes and gave this a moment's thought before shrugging, "At least you'll have something to do."

"You won't," Reist said. "You'll be dead. I have no experience with that, but I have it on good authority it'll suck pretty bad."

"Only very briefly. Then I'll be immortal and we'll do you." Eira had a fistful of candles and paced around the room. "Gods, your room sucks for this. I'll have to move some of your furniture around to make this work."

"Trying to make the ten points?" Reist said, skimming through her notes.

"Yep," she said with a grunt, pulling his dresser at a different angle, and placing two candles on top. "This way, the god we're trying to invoke will notice us. Sorta like an optical prescription."

"Candles are spectacles," Reist muttered, trying to pierce logic through the nonsense.

"Theoretically," Eira replied. She put another candle on his windowsill and looked at the curtains. She pulled his chair to a better spot, placed two of his hardcover textbooks in the seat, and positioned the candle so it would stand on its own.

"Oh, well, if the only way to bring you back from the dead is a theory, then lemme strangle you right now." Reist rubbed his eyes.

Eira paused, arm outstretched and held the last candle. It hovered an inch off of Reist's writing desk. She blinked and placed the candle down softly. "That..." she started. Turning to face him and lifting her chin up, "Grab it."

"What?" Reist asked.

"Grab my throat," she repeated. "You've never choked me during sex, and I've read some people are into it. I want to see if I am. If we do it now, with our pants still on, then there's no crazy hormones messing with the results."

"Uh...ugh, fuck it," Reist said, shrugging. He reached out and grabbed Eira's throat. The diameter of her neck was small enough that his fingers nearly met on the back of her neck. It was...soft, tender, and warm under Reist's grip. "Hm," he mumbled and brought the other hand up to join the grip. "I'm..."

There was a sparkle in Eira's eye. "Me too." She grinned and rushed forward to peck Reist's lips. "I'll light these. Go over the kit. Where's your knife?"

"In that drawer." Reist pointed and turned to pull the defibrillator kit from the bag. As far as he can tell, it hadn't been touched since the last time she pulled it out. He went over the inventory list and function checked the paddles. "It's all set," he said.

Reist put the kit on the floor by the bed, so he could easily grab it. He paused while standing back up. Eira was set on dying tonight, but clearly wanted to be brought back. Or did she? She forgave him so easily, and shortly after insisted on retreading an unproven ritual.

"Babe, listen," he said.

"What?"

"Run me by this ag-" he turned and Eira was naked in front of him, blade out, and looking up at him.

She held the knife by her teeth, rolled her eyes, and started undoing Reist's trousers and pulling his shirt off. "Hand," she said.

She pressed the blade coldly against the nearly healed scar across Reist's palm. She re-opened it and handed him the knife and her scarred palm. Reist paused again and Eira lifted his bleeding hand to her lips and licked the blood. She winced and bit on the base of Reist's pinky when he sliced through her scar. Taking her bleeding hand, they both stood there, naked and lapping at each other's cuts. Lips wet, tongues red, they came together, their bodies illuminated only by the candles. They moved to the bed and continued their embrace.

This evening had a more unique sensation than last time, at least it did for Reist. There was a stronger fire smoldering in his core, fueling him on. It linked and joined with one he felt in Eira. Passion met passion, and his hands gripped the warm tenderness of her throat.

Their hips rolled into each other and Eira slapped Reist's face to coax him into squeezing harder. One of her hands was on his forearm, nails digging into his skin. The other grabbed a fistful of the blanket. Her hips rose to meet his thrusts, chasing her climax the same as him. He told her he was close, and she nodded, her warmth tightening around him.

In the flickering light, they maintained eye contact. Then Eira's eyes rolled back, and her grip slacked on Reist's arm. His completion came when she went limp. He let go of her throat and felt the high. The elation flood from his system only to be replaced by shock and terror.

"Shit," he muttered. "Shit, shit, shit." He shook her and slapped her face, then checked her pulse. It was steady. Eira only temporarily lost consciousness. Relief flooded over his senses, "Oh, gods."

Panic subsided. He leaned away from her prone and limp form. The nearest candle was too far for him to reach without getting off the bed, so dripping hot candle wax on her was out. With the defibrillator case in arm's reach, and the knife was directly next to it. A sinister part of Reist's brain pushed his hand to grab it. He unfolded the icy blade and pushed it down onto the slope of her right breast. The thin crimson line bubbled out, beads of blood pushed through and painted down her pale skin. Reist leaned in and licked them, suckling on the red line, one inch at a time.

With a sharp inhale and a jolt of her body, Eira was flailing her arms and grasping at Reist's shoulder and back. She gasped and panted, "What the fuck..."

"Welcome back to the land of the living." Reist kissed along the cut he made and back up to Eira's lips.

"Fuck," she gasped. "Did it work?"

"You lost consciousness," Reist said. He stood up to get a cup of water he had next to the candle on his desk, blowing them each out as he went. He handed her the water. "Scared every kind of hell out of me."

She accepted the cup and sipped. Her eyes bounced from one corner of the room to the next, studying the flickering shadows and altering darkness, as if trying to remember where she was or how to be alive. "I passed out," she muttered.

"Yeah." He took the cup when she lifted it to him and drank it himself.

"Fuck, my throat," she gasped, tendering touching the front of her neck. She motioned for him to lie down next to her. He climbed into bed. Face buried into her hair, and arms around her waist, they laid there silently in the darkness.

MORNING LIGHT CREPT in through the curtains and landed directly on Reist's face. It nudged him into consciousness. He groaned and stretched into an attempt at wakefulness. Eira wiped loose strands of hair out of her face. "Mornin," she moaned.

"Mornin." He leaned in to peck her lips.

"Really digging the morning breath, big guy," she replied.

The best response, Reist felt, to that comment was to pepper her entire face with further, longer kisses. She stifled a giggle at this and swatted her arms against him, fighting the rank smelling onslaught. Clanging and clacking echoed from beyond the closed bedroom door. With it came the shock and realization. "Shit," Reist muttered, covering Eira's mouth. "You stayed over."

"I know," she replied. "I was there."

"My parents don't know you're here," Reist said, trying to get the point across.

Eira shrugged, "You dad might not, otherwise he would've stormed in here by now. Your mom? She's pretty quick. I think she's had some sixth sense tingling when she woke up."

"Your parents-" he started.

"Neither of them were home last night," Eira replied. She sat up and started collecting her clothes and the contents of the bag she came with. "I'm pretty sure dad's cheating and I think mom is hung over in a ditch somewhere."

The typical noises of a peaceful morning were still causing a commotion in the kitchen. Reist was still standing by the window, waiting for his brain to return to the proper speed it needed to go at following what Eira was saying.

"Wait. So." The mental gears picked up momentum. "Your parents?"

"Are assholes." Eira had everything on and was tying her shoes. "Just like you. It doesn't mean I love you all any less, but with all that's happened, I need some emotional distance."

"Wait, what?"

The bag made a thick lugging sound when Eira hoisted it up over her shoulder. She stopped to gaze up at him. There was no anger or ill meaning behind her gaze, just waiting.

"Are..." Reist started, "Are we breaking up?"

"Do you want to break up?" Eira asked.

"You first."

With a sigh and slumped shoulders, Eira muttered an "Okay." He never made things easy for her. "I want us to still be partners," she began. "We've busted our asses training for Recon and I think we should give it a serious shot. But this boyfriend and girlfriend stuff? That's pri-ed shit that we'll not have time or energy for on this path. We love each other. We love each other's company. We push each other and better each other. We are partners until one or both of us decide we're not. I think that'll be the best thing going forward until we figure out how military life works, and we go from there. Deal?"

No answer came out. Reist stared, confused.

"Throw on some pants and get some breakfast," she sighed. "I'll drop this off at home and message you in a bit. I was thinking we could go to the recruiter today and get started, finally." She leaned up to peck him on the corner of the mouth and went to open the window.

As if by instinct, Reist followed and bid her a mumbling farewell. He shut the window, got dressed, and had breakfast. Pari and their dad wished him a good morning with a tone that said they were oblivious to what happened last night. Their mom, however, had a knowing look behind her eye when she handed him a plate of breakfast.

Chapter 20

THERE WAS A COOL BREEZE on the bike ride home, mingling with the warm air of the rising sun. It was the start of a lazy day, perfect for starting a new home project, perfect for Eira to begin her life. One neighbor she passed was starting his hover mower and adjusting the height. He gave Eira a little wave. Soon, she may never see him again. Eira would be on another planet, training to kill. Surrounded by others, training to kill. In another year he'll still be here, mowing his lawn, coming home from work to dinner with his wife. Day after day after day after day. It was haunting to think about. *I can't be the only one with this dark drive inside,* she thought, waving back at the neighbor. *How does he address his?*

Her father couldn't be the only one on their block having an affair. Her mother wasn't the only alcoholic everyone was too embarrassed to confront. Out in the cold of space, tit's deep in the mud of a faraway planet, surrounded by the smell of gunfire or rumble of explosions, was as far from here as Eira could go. *At least out there. It'll be honest,* she thought. *Upfront, direct.*

With Nana dead, there was nothing keeping her here. Reist's lack of emotional support showed they had no chance of being as close as his parents; they were the outlier. Though he *did* watch her back when explosions and gunfire blasted around them, not on some faraway planet, but at work. This, done before either of them had any training, proved there was *something* there she could rely on.

It wouldn't be happily ever after for them. It would be something else, something unique and legendary. And if it turned out Reist was incapable, or unwilling, of pushing on through to the end with her, that was alright. He got her this far and she can be thankful for that and wish him the best. He was capable of finding his version of what his parents had. It wasn't with her, and he needed to understand that before they continued forward. Either way, he was just like her enough to speak on the same mental frequency. And that was the rarest thing in the universe.

As it turned out, Eira was half right. Her father was not home, but her mother had driven the car over the lawn. Patches of grass torn out through muddy trenches from the tires. The driver's side door was still open. Eira pulled her bike up to it and shut the door before going into the house.

Various knickknacks set up in the foyer and up the main hallway, all littered the ground in pieces. Eira followed the path to her parents' bedroom. Her mother, still in a cocktail dress, with one heel on and the other on the floor, was snoring loudly. She was face down in the pillow when Eira walked in. She turned her mother onto her side, propping her there with the decorative pillows they never used. The car keys were under the bedside table. Eira grabbed them and stopped by the kitchen for a quick breakfast. "Young lady?"

Eira turned from the open cupboard, bowl in hand. Cuquas was standing, arms folded behind his back in his classical, subservient way. He bowed his head slightly. "I am glad you are unharmed. With the house empty the way it was last night, I feared for the family."

"I'm alright, Cuquas," Eira said. She poured herself cereal. "Do we know where my father is?"

He shook his head, "I'm afraid not, young lady. Mrs. Filodoxia was the first of the family to return home. She entered approximately an hour ago. I am in the process of providing the lady with a medicinally hearty breakfast that will combat the headache she will have when she wakes up."

Eira propped herself up on a barstool along the kitchen countertop and began eating. "You're one of the good ones," she said.

"Thank you," he said, bowing again. "Is there something more substantial I might provide for you this morning?"

"No, thank you." She raised her bowl slightly in the air. "I'm good with this. And I won't be staying long. I'm going out with Reist today. So, I don't know about dinner yet."

"Then I shall be flexible, young lady," he said, offering another bow. They continued with idle chatter until Eira finished her cereal. She jumped to her feet and Cuquas held out a hand to take the bowl to clean. Eira said thanks and left.

The flashing neon lights grabbed her attention first. There were two police vehicles in front of the house. An officer was walking around mom's car, gazing in through the windows. Eira could only imagine the trouble her mother got into on the drive home last night. Deciding she was having nothing to do with it today, Eira left the keys on the table by the front door, messaged Reist to meet her at the entrance of the neighborhood, and told Cuquas about the police outside. As the chef gave yet another bow in acknowledgement, there came a loud *screech* outside.

Eira heard the police speaking loudly to someone to calm down. A separate voice responded he would *not* calm down and demanded to know who the *fuck* they thought they were going through a car *he* paid for. Eira's father pushed that attitude against many people, and they always buckled under the weight of his gaze, but this time it would not work.

While the argument escalated in the front yard, Eira snuck into the garage from inside the house to grab her bike. She walked it through the living area and nodded to Cuquas. "I'm going out the back," she said.

The stoic Zentharan stood still, eyeing the wall as if he could see through it to the scene happening outside. He gave Eira a momentary glance before nodding. "Please be careful," he said.

As a company-funded servant, he had no authority over any member of the family he was assigned to, not even the children. But he still had to take responsibility, even if the bylaws were annoyingly unclear about it. But these rules didn't say anything about his family falling apart.

Easing her bike down the balcony, Eira flanked around two neighboring houses before coming out to the main road. Everyone who was awake and outside was paying closer attention to the altercation between her father and the three officers in front of her house.

THERE WASN'T A PLACE for Reist to park, so he pulled into the grass and waited for Eira. He messaged her and waited. That morning's talk hadn't stopped jumbling through his mind. Not being boyfriend or girlfriend gave him pause, but it didn't mean they weren't together. 'Partners,' she had said. It made it sound like a business venture. *Our business will be death, and we will be rather good at it.* Reist shook his head. Where'd that come from?

The more he thought about it, the more it made sense. Hi-ed was ending and everyone was moving on with their lives. He had classmates who had gotten together and broken up dozens of times over the years. Some seemed solid, and some were getting married right before starting their new jobs. It was like the wedding was more a celebration of landing the job than it was celebrating their relationship.

People were weird and didn't always make sense. Eira did, though. She wanted to be better. She saw the wrongness of the mundane and wanted to step out of it. That was the sort of thing Reist could grow with and benefit from. All this time, he thought there was something wrong with him because of how little he felt about the average person or whatever event was taking over their lives. Because of this separation as an "other", Reist kept his head down. Eira saw something similar in herself and did the exact opposite. Why fight against the waves when they could fly?

In the rear mirror, Reist spotted Eira pulling up to the nearest street sign. She secured her bike against the metal pole and walked over to him. With an exhausted exhale, she fell into her seat. "Can we stop off and get coffee on the way?"

"Yeah." Reist pulled off onto the main road.

"Right at the light," she said. Her device beeped. She looked at it and clicked it mute. "Today is going to be interesting. Keep going straight."

"First day of the rest of our lives," Reist said. "It's a big deal."

"Yeah, there's that." They stopped at a traffic light. Eira gazed out the window at the little storefronts. People went about their day without a care. Or what if they did? How many of these scattered people were hanging on by a thread? Maybe that one over there found out he's terminal and was trying to put on a happy face. Or that other one right there could be high out of his mind and enjoying an ice cream. "But I mean for after," Eira said. "I think one or both of my parents will be in jail before lunch."

To his credit, Reist didn't act shocked. An average person would've been shocked. Instead, he gave a more controlled, "Okay." but the gears still turned behind his face. He preferred to figure out how or why of something before asking questions. "Were you right about your dad and mom found out? A domestic?"

"Oh, that will definitely come up later." They pulled forward through to the next intersection. Eira's side of town was nothing but shops. "And even if they don't," she continued, "it can be something I can use if they ask where I was all day."

"They're gonna think it was my idea," Reist said. He gave her a sideways smirk.

He probably didn't even know how much his smirk affected her. When they first met and his blank facade fell and he finally loosened up. She thought it was irritating. It was a target for her to punch, but now Eira wanted to kiss her fist first.

"That's because it was," she said. "And I will tell them so."

"I recall us talking about it together," he said.

"Turn right up here," she said. "And we did. But *you* brought it up. Now this left."

"You had already been researching it though."

"This parking lot here," she said. "And? A girl can't research anything for the sake of curiosity? I researched anal sex before. Doesn't mean I plan on partaking anytime soon."

"Jilling yourself off to porn isn't research." Reist parked the car and undid his seatbelt. The 'filth' was coming seamlessly now. He leaned towards Eira, an inch away from her face. "And you're only saying you wouldn't do it because you're too scared to try it."

With a peck to her lips, he reached into the back and grabbed their documents before climbing out of the car. Red, embarrassed frustration bubbled through to Eira's face. She got out of the car and rushed after him. "I'll try it if you do."

Without looking back or even acknowledging they were discussing anything untoward, he said, "Deal."

The coffee shop she had picked was a block away from the recruiter's office. Once inside, Eira ordered their drinks and joined Reist at a table he picked out. They spread the papers out on the cool surface. They likely didn't make any mistakes in the forms. But they wanted to check, anyway. It was nice, for Eira, to not be the only insane one when it came to double and triple checking her work. She often was, but when Reist did it too, it made everything feel important.

Their order was up. Eira went to get them and realized something on the way back. They had never decided on who was to order the drinks and where to sit. When they walked in, they simply split and rejoined. Even how they were sat revealed a subtle layer of efficiency. The table Reist picked wasn't in some back corner, out of sight and so obviously filled by a cop or someone paranoid.

No, he had picked one that was in the middle, but still off to the side to take cover in the bathrooms or retreat out the back entrance if necessary. Reist sat himself facing the front door and she the back door. Coasters laid out for their cups when Eira sat down. She was still processing this realization. The more it calculated, the wider she smiled.

"We got this," she said.

"Yes, we do," Reist replied, not looking up.

Did he realize this as well? And when? It didn't matter. She reached out and took his hand. He looked up and met her smile with one of his own. Reist had once confessed to her he didn't like his smile and he was an idiot for believing this. His was a rare smile that lit up his face. Far too many smiles were fake, but his never was.

They sipped their coffee, chatted about the forms, and filed them away. For just a few minutes, the rest of the world didn't matter. It didn't matter if her parents were probably being arrested as they sat there. It didn't matter if they were about to push their lives into the most dangerous path there was. That bit was exhilarating. It would have been nice if Nana was around for Eira to tell about this afterwards. She'd worry about Eira, but it would've been nice to see the little twinkle of pride she'd gotten whenever Eira accomplished something impressive. She'd do anything for that twinkle again.

For Reist, the freefall they teased themselves with was equally intoxicating. From where he was sitting, he could see the recruiter's office. It was less than a five-minute walk away, and inside was a cavalcade of unknowns. He sipped his coffee and beamed at Eira. He couldn't keep a straight face. This was too much to *not* feel anything about.

In a deeper cabinet of Reist's imagination was the trepidation about basic training and beyond. The fear of failure still petrified him. What if there was something they hadn't accounted for, and it made him crumble before they began? She'd continue. Eira was strong and since they weren't technically together, she had no reason to back out with him. And nor would he encourage her to. If she could make the cut when he couldn't, then good on her. He only hoped that she'd remember him while she was killing pirates and aliens.

Eira's foot was gliding up Reist's leg. All fears fell away. The fight to come, the struggles, the firefights they would endure. None of it mattered. The only thing that did, in that instance, and hopefully for the rest of their lives, was each other.

The front windows of the recruiter's office were obscured by vertical blinds, opened just enough to let the morning sun in. Adorning the windows were the various Confederate Defense Force insignias they had been staring at for months.

Reist and Eira stood and stared at the door. Nervousness tingled down to their fingers and shuddered their insides. They gave each other a look and a timid laugh. After a deep sigh, Reist opened the door for Eira. One last roll of her eyes, and she stepped into the office. She was about to call him a coward, but her brain went quiet from a sharp jolt of pain from her backside. She turned to glare at him but, like before, he gave no indication he smacked her ass on the way in. *You'll get yours,* she thought.

THE MEETING WENT SMOOTHLY. A sergeant greeted them inside. They sat together in silence while he went through an obviously rehearsed speech about the benefits of joining and how elevated Eira and Reist were to their peers for even stepping through the doors. He slid a tablet across the desk and asked them to fill out their basic information to get the process started. He was surprised when they whipped out their forms.

Pride bolstered in and spun through Reist and Eira as the sergeant read carefully through each of their forms and had no corrections. Instead, he said, "Wow. Okay, yeah. I'll, uh, I'll get this plugged right in. And just so we're all on the same page: you *are* asking to be considered for Special Reconnaissance?"

As one, Reist and Eira nodded, "Yes."

"And you both know what that means?"

They went back and forth, listing off details about it.

"Special forces job," Eira started

"Three years of heavy training across a dozen different locations," Reist continued.

"Combat specialty, often fighting against rebels, pirates, terrorists, and some creatures that are totally not aliens but absolutely aliens."

"Ninety-something percent washout rate."

"Okay, okay," the sergeant said, holding up a hand. "Let me get your information in and we'll talk about days to ship out. We won't have a set date down for another couple of weeks, and we'll need you both to come in a few times between now and then to get your physicals and some IQ and training tests done. But after that, it'll be quick. And you two want to go in together?"

They both nodded again. "The buddy program," Reist said.

"Got it ticked on subsection 17 at the bottom." Eira pointed to the paper in the sergeant's hand.

"Just checking. I'll be right back." The sergeant shut the door softly when he left.

"He's more used to people coming in who don't know what they want," Reist said.

"See how much easier it is knowing what you want?"

It was a few minutes before he came back, and they spent that time studying the paraphernalia around his office. On the back wall was a university diploma and another from a trade school. Next to them were plaques showing bases where the sergeant had been stationed. On the desk were photographs of different platoons. Reist tried to pick out their recruiter in them. It took him a minute. The caption read "12th Combat Engineering Corps, CDF." The man next to their recruiter had eye-dye implants popular among punk groups. It made his eyes a solid white. Reist's parents always disapproved of them. They looked scary, and that was clearly the point. Parental disapproval is another strand of Reist's motivation to be here today.

There was something Reist hadn't thought of. He never stepped out while growing up. In fact, sneaking out for his and Eira's javelin competition was the first time he had ever done anything 'bad.' And he had thought nothing of it or living the lie every day by not telling them. He just didn't think about it. Was everything he did with Eira just teen rebellion rearing its ugly head so late into the game? Reist turned to her. She met his gaze with excitement exploding out of her eyes like invisible lightning bolts. They ignited something inside him.

No, he wasn't here to rebel against his parents. He was here because one day he would die, and no one would remember his name. This way, there was a greater chance of a legacy; a real legacy, not a child carrying his name. The poor boy would only feel the same existential devastation. In a way, he was protecting his would-be son the same way he was protecting Pari.

Pari. That would be the hardest part. He knew she would try to follow him into the CDF, even try out for Recon. But by then he'd have ascended the ranks high enough to have a say, ideally. Perhaps he could make it so her request would be lost. There were other jobs in the CDF. They're basically a nation to themselves. There're kitchen workers, financial workers, and communications or some other such safe job. His parents may react poorly, no doubt. But one problem at a time.

Eira didn't have such inner contemplations to worry about. With Nana gone, she had no one to leave behind. This was only the way forward. Her parents' disapproval was a bonus, but ultimately meant nothing. With such a long road in front of her, it was hard to even notice the path she was leaving. She grabbed Reist's hand. When he looked at her, she could barely contain her excitement. This was it. The first step. This was all they needed to do to begin their new life.

The sergeant returned with the documents. They set their next appointment for in-processing and got contact information for the medical office for their checkups to the CDF's liking. And that was it. They were in such a daze when they left the office that they didn't speak until they got to the vehicle. Reist turned it on and sat there. He and Eira stared into a distant point in another plane of existence, somewhere off in the far-flung, potential future. Silence shattered into several hundred world ending pieces as Eira screamed into the ceiling. The excitement brought her legs up, and she kicked into her seat, hugging herself and punching the air.

Reist's laughed, loud and booming like an earthquake. He turned to her, and she brought their foreheads together, causing another link to bind them tighter together. The voltage from their gaze pushed up several more volts when their lips met. The next few hours were spent behind the shopping center, in the shade of an overhanging tree. They moved to the back seat. More room there.

Chapter 21

REIST DROVE WITH THE windows down. The cool breeze was the best sort of refreshment he and Eira could ask for. He held her hand while he drove and occasionally brought it up to kiss or suckle on a fingertip or knuckle. Safely returned to their meeting point, he waited until she unlocked her bike and rode off. She gave off a shrill scream of excitement on her way. Reist drove home, elated and smiling so much his face hurt.

Reist made it home and dropped the empty coffee cups into the kitchen trash can. His dad was watching the news, his mom was in her high-backed antique chair in the corner, reading, and Pari came bouncing out of her room. She and their dad asked if Reist could drive Pari to her friend's house. There was a sleepover she was in danger of being late to. There was takeout already ordered and Pari was quite insistent she didn't want to miss any of the good food.

It was like a portrait. This house, this moment, in this place in the galaxy, frozen in time. This is what Reist was walking away from. Parents who loved him and a baby sister with friends and sleepovers, but still adored him. One way or another, he was going to leave here. There was no bile or ill will. Everyone left home eventually. His parents did, and in time, so will Pari.

"Okay, little wing," Reist said with a slight chuckle. He put a hand on top of Pari's head. She was so small. His palm nearly covered her whole scalp.

The tiny gap between Pari's front teeth came through in a beaming smile before she sped back to her room. She came back out a moment later with her overnight bags and made towards the garage.

Reist hoped her energy and excitement would never go away, but he knew it would.

WHEN EIRA ROUNDED THE corner to her street, Cuquas was in the front yard with a wheelbarrow. Dressed in light clothing, thick gloves, and a wide hat that made a perfect circle of a shadow around him, the chef was ripping up the old grass ruined by her mother's drunk swerving this morning. In the wheelbarrow was a stack of replacement squares of grass. Her mother's car was missing, but her father's was at the base of the driveway. It hadn't moved from where he pulled up to shout at the police officers.

"Welcome home, young lady," he nodded to Eira as she pulled in.

"Thanks, are they in?"

"They have not returned from the police station yet, I'm afraid."

"Alright," she said, pushing her bike up the slight slope of the driveway and into the garage. She came back out. "So how'd the rest of it go after I left?"

"Well," he said. He paused between pulling up the first bit of grass, trying to find the more polite way to explain. "Despite your father's insistence, the officers determined his outbursts towards them were unruly and a public nuisance. A few minutes after your egress, your father was on the ground."

"*What?*" Eira sat on the ground, taking in the story.

"It was quite an impressive throw." He cut up another bit of grass to make it more, even for the next square. "The police officer stepped towards him, and your father's face was in the dirt right there next to your foot. When he was placed into their vehicle, the other two requested to be admitted inside. Legally, I could not stop them and opened the door.

"I don't suppose the gentleman and lady will take kindly to this when they return," Cuquas continued. "So, I hope to gain some small favor when they see their yard repaired in their absence. I must admit I am not so good with landscaping, but my uncle was. I spent my days off with his company when I was a lad. Never applying the trade, of course. I was more of a runner for the workers. My mother had never fully recovered from the Mier internment camp. I apologize, I'm babbling."

"It's okay," Eira said. This was the most the Zentharan had ever spoken in a single instance, at least when it didn't involve their dinner. Much of her training was going to take place at several locations across his home world. And, she had to admit, Eira knew embarrassingly little about Corvus' planetary neighbor.

"Well, as I said, the other two officers came in and pulled your mother out of bed," Cuquas said. He placed another square down. "She was of equally foul mood."

"I bet she was."

"She was demanding I force the home intruders to unhand her. I don't think she heard me, or the officers, for that matter, when I told her they were the police. I *do* apologize, young lady. I am a servant of the state first and I *must* abide by the laws, regardless of my loyalties to your family."

"It's okay, Cuquas. I'm not mad. You're a good man." Eira stood up and brushed her hands off her shorts. "How can I help?"

"With this?" He paused and finally looked directly at her. He stuttered for a moment, "I-well, I'm-I...I'm sorry, young lady. It would be most improper to let you sully your hands with common work like this. Your status demands."

"Cuquas."

"Yes?"

"Fuck my status." She shoved him gently aside and took the handles of the wheelbarrow. It fell on its side as soon as she attempted to turn it toward the garage. "Ugh, shit," she said.

Mute and dumbfounded, Cuquas gave a small snort and doubled over in laughter.

"*Whaaat?*" Eira turned, unable to stop smiling despite herself.

"I...heheh, I apologize, miss, again." He pulled a glove off and wiped his face. "I have been assigned to your family for several years, and your assured attitude never ceases to inspire and, in some cases, entertain."

He went over and dumped the squares back in the wheelbarrow and pushed it up into the cool shade of the garage. Clear bags of yard waste hung from the wall next to the bike rack protruding from the walls. Eira took one and held it open for Cuquas to drop the dirt compost inside.

"Thank you, miss," he said. "In truth, if I am not being out of line for saying so, you remind me more of the dowager than the lady or the gentleman. She always insisted on helping me while I work. I think she missed cooking. Several of the meals I have cooked over the years involved tips and suggestions she had made during my first days in your home."

Eira said nothing. On seeing her smile falter, Cuquas began apologizing. "No," she said, dropping the bag to wave his words away. "No, really. It's okay. I miss her. But I think I did her proud."

"Of course you did," Cuquas said. "She was very vocal about this."

"No, I mean today. I enlisted."

Cuquas paused at this, "The Planetary Militia? It is a bit below your station. If you don't mind my still saying so, miss. From what I hear, it can be a bit of a boys' club, but there are several useful contacts to make and networking to begin for future work."

"CDF, Cuquas."

Another pause. "Is that right?" he asked. The usual formal tone dropped momentarily. "What SDC?"

Eira was taken aback. "You..."

"I had a life before working for your family, miss," he said. Eira could not place what was different about his tone. Rougher? Deeper? "Please, assuage my curiosity."

"I...Recon."

"Oh." His eyes went wide and took a new stance. A series of slight changes transformed the meek cook into a much older, wizened, and worldly man Eira didn't recognize. It was like a different person suddenly appeared. He looked her up and down, measuring her. As if pleased with his assessment, Cuquas nodded. "Very well. I hope you make it through."

"Were you..." Eira began.

"Oh, lords no," Cuquas laughed again. He seemed freer now that her parents weren't home, and he didn't need to be 'on' so much. "I worked in the kitchens even then. It is where I began learning my own trade that I continue to this day."

"Oh," she replied, trying to hide the disappointment in her voice. Having someone with firsthand experience in the field would've been helpful.

They returned to the front yard and finished the work. It was still shabby, in Eira's opinion. But it was still a damn sight better than it was before. Cuquas propped his fist on his hips and beamed at the front yard. "It's still ugly," he admitted without the smile faltering. "But it's something I wasn't very good at, and I got to learn something. That's always good, I think."

It was refreshing seeing the usual stoic and serious Zentharan smile. The afternoon sun came down so beautifully, only for a cloud of overcast to slide over their heads. Eira's mother's vehicle turned the corner at the end of the street and halted shakily into the driveway. Her father was driving with his foul mood was visible through the windshield. As soon as the vehicle parked, Eira's mother emerged and rushed inside without a word or a glance in her daughter's and chef's direction.

By contrast, Eira's father stepped out of the driver's seat and slammed it shut. He gave out a groan and rubbed his face. Then he scanned over the work Eira and Cuquas had done with a steady eye. He gave them both a nod before wearily following his wife inside. *Probably the nicest thing he's ever said,* Eira thought. Her father was a hard man to impress. Cuquas had been with the family for a little over a decade and he rarely complimented the man or his cooking. Their state issued house servant had stepped beyond his area of responsibility for the sake of the family and its reputation. A nod spoke volumes that some people are incapable of putting into words. Cuquas was also such a man, as are most Zentharans from what Eira understood.

Growing up with two such quiet men, it became easy for Eira to understand nonverbal speech. It might've been what made Reist so easy to read. Unlike her mother, Eira was uninterested in sitting quietly by and letting her man continue in such a manner like it was a cute aspect of his personality. How was he supposed to grow, and which would push her to grow, if he never changed?

SEVERAL MILES AWAY, Reist was pulling into his parents' driveway. Compared to Eira's return home, his was uneventful. He went inside and returned the vehicle keys to his mom with a kiss on her cheek. She smiled at this, but squinted at him. "What do you want...?" Her tone was half playful and half curious.

"Just wanted to say thank you is all," Reist said. The little lies were always the easiest.

So, when are we gonna tell them? He messaged Eira after dinner.

I think wait until we have a date to ship out, she replied.

A bit cowardly, he messaged back.

Maybe, but I can't find a fuck to give. I just want to avoid unnecessary shit.

Yeah, he replied. *They won't accept we're leaving until we've gone. Exactly.*

Are your parents okay? Reist messaged.

Yeah, they got back a little after I did. They have court summons they have to get to, so I'm thinking we schedule the medical checks during that time?

Good with me. We'll need a cover story for it though.

Trade school interviews, Eira messaged simply. *Put on something nice whenever we go in. Parents will be none the wiser and it makes us look more professional than everyone else whenever we go in.* Reist read this and went into his closet, searching for his business clothes. As if she was reading his mind from home, Eira sent another message, *We'll go shopping for interview clothes.*

Thank you... he said.

THE NEXT FEW WEEKS passed in a single-minded blur. Graduation came, and while the rest of their student body was awash with emotions, Reist and Eira were getting tired of faking emotions. With diplomas held high and smiling as wide as they could, they posed for several photos together with classmates and teammates. There was one classmate that caught both of their attention, however.

By this point, Reist and Eira had attended two meetings with the recruiter. Nearly all the other hopefuls were students like them, with a few older ones hoping for a new life after hitting a low point. One of them was a classmate they had recognized but didn't know, so they had chatted in the recruiter's office. His name was Gareth, and he was interested in seeing the stars.

There was a knowing, and embarrassing, look Reist and Eira gave each other when Gareth revealed he was on the javelin team. He asked about Recon, mostly to see if he could do it. But other jobs stood out to him more than that, like Logistics or Engineering. "That way," he reasoned, "I have something to fall back on whenever I decide to leave."

At graduation, through the sea of other students, now full-fledged adults in the eyes of the state, Gareth was the single needle in the haystack under sunlight. He stuck to his parents and the circle of friends. When the crowd cleared just enough for them to see each other, both Reist and Eira gave their soon-to-be comrade a nod and he returned it. He shipped out to basic training a week after, and Eira kicked herself for not getting his contact information. Then kicked Reist because they waited too long to sign on.

"I have *so* many questions!" Eira hissed at Reist in the hospital waiting room.

Eira's outburst pierced through it the low murmur of quiet conversation, but she didn't care. A few years ago, Reist might've glared at her, but he didn't care either. The hospital they had requested for their CDF medical screening was one further inland, on the opposite side of the region as the one they interned in. Eira specifically requested it and Reist backed up this choice with a lie. He told the recruiter this one was closer to their houses. It was almost an hour away, but that didn't matter. Though theirs had been rebuilt since the attack, Eira didn't want to see those walls ever again. The emotional masochist in her would take control of her legs, walk to where Nana's room was, and stand there until she saw Nana's spirit.

Another few lies, some coffee, and a road trip later, and here they were in the waiting room. Eira couldn't contain herself, be it excitement at the potential future or the caffeine. Reist suspected it was a combination of the two. His hands were shaking, too. "He could've given us a week-by-week breakdown of basic," Eira continued.

"We already have that," Reist said. They had dropped hundreds of questions, ranging from the average day to the type of food served in 'chow halls.'

"Yeah, but those guys went through years ago," Eira said. "Who knows how much has changed now?"

"And you're thinking it'd be nice if someone gave us a definite answer as to what 'Hell Week' actually is."

"I don't like how, whenever we ask about it, people just titter and say 'you'll see,'" Eira said the last two words with a mock deep voice she used to make fun of her male peers, including Reist.

"There's nothing wrong with there being *some* surprises," Reist said.

"I know, but I don't care. I want to know," Eira said. Her knees bounced. "What if it's too much?" she whispered. "How're we supposed to make it through years of Recon if it turns out I can barely handle Hell Week?"

"We'll be fine."

"*You* might be," Eira said.

Reist put a hand on Eira's bouncing knee. His grip was firm and pressed down, steadying it to a halt. "Look at me," he said. She met his gaze. "Do you honestly think I'd let you give up?"

An invisible weight fell away from her shoulders. Eira buried her face in Reist's neck. Though she continued with the jitters, there were fewer outbursts while they waited. They were called in by separate doctors. When the evaluations and checks were over, they met outside. Reist was sitting on the dry spot of a massive fountain that overtook the hospital's front steps. He looked up at her as she walked to him and gave her a smirk. "One less thing now."

With their new medical documents in hand, they drove back across town to the recruiter. They were instructed to hand deliver the medical forms to the sergeant as soon as they were done. Reist didn't question it. Eira did.

"It has to be some kind of test," she said. "Why bother with this when the doctors can just send it to the sarge themselves?" Lately she had taken to shortening the recruiter's rank. Reist followed suit.

"Oh, it totally is," Reist said. "Maybe they're timing us to see how long it takes to accomplish it."

"That's dumb, that'd be so..." Eira thought about it. "Shut up."

"Or maybe it's just a mind game," Reist said. An alternative theory would make the drive go by faster. "Getting us used to following orders, even if they don't make sense."

"Why do the orders not have to make sense?" Eira said. "Hey, could you step on it a bit?"

He did. "I'm just saying that is another consensus I'm getting. Sometimes leadership will hand down stupid orders and we'll have to follow them."

"If the orders are stupid, then don't follow them." Eira looked out the window. "Seems pretty obvious to me."

"Part of the service oath includes swearing to obey all orders given to us," Reist said.

"And if the order counts as unlawful?"

"If it's unlawful, then we don't follow it. But it doesn't say anything about it being dumb."

"Then dumb orders should count as unlawful," Eira said. "A good leader should listen to her people and admit when her decision is dumb."

"You don't."

"I don't what?"

"Admit when you make a dumb decision," Reist said.

"Well, when it happens, which it won't, I will."

"I bet you wouldn't stop yourself from following an order even if you knew it was stupid," Reist said.

"Are you actually going to challenge me or just chat shit in my direction?"

"I bet that, well. Hold on. Okay, say we're Recon-"

"Which we will be."

"-which we will be," Reist said. "If we were on a mission, deep, *deeeeeep* behind enemy lines and we were given dumb orders, you'd follow them because of how far from home we were. You'll talk a big game now, but that's because you're safe in the car with me. But you will go along with whatever is being touted your way just so long as you can get home."

"Yeah, that's not what would happen."

"No need to be defensive about it. I mean, it's only human nature. We want to-"

"Don't be pulling that psychobabble shit on me. I know just as well as you about our stupid primate brains. We have this underlying obsession with comfort because comfort means our survival is established and affirmed. But Recon is meant to push us *out* of that. So, no. Being stuck in the middle of ass end nowhere would not freak me out to the point of blind faith and complacency. If the orders are dumb, they're dumb no matter where they're being given. Asshole."

"Time will tell," Reist said.

"Time will tell plenty. Right now, time is telling me you're an asshole. Let's just be excited for a minute. We're another step closer to this and you're poking holes," Eira said.

"Better to poke holes now and make sure it's seaworthy before discovering it when we're too far gone."

"I know, I know," Eira said. "And I like, but also don't like, that you're doing that. You're thinking ahead, which I like, but you're also messing with my high. Which I don't like."

"So, what would you have me do?"

"Be you, stupid."

Chapter 22

REIST WATCHED EIRA walk up her driveway and pulled away when she walked inside. Her absence was instantly noticeable. The air felt heavier. Reist took a deep breath and drove home. The vehicle fit in snugly beside his dad's in the driveway. Reist walked in and returned the keys to his mom, leaving a peck on her cheek as he did so. She smiled and went back to her book.

"Hey, kid," Reist's dad said from his home office. "I need ya for something."

"What's up?" he asked, coming in from the hall.

"Get the door for me?"

Never a good start, he thought. Reist shut the door behind him and stood before his dad's work desk like he was facing the principal. "What's up?" He repeated, though with a more serious tone. He did his best to mask his uncertainty and paranoia.

"Where'd you say you went to today?"

That was it. He'd been found out somehow and now his dad was asking him to come clean, just indirectly. But he didn't ask Reist where he was. He asked where he said he had gone today. There was a loophole to use.

"Trade school interview," Reist said. "An admin academy was having mass interviews at the community center." Loophole found. He never specified where he went. Reist made sure to say that's where he was going. By saying where the interviews were being held, the brain would interpret that as the answer.

"And did you go there?"

Shit. Reist paused and conceded. "No," he said. "I didn't."

"Okay. And where were you instead?"

"Hospital. The hillside one," Reist said.

His dad nodded and asked, "Why were you there?"

"I was getting a physical."

"For?"

"CDF enlistment."

The mood of the room worsened, like a dark cloud formed at the ceiling. When Reist shut the door, the air got heavy and humid. Now, with his dad's gaze hardening, heat rushed to Reist's face. He kept eye contact with his dad, regardless of how difficult the room felt to be in. "And when were you going to tell us?" He was whispering now.

"When I got a ship date," Reist said, equally quiet.

"I see. Please go get your mother. We'll be discussing this together now."

Reist did as he was told. He was found out and there was no need to dig deeper to hold up a charade that had fallen apart. Confused, his mom followed him, confused, to his dad's room. His dad motioned for the door again and Reist shut it.

"What ...is going on?" His mom asked.

"You're up, kid," his dad said.

"I lied, Mom. I wasn't at a trade school interview. I was getting a physical for CDF enlistment."

She stared at him. Then she looked back and forth from her son and husband. "How long has this been going on?"

"I only just found out," his dad said. "Kip from work messaged me asking if you were okay because he was taking his son in for a flu shot and saw your vehicle there."

"The bumper stickers?" Reist asked.

"Yep," his dad said.

"How long has this been going on?" his mom repeated.

"Since my resumes," Reist said. "That was the plan, but I didn't go into the recruiter's office until a month ago."

"And have you signed anything?" his dad asked.

"Yes."

"*What* have you signed? Maybe there's a way to still get you out of it," his dad said.

"He's not a minor anymore," his mom said. "If he signed after his graduation, then it'll be harder to argue against it."

"I'm not getting out of it." They both paused and looked at Reist.

"Yes, you are," she said. "You need a job here, away from all the craziness happening. You'll be in a safe and secure building *here*, on Corvus, and not out fighting someone else's war."

"The Confederacy is going to break up, son," his dad said. "Efferus is making too much noise for Zenthara and Corvus to ignore, and there will be a war."

"There're always wars, Dad. If it wasn't this, it would be something else."

"And if it weren't for the last war, you would've had another uncle to go visit during the holidays," his mom said. "My little brother ran off with the CDF too and was killed fighting the Mier Republic."

Reist paused. He had never known this. Reist thought his mom was an only child.

"He and my parents had a falling out." She always had a way of reading his mind somehow. "That's why he's in none of the photos of grandma and granddad. Now it would be *very* nice if you did not go down a similar path."

"I don't want to leave on a bad terms, Mom. But I'm going."

"Please." Tears rose in her eyes, but she didn't look at Reist. There was a sternness in her shoulders, like she was trying to force them back down. His dad rose from behind his desk and started pacing.

"Dad. Think back to the riot. We were stuck on that overpass. There was gunfire directly below us. Then there was the murder on the bus." His dad stopped pacing and looked at him. Tears broke through his mom's eyes. But they were listening and trying to steel themselves to the point that they knew he would make. "And I did not know how to react," Reist said. "I didn't know how to protect myself or anyone around me. If I stay here and get an office job somewhere, then I'll stay as helpless as I am now. There're millions of Efferans living here. And a lot of them are very vocal about which kingdom back on Efferus they answer to. If war is really going to break out, then it will come here and it will be worse. We're not safe anywhere and I will have a greater chance of survival by being taught how to fight and defend by the CDF.

"I can't stay here," Reist said. "I love you guys and I love Pari. But I need to go." He put his hand on the door. "I have to go and explain this to her now."

Comparatively, it was harder to explain to his little sister than his parents. Though Pari didn't grasp the minutiae of interplanetary politics and the centuries of history leading to now, she understood enough to know it wasn't good. Reist sat on the corner of her bed and explained it as plainly as he could. She didn't cry. She didn't ask any questions. Instead, she scooted over and hugged him. The contact erupted tears out of Reist's eyes as he hugged her back. He hadn't prepared for this at all.

EIRA'S PARENTS DIDN'T ask where she had been all day. Instead, they went on about their court hearing. Cuquas looked up from the stove and offered Eira a nod. She returned the nod and a little smile. *It went well and I'm excited*, the little motion said.

"This is disgusting," her father said, staring at the news report. Riots were breaking out on the other side of the continent. "I get dragged in for pulling into my own driveway and these beasts destroy state property, and I bet they won't even see any jail time."

The video panned to a wall of black uniforms. Platoons of police in heavy riot armor, clacking thick clubs against riot shields, shuffled towards the rioters. The two groups faced each other in a moment for a tense standoff before the rioters sprinted forward, into the wall of armor, and death.

"They might not need jail time, dad," Eira said. "Doesn't look like a lot of them will walk away from this."

"Good, they should've known better before coming here and roughing up our homes."

The news said it was a charity outreach center. Eira pulled up her personal device and researched it. The organization who ran it was currently under several audits and investigations for fraud and embezzlement. She showed this to her father. He waved the new information away. "Ah, none of that should matter. If they want to make it so bad, they can start from nothing and work up. That's where the real pride comes in."

This left Eira conflicted. She agreed with the concept of building oneself up from nothing and couldn't wait to do it herself. But her father didn't start from nothing. His late uncle had left him this house, and they made a fortune by selling his childhood home and having Nana move in with them. Her father would brag that was how he had bought the renovations for their back porch overlooking the lake.

The telltale jingles of the cheap jewelry her mother wore echoed from their bedroom. She stepped out into the living area, attaching her earrings. "I'm going out."

"Woman, we *just* had probation handed to us today," her father grimaced.

"I won't drive." She didn't look at him and instead went into the kitchen, snapping her fingers to Cuquas. The chef produced a chrome shaker from the corner of the counter and poured Eira's mother a glass. Eira recognized the smell of rum; sharp and tangy.

Her mother took it back in one gulp. "Thank you, dear." She put the glass back down and made for the front door.

After the door opened and shut, Eira took in the feel of the living area. It was freeing, in a depressing sort of way. She was a legal adult now and wouldn't need her parents to know she was enlisting. She went to her room and allowed herself a few minutes to wonder how long it would take either of them to notice she was gone once she shipped out.

Eira's device buzzed as soon as she sat on the bed. It was their recruiter, giving them a day to ship out. He wanted them at his office that afternoon, with the other hopefuls, and they'd take the bus to the transport depot. From there, they'd take to the sky and fly to Zenthara for basic training. Eira, almost squealing with excitement, called Reist, whose voice was shaking uncontrollably.

THE ADEIO FAMILY HAD invited Eira and her parents over for lunch. She had packed two bags, knowing they'd go straight to the recruiter's afterwards. Eira had contemplated taking her bike but thought it bad manners to leave it at her boyfriend's parent's house (...*not* '*boyfriend*,' she thought, *partner*). The bus will do, she had decided. When she made to leave her home for good, Cuquas had been the only one to notice.

"Is today the day, young lady?" he asked.

"This afternoon." Eira looked over her shoulder at the back patio. For a brief and horrifying moment, she thought Nana was sitting out there, admiring the lake like she always had. But it was her father, cradling a glass and an empty bottle of whisky on the table next to him. Her mother hadn't come back yet since last night. "I haven't told them yet. Sorry about that."

"Oh, I am just a lowly cook," Cuquas said. "How could I know the goings-on of everyone in the house? My purview is the meals, all of which of today's are prepped. So, I think I have some time to, say, take a bus ride?"

Eira gave him a look of almost sad relief. "I'd like that."

EIRA HAD NEVER RIDDEN on the bus before. Cuquas had, and she told him Reist's address and followed his lead. The whole ride, they didn't speak. It was like he knew she needed the time to reflect on this new chapter in her life. All the other passengers, coming and going from wherever to somewhere; just a day in their life. In a couple of hours, all of them would go home and have dinner, and she'd be leaving the planet. She wondered if this was the same bus Reist had been on and was glad for Cuquas coming with her.

Map in hand, Cuquas nodded out the window when the stop for Reist's house came up. They rang the bell and stood. "May I help you to the young man's house?"

"That's alright," she said. "I got it from here."

"Very well," Cuquas said, and he stuck out his hand. "Good luck, Eira."

She shook it, her whole body still rattling. "Thank you." Eira strode past the impatient faces of the other passengers and down off the bus. Straps dug into her shoulders, and she texted Reist that she got off the bus.

You took the bus? He texted. *Hold on, meeting you halfway.*

He didn't have to, but she didn't have the mental faculties to argue right now. True to his word, he came around the corner a few minutes later and took one of her bags. "No parents?" he asked. She gave him a loud and sarcastic cackle. "Fair enough," he said.

Emotions bubbled through the air the minute they walked through Reist's front door. Reist's parents welcomed Eira as they always had and were kind enough not to ask about why she came alone. Instead, they took her bags and put them by the door, next to Reist's. His parents fell into the role of host and hostess, but Eira could see the change they hid underneath.

There was the ever kind face of his mom, her smile masking the trepidation below, like painting over mold. She had spoken her peace to her son, and Eira suspected the woman wished it was still possible to scold her son into compliance, just one last time. Reist's dad displayed a stoic acceptance. When the topic of the CDF enlistment came up, he made it sound like it was just a phase Reist would work through. It was just one chapter of his life before he settled down with a decent job and a unique resume that would certainly open all the doors that lay before him. This was how Eira knew that, though Reist's parents knew he was enlisting, he hadn't told them he was trying for a combat position.

Those are the parents, though, she thought. *What did Pari think?* Reist's little sister was uniquely silent during the visit. The first time Eira joined them for dinner, months and months and eons ago, she had attempted to talk to the little girl. She'll be a teen in a few short years, and a relationship with one person is a relationship with their family as well. But Eira decided against it.

Her shell was still hardened from Nana's death, but the warmth from her partner's family was a welcomed kindness. There was still a failsafe of sorts in the back of Eira's mind because of this. Reist's upbringing had been much kinder than hers. Her father would politely look down on them for being of a lower class. Though they were still well off, they lacked the flashiness her father implemented in an eternal pissing contest with anyone within the splash zone.

The Adeio family had apparently decided this mentality wasn't worth thinking about. The peculiar mindset of his family had fascinated Eira from the very beginning. Especially with how it ran counter to the competitive side Reist hid so deep inside himself. It would've been a lovely family to join if things had gone differently.

But they hadn't. They had gone as they did and would continue. Her father may've viewed himself as above his peers, but he was still a man. He was still flesh and blood, tethered to corporeal things and societal mores. He cloaked his shortcomings as strengths. He used them the way a flamboyant bird used its rainbow feathers to showcase its own talents and benefits.

No god had given him these things. He was born lucky, and Eira was as well. She'd rather have been born to the dirt, and she might've been tougher. Instead, her privilege might always prevent her from being anything more than a soft pretender. It was best to strip herself of it as soon as possible. Hopefully, among the rank and file, and mingled in with all walks of life along the Confederacy of Planets, her birth defect of privilege won't matter. She will be in the dirt and mud like all the others and be a part of something greater.

She eyed Reist from across the table. He focused on his meal, eating as if his house wasn't about to collapse. He ate as though his little sister didn't move with hesitant slowness. The poor girl looked so scared, like she thought one wrong move would ruin whatever normalcy leftover.

It was hard to read him sometimes. Easier whenever she punched him or pushed him into tough spots. But even then, he was calm. Eira was eager to find out how well he'd deal in a firefight with actual training. From what she had seen during the hospital attack—much of it all locked away in sections of her brain she'd rather leave untouched and unopened for the rest of her days—he had kept a logical mind. In a flight or fight situation, he had chosen flight. But it had been a calculated flight. And as soon as the gunfire had started, he had run straight to her.

Eira can trust him to keep her alive. The elegant simplicity of that fact was too beautiful to put into words. So, it was only fair to pay back this when she could, however she could. In this instance, it was reassuring his parents. She addressed the topic in the air with his mom and focused on the good things waiting for them. She talked about the interchangeability of career benefits. Every CDF duty position had a civilian equivalent with each Confederate Planet. It was one of many such topics they had compiled into a list they wanted to use to sell their families. It was a moot point, but Eira was salvaging as much as she could with her winning charm.

"-and really, a lot of these are certifications we would achieve right out of basic training," Eira said. "Some of it isn't much, but it's all a good foundation to work in any direction, really."

"Opens a lot of doors then," his mom said. She turned to Reist, stepping back towards the table as his dad was pulling out his latest dessert project from the fridge, "I'm glad the trade schools pick you kids up quick, but you're still so young to know what you want to do with your life. Maybe this could help you get, like you said, honey, a firm place to start when you're a little older...a little wiser...been around the block a few times to know what you want?"

"That's the idea, Mom," Reist said.

When lunch was finished, Reist went to handle the dishes, as he always did, but his dad stopped him. "Leave 'em," he said. "I'll take care of that later. You two have somewhere you need to be." He tried to add levity to his voice but had a noticeable crack.

His mom also choked back a gasp and flexed her fist to fight it down. "Big day," she said, standing up.

Reist and his dad carried all the bags to the back of the vehicle, with his mom, sister, and Eira following behind. His mom fiddled with Eira's hair before they all climbed in. Reist sat in the middle, between Pair and Eira, in the backseat. They were silent the whole drive. The only sound he could hear was his and Eira's shuddering heartbeats.

Every night after he had told his family he was enlisting, he had heard his mom crying and his dad whispering softly. Pari had asked for more sessions of Alien Hunter and Reist had obliged every time.

Though it had been getting rather draining on him. It was a selfish thing for him to do, but it was also the only selfish thing he'd done all his life. Surely, they can let him have this.

They pulled into the parking lot the recruiter shared with the small shops. When Reist and Eira had come the first time, it had been half empty. Today, it was bustling with families, all gathering around the recruiter's window front. Reist's dad found a spot to park. They gathered up the bags and went to join their new peers. Eira's personal device went off. She looked down at it and shot her head back up. "I am so sorry." She clicked it and it stopped making noise. It went off again. She clicked it into silence.

"It's alright, honey," Mrs. Adeio said. "It must be important. Go on." She said it with a smile and the usual twinkle in her eye that reminded Eira of Nana. Reist's dad introduced himself to the recruiter.

"I am so sorry," Eira said. She bowed slightly and stepped away from the small crowd to answer the call.

"Where'ssh your mother?" her father asked.

"Haven't the foggiest," Eira replied. "Did you lose her again?"

"I, I, I didn't losshe no one," he said, the slur blatantly obvious now.

"Well, I haven't seen her today," Eira said. "Or much of yesterday, really. Her being your wife and all, aren't you her keeper, or did you want to take a few swings and defend her honor?"

"S-s-sh-she had called some guy today," he muttered, more to himself than to her. "I asked who she was talking to, but she said it was Betany. That wasn't no woman's voice. I, I, I could tell..."

"Congratulations, Dad. I'm so proud of you for being able to differentiate a person's sex over a call."

"She prolly havin' sex now..."

"Her or you, Dad? What's this one's name?"

"You leave her outta this, stupid child. I needa talk to your mother. Where are *you*, anyway? No one's home."

235

Here it comes. "I'm at the CDF recruiter's," Eira said. "I'm flying out to basic training today."

He was quiet for a minute. "What in all the bleedin hells are you talking about, stupid child?"

"I was thinking I didn't like being called a stupid child by an alcoholic cuck. This was the most reasonable thing I could think of."

"....The fuck did you say?"

"I said it's rather embarrassing that, instead of owning up to your own cheating or the fact you're being cheated on, you drink. And your only child wanted to get as far away from that as possible, so she signed up for a combat job to kill every motherfucker who looks like all the people that fucked her mother for funsies, daddy," she said. "Did you hear me that time?"

"Ble....you...well.."

"Captivating," Eira said. "Well, I must cut this short '*dad*' if you really are my father, but who honestly knows? I'm attending a pre-gang bang dinner and they're calling for me to hurry up. I'll lift a hallucinogen cocktail to toast to you, my good man." Eira shut the device, her heart racing, still.

With a deep breath to compose herself, Eira stepped back towards the crowd. A couple of people looked away suddenly when she turned to them, except Reist. He had his arm around his sister's shoulders while she hugged his waist and had his damn smirk on again. "All good?" Reist asked.

"Yep," Eira said, keeping her tone light and unbothered.

"Excellent. We wouldn't want you to feel like you had to hurry up." Eira glared at him and glanced at his parents and Pari. She snuck him a rude hand gesture. He blew her a kiss. "Legit though," Reist whispered. "Are you good?"

"Yeah, I'm okay," Eira whispered back.

A rumbling like a beast from a deep, dark corner of the wild lulled everyone into a dull hush. The bus that would take them to the depot came roaring around the corner and inched its way through the parking lot, stopping at the curb. "Right," the sergeant said. "Recruits! Here's our ride. Give one last goodbye and we'll head out to the depot." He climbed onto the ancient, rusting transport to talk to the driver.

The crowd turned into a pile of emotions of teary hugs. Reist's mom wrapped herself around him and squeezed before littering his face with kisses. He took it all in stride. "Love you, Mom." His dad hugged him next and told him to be good. "I will, Dad. Love you." He spoke so effortlessly, and Eira was speechless when his mom embraced her.

"I'm glad he's not doing this alone," she said to Eira.

His dad came over to hug her as well. "You watch his back, yeah?"

"Of course," Eira's voice felt so feeble coming out of her mouth. A line formed up onto the bus.

"Alright, little wing?" Reist asked Pari, giving her a little half armed hug. She hadn't moved from his side. Other parents were crying and waving to their children through the window.

"Uh huh," Pari said without looking at him. She gazed up at Eira. "You're going with him, right?"

Eira looked at Reist, who nodded and was anxious to get in line himself. She bent her knees slightly and leaned into the conversation. The line could wait. "Yes," she said. "I am."

"And you're his girlfriend," Pari said. "That means you'll look after him?"

"I'm not his girlfriend," Eira said bluntly. There was a slight but noticeable dimmer in Reist's face. But he said nothing. Eira thought back to the hospital. The rounds punching through the walls and blood exploding out of the patient's chest. She never learned that man's name. She had forgotten him until now. It may have been for the best. "No," Eira said. "He doesn't need me. He'll be just fine."

And with that, she let go of her brother. Pari didn't look happy with that answer, and Reist pondered her exact words as they climbed onto the bus. They stowed their bags in the overhead compartment and sat together. The bus roared again as they pulled away, Reist and Eira waving to his family until they were out of sight.

"I don't think she understands 'partners,'" Reist said. Everyone was talking amongst themselves.

"I'm sure you'll explain it to her," Eira said. Her eyes focused in front of her. This was the next step, the next chapter.

"I'm sure I will when she's older," Reist said, matching her energy.

The city of Urbis passed them by, as if waving farewell too. Sunlight reflected off the mirrored skyscrapers. Large, angry, red eyes spray painted on the side of buildings glared at them, boring into their backs as left the city limits. Golden sand gusted up into clouds around the bus as the glass perimeter of the spaceport winked at them. The black form of the transport ship grew larger with every passing second. Eira grabbed Reist's hand as the bus passed through the security gate. They only let go to grab their bags and climb off the bus.

Their recruiter was talking to another sergeant by the transport ramp. "Recruits!" he called out to them. "This is Staff Sergeant Kheiron. He'll be taking you guys from here to basic training. Good luck." And like that, he was back on the bus and riding away.

Sergeant Kheiron clicked his device on. His wrist glowed green as the hologram formed a box above his wrist. "If you hear your name, say 'here,'" he said, before going down the list and marking off everyone who answered. "Right. Form a single file line. Let's get going."

Everyone stood still, their eyes squinting in the late afternoon sun. Eira looked around at the gaggle they had made. No one wanted to be the first to step on the ramp. She looked at Reist with a sinister look in her eye he couldn't say no to. She made for the ramp, him at her side.

Game on.